Somebody was running his way. Catherine. And there were tears streaming down her face.

Something was wrong. He thought of the baby first, for some reason. Or Joe Banker.

"Honey, what's wrong?"

She tried to tell him but it wouldn't come out.

"Calm down, honey. What's happened?"

"It's Little Joe!"

He held her away from him and looked into her face.

"He's gone, Jodell."

"What?"

It still didn't make any sense. He had just seen the little cuss a while back in the race. It looked like he'd hit the wall pretty hard, but he had surely hit many other walls a heck of a lot harder than that before, and he had lived to brag about it.

"The wreck. He was killed, Jodell."

Follow all the action . . .
from the qualifying lap
to the checkered flag!

Rolling Thunder!

Rolling Thunder
STOCK CAR RACING

RACE TO GLORY

Kent Wright
& Don Keith

TOR®

A TOM DOHERTY ASSOCIATES BOOK
NEW YORK

This is a work of fiction. All the characters and events portrayed in this book are either products of the author's imagination or are used fictitiously.

ROLLING THUNDER #3: RACE TO GLORY

A Tor Book
Published by Tom Doherty Associates, LLC
175 Fifth Avenue
New York, NY 10010

www.tor.com

Tor® is a registered trademark of Tom Doherty Associates, LLC

ISBN: 0-812-57508-3

First edition: August 1999

Printed in the United States of America

0 9 8 7 6 5 4 3 2 1

"No other man-made device since the shields and lances of the ancient knights fulfills a man's ego like an automobile."

—Sir William Rootes,
British automobile manufacturer

*This book is dedicated to those who have raced to glory,
and to all those who watched and cheered them on.*

The night had turned even colder. The chill and the humidity from the off-and-on rain seemed to climb inside a man's jacket and make itself right at home. At least the storms and downpour from early afternoon had finally weakened to only misty haze, not enough to postpone the festivities, just enough to give it a haunted feel. And the only thunder now was that which reverberated around the lightning-bright racetrack as the cars roared again and again past the Atlanta Speedway sign down the backstretch. It was almost midnight by then and the drivers were finally, mercifully, on a mad, twenty-five-lap dash to the long-delayed finish of the last race of 1998. The contest, scheduled to start in early afternoon, was finally getting itself resolved through a dark, ghostly mist and damn near the witching hour.

Down in the infield, perched high on the roof of one of the team-hauler trailers, an older man sat quietly in a director's chair, all alone, his gray head swiveling as he watched the cars flash by. Finally, near the end, he stood slowly, careful to get his balance, and then reached to grab the railing that framed the top of the semi-truck trailer. He shook his head and smiled in appreciation as he watched the cars approach the starter's stand, where the white flag was already in the flagman's hand, ready to wave, even though there were yet three laps left. It looked as if the flagman, too, was ready to call it a season.

But late, wet, cold, exhausted, back-of-the-pack or not, the old man admitted to himself that he would still have loved to have been out there amongst them again, banging and knocking and jockeying to bring his mount in somewhere closer to the front of the field.

He got himself into these moods sometimes, more so in the last couple of years, and especially when he found himself alone with the time to think, temporarily relieved of the pressure of managing his team. The race had ended early for his crew this day, and even earlier for his wife, Catherine. She had packed up the grandkids and gone on back to the hotel hours ago, when it had looked for certain that the rain was going to be the only winner this day. Being held captive, out of the weather in the crowded motor home, had made the kids rowdy, then tired, and everyone else nerve-jangling irritable.

The rest of the crew was down below him now, cussing and banging as they tried to load a busted-up race car into the back of the hauler. An overly anxious rookie had shoved his driver into the wall and murdered a perfectly good car. Now they had no option but to strip away most of her mangled front end just so they could get her to fit into the trailer again. Jodell Lee knew he should be down there with them, overseeing every turn of a wrench on his car, but he felt a strong need to see the race through, to watch the last checkered flag of the season. And it was the cold solitude on top of the hauler that had given him the opportunity to think, to remember.

He could hear the race cars roaring out of the fourth turn, then here they came, lined up tightly as they flashed by in front of him with two laps to go now. The cold wind almost flipped the sponsor's cap off his head as he turned quickly to watch the lead pack dive hard into the first turn. As he twisted around in the damp chill to follow the cars, he could feel all the various aches and twinges his body had picked up over the years like souvenirs from some of the great racetracks in America.

He had named each of them for the places where he had acquired them: the Darlington knee, where he had finally had the inevitable tangle with the famous wall there; the Talladega shoulder, from when he had barrel-rolled the car and had been lucky to be able to walk away with only an arthritic shoulder socket and the memory of the car coming to pieces all around him; the Dover hip, that just as easily could have left him piloting a wheelchair for the rest of his life instead of some brightly adorned race car. Endless, tiring days followed by cold, rainy nights like this one only seemed to make the pangs worse.

As he watched the darting cars, he drank in one more time the expanse of the huge Atlanta track that flowed around him like a shiny asphalt river. The magnitude and glory of it all still took his breath, even after all these years, and it made him dizzy until he finally remembered to inhale again.

Now it was almost over. The thirty or so cars' engines grumbled like one big monster as the field came by to take the white flag for the final mile and a half. The lead car wore a multitude of colors and sponsor decals, like peacock feathers, and it shimmered in the hazy light as it moved around to boldly claim the win, bottoming out one more time in a shower of sparks at the entrance to the first turn. Its driver didn't back off at all when he took the checkered flag. It almost seemed he wanted to keep running all night, whether anybody else did or not.

"Gordon," Lee whispered.

His breath fogged in the cold air and he shivered once, smiled again, then finally began to climb down the ladder and off the top of the trailer.

Jeff Gordon. The kid had just won the championship yet again, prevailing in style, claiming his thirteenth race of the season in the process. He'd even taken the last few contests outright, when he had really only needed to show up and play it safe and finish the races to get the bigger prize. He was too driven to win to ever consider dogging it on a racetrack, though. That feat, winning a baker's dozen races, had tied Richard Petty's modern-era single-year record, and Petty had been the best the sport had to offer. Gordon would be in New York at the Waldorf-Astoria in a couple of weeks, all decked out in a tuxedo with a rainbow cummerbund, with his toothpaste commercial grin and his perfect hair and his too-pretty-to-believe wife, to take delivery of his title once more.

The old man paused on the ladder and watched the kid direct his car down onto the pit road, then aim it toward Victory Lane once again. The throaty baritone of the single powerful engine idling along had replaced the angry chorus of all the cars at full song.

Some didn't like Gordon. Even the fans, who normally sided with winners. They said he'd had it all handed to him, the best cars, a flawless crew, and that all he had to do was to steer the thing around the racetrack and he'd win.

Jodell Lee knew better.

It took somebody like Jodell Bob Lee to appreciate the kind of pure talent and dedication the kid had. He saw it in the way the Chevy's rear end wiggled slightly coming down off the banking in the fourth turn, pushed to the limit, on the raw edge of letting go its grip. And it happened whether Gordon was leading by a half lap or in those rare times when he was down too far to ever hope to catch up. Gordon had the same almost manic desire to win regardless of what track he was on or who the competition might be. Whether he was racing side by side with Dale Earnhart, Rusty Wallace, or Mark Martin, zooming for the checkered flag, door handle to door handle at close to two hundred miles per hour, or simply testing tires all alone on an otherwise empty track somewhere. Jodell liked to think sometimes that the kid might actually he racing the ghosts of Fireball Roberts, Little Joe Weatherly, Davey Allison, Alan Kulwicki, or Neil Bonnett out there, competing for some kind of immortality that only the men who navigated such powerful machines could understand. Men who drove as much for the glory as for the money.

Jodell Bob Lee understood. He had raced for glory for the better part of forty years. Now he was in the final laps of his own career as a car owner. But he still felt that tickle in his chest when he saw someone defy the basic laws of physics like Gordon was doing out there, with a hundred thousand people cheering him on. These were the times when one old, sore race car driver most wanted to pull his driving suit out of the

*mothballs and get out there and rub a few fenders with
the rest of them. Then he could see for himself if Gordon was really as good as he looked from the top of the
hauler.*

The kid was driven. That was for sure. Whether he
was squared off against Bill Elliott, a stopwatch, or his
own nerve, there was nothing else but flat-out for him.
Jodell made his way along the wet pavement, ignoring
the throb of pain in his Talladega shoulder, making
his way past Victory Lane, where Gordon and crew
were taking their congratulations.

It had been a good race! And that's what Gordon
and Lee and men like them lived for: good races, and
especially ones when they finished in front.

Jodell Lee slapped a few backs and shook some hands
at the fringe of the victory celebration, and then, ultimately, turned away and headed back to help his own
crew. He had a few more things to do back in the
garage before he could call it a day, a season.

And besides, he knew that if he stood there much
longer, as the fog settled in and some of the arc lights
began blinking off, as the last crew members deserted
the pit road, he might start seeing the ghosts again
himself. Fireball and Little Joe Weatherly and all the
rest of them, walking, laughing, bragging, driving,
winning. Their spirits were still there, of course, as big
and as alive as ever. The ghosts of all the ones who
had raced before.

All the ones who had raced for glory.

RACING TO RACE

The sky was clear and bright deep blue, the weather hot as a two-dollar pistol. The calendar promised that fall was imminent, but somebody had forgotten to tell summer it was already mid-September, time to kindly step aside. There was no hope of a cooling shower either. It had not bothered to rain for almost a month, and the billowing dust was having its own way; the grass had long since surrendered and turned brown, and the creeks had gone into hiding.

The people who had lined up and were already filing through the gaps in the chain-link fence didn't care, though. It was perfect weather to watch practice and qualifying for the stock car race the next day. No threat of rain to cut the festivities short. Lots of heat to keep thirsts whetted for more beer or soda. Not much wind, so maybe the dust would stay in its own place for the afternoon.

As they found a place to rest in the old wooden bleachers, they could survey the track itself, a tight, half-mile, freshly paved oval. Out there on the asphalt, a dozen or more cars circled, dodging and darting about, getting a feel for the track and how the machines handled. Their unmuffled pipes roared menacingly, the constant drone punctuated here and there by the boom of a backfire when one of them decelerated for a turn. Cars constantly dashed off the track to the pit area for adjustments, while others, duly tweaked, eased out to rejoin the practice. The area in the middle of the oval was a squirming collection of frenzied activity.

Down there in the midst of the melee, beneath a nearly new Ford race car, two men fiddled feverishly at the bottom of the engine block, only their feet protruding from either side of the vehicle. Directly above them, another man, a bearish mountain of a man, was busy with both hands, working on the motor from the top, frantically trying to get it loose and free so they could lift it out of the automobile. Tools and parts lay everywhere, as if there might have been some kind of recent, tragic explosion inside the tool chest. Above the grumble of the cars out on the track and the first hurrahs from the crowd, anyone standing nearby could hear a steady stream of some definitely un-Christian language from underneath the car.

Time was running out. They had to get the motor free, then lift it out of the car and onto a stand so they could cure what ailed it. Then they would have to wench it back into its mounts, buckle it down, and get it going again, hopefully as good as it had been before. But they had to get it running well enough to qualify or there would be no win at this hot, dusty place. No race tomorrow for the blue Ford race car. No glory. No money.

Then there was a sudden boom out there on the track, as if someone had tossed a stick of dynamite amidst a pack of practicing cars. The spectators came to their feet as one and watched as a bright red-and-white car spun several times coming out of the second turn, maybe simply losing traction, maybe getting nudged by another car, maybe having something vital break under stress beneath the vehicle. Whatever it was, the car was pinwheeling around the middle lane of the track directly in the path of others who were quickly bearing down on him. Sure enough, a second car whose driver had apparently not seen the tire smoke from the first, nor spotted the whirling vehicle in front of him, bulldozed directly into the side of him. "T-boned," the drivers liked to call it, though they, to a man, hated the thoughts of such a thing. A fellow could get hurt.

Whatever, it was a vicious coming-together. Both cars were heavily damaged, and the thunk of the impact left the crowd suddenly hushed.

But then they screamed their approval as both of the drivers crawled from what was left of their shattered, smoking race cars, each a bit wobbly on his feet but apparently none the worse for their wreck. Amazingly, each danced around the wreckage of his own car, trying to find some sign of life, to decide if it might still have enough breath left in it to race the next day. Only when the wreckers arrived to tow away what was left would they finally concede that their horses were dead, more ready for burial than for galloping.

The three men performing surgery on the Ford's

engine did not even pause long enough to look up from their operation, even when the screeching, booming demolition took place not a hundred yards from where they worked. Whatever happened out there during the practice was of no consequence to the pickle in which they now found themselves. Getting this engine out of the car and healed was all that mattered.

This was their third race in six days. The engine that suddenly developed a bad case of "blowed-up" had already run more than a dozen races before it had finally rolled over and died the night before. The 250-lap race would be run the next day, but that wouldn't matter to the three men if the motor was not ready to go by qualifying time. A quick trip to the supplier had gotten the parts they thought they needed for the broken motor. Now they had to get it yanked out so they could fix the damage from the faulty cylinder. Luckily, the motor had apparently been shut off before any terminal damage could be done to the block itself. Otherwise, they would have simply made a ninety-degree turn and started a long, disappointing ride back home with a wasted couple of races, a sour motor, and damn little money to show for this particular trip.

The car's driver, at the moment the set of feet sticking out from under the passenger side of the Ford, had been the one with the foresight to cut the engine off at the first hint of trouble. That had left the car in thirtieth place and had netted a paltry fifty-dollar payday. All of that and then some went toward the expense of trying to fix the damaged motor.

Finally, the engine was hauled up onto the makeshift stand, where the three of them could get to work on it. They had only a little over three hours left to get it fixed and put back into the car before the late-afternoon qualifying session began. And even at that, they would probably miss all the practice laps before qualifying. That meant they would have to qualify blind, never having driven on this track before.

"Hey, Bubba! While you're restin' why don't you hand me that nine-sixteenths wrench?"

It was the driver who had spoken. Beneath the grime and grease on his face, he was clearly a handsome man, his hair long and dark, and despite the feverish pace of their work, somehow it had managed to stay neatly combed back in a swooping cowlick. Anyone could see he had been and probably was still an athlete. But his most prominent feature was his eyes. They were dark blue and expressive, and immediately conveyed determination and intensity. And anyone who knew Jodell Bob Lee knew he was both those things. In spades.

The big man he was talking to was up to his elbows in the motor at the moment.

"Hold your horses, Jodell. Let me get to a turnin'-loose place."

Bubba Baxter was a man among men. From behind, his shoulders seemed as broad as the Ford's rear bumper, his neck thick as the car's axle. He could easily have been a pro football player or professional wrestler. He had, in fact, played ball in high school, shoving aside would-be tacklers so Jodell Lee could loft passes downfield or dance to first downs. He still showed the way for his best friend, in a manner of speaking. The big man had a natural acuity for setting up the frame of a car, its front end, the wheel alignment, and the thousand-and-one other tiny adjustments that helped a race vehicle run straight, true, and fast.

And the third man, now digging into the engine with a vengeance, had been a halfback on that same squad with Jodell and Bubba, the Consolidated High Eagles back in Chandler Cove, Tennessee. Joe Banker was a first cousin to Jodell Lee, his mother the sister of Jodell's late father. The three of them, Jodell, Joe, and Bubba, still made a very effective team.

"Y'all want to quit passing the time of day, you could help me back here," Joe growled.

He was the engine man. Few people knew more about what made an internal combustion engine turn than did Joe Banker. It was a self-taught skill that he had assimilated while working on cars and other machinery since he had been big enough to hold a Crescent wrench. It didn't take long for anyone to pick up the family resemblance between Joe and Jodell either. Especially the women. He, too, was Elvis-handsome with his dark hair, smooth complexion, and blue eyes. But where Jodell Lee's eyes shouted of intensity, Joe Banker's hinted of mischief and flirtation.

They worked quietly for a while, concentrating on the business at hand, ignoring the last of the cars that were still circling the track, getting the most from their practice. It was Bubba who finally spoke, not necessarily to anyone in particular.

"Boys, I was just wondering what I was going to have for supper," he said. The man's appetite was already legendary on the stock car circuit. Curtis Turner, a driver they had run with in the past, had once sworn to everyone who would listen that he had watched Bubba Baxter eat three whole chickens, bones and all. And then the big man had allegedly asked for more gravy and biscuits.

"And I was wondering if that brunette waitress at that diner might still want to get a moonlight tour of a real live racing pit tonight," Joe said wistfully. Another of the drivers, Little Joe Weatherly, had said of Joe, "That Banker is real particular about the kind of women he goes after. They gotta have at least one eye, some of their own teeth, and be breathin'."

"If y'all would work as hard as you jaw, we might get this engine fixed in time to actually qualify for this darn race," Jodell growled. Turner and Weatherly had both made the same pronouncement about Jodell Bob Lee: "That boy's wound so tight he'd put his own grandma into the wall to win a race."

"Jodell must not have got his nap out," Joe offered.

"Probably just needs to be fed," Bubba suggested.

Never mind that they had not had a night's sleep in a real bed in days. Nor that their best meals had come from a sardine tin.

Still, the trio had come a long way from their moonshining and drag racing days in the mountains of northeastern Tennessee. Three and a half years of running the Grand National Stock Car circuit had been both frustrating and educational for them. Success had been so close they felt sometimes like kids on a merry-go-round, the brass ring only inches out of their reach as they spun past. They had run a good portion of the races on the tour over the last three years, had consistently finished in the nickel-and-dime money, but so far that first win, the glory, and the serious purse that went along with it, had still eluded them. And for that reason, the primary sponsor they had worked so hard to reel in back in the beginning was now threatening to spit out the hook.

The sponsor, a bottling company that distributed Bubble Up soda, was feeling the pinch from the competition. They needed a winner to help them sell more soda, to justify the advertising dollars they were spending on the race team instead of in the papers and on the radio, like all the other sodas did. Homer Williams, the company's president, would tell anyone who would listen that he was getting more than his money's worth from Jodell Bob Lee's racing team. But it was also getting more and more difficult for him to justify the cost to his board of directors and stockholders without a big-time win to show for it. Seeing the car with the big Bubble Up logo out there riding around, even in the lead pack with all the big names, wasn't the same as having it front and center in the winner's circle. And all the other non–Grand National races they had won didn't count for much when it was the big-time contests that everyone listened to on the radio and read about in the newspapers.

Nobody ever actually came right out and said it, but it was clear that Mr. Williams needed to have a victory before the end of this Grand National season, a trophy to show the boys back home. And the laps were quickly ticking down to the end of the year, maybe the end of their racing.

Without sponsorship for the upcoming 1964 season, their racing careers would certainly be over. Most likely for good.

The three of them had been living a dream, and on the practical side, they had been winning enough money to go with what Jodell's and Bubba's wives brought in to make ends meet, taking care of themselves as well as Joe and Jodell's grandmother. But without the soda company's money to cover the cost of the travel and upkeep on the car, the fantasy could quickly vanish. They would be back to working in one of the mills or plants back home or again trying to scratch out a living plowing the rocky hillside farm where Jodell had been raised by his grandparents. But

even back then, Grandpa Lee had relied on his moonshine whiskey he cooked up to get by, and on Jodell
to deliver it. Without the whiskey, the farm could not
have fed them then, and was even less likely as a
source of income now.

Whiskey-running was no longer an option. Times
had changed.

They simply had to make the racing work. It had
become an obsession, a gnawing hunger made even
more intense by the limited success they had had. But
it seemed that every time they had been in a position
to win, someone else either wrecked them or something in the car broke. Once, Jodell leapt out to a
three-lap lead on the field with five laps to go, and
Joe and Bubba had already started celebrating in the
pits. But then the rear end had given out in the car
and he had had no choice but to coast into the pits
while the rest of the field made up the laps. Somebody
else had rolled under the checkered flag first. Somebody else had gotten his picture taken in the Victory
Lane and had had his sponsors' names emblazoned
across the sports pages the next day. Somebody else
had cashed their winning check.

The blown motor they were frantically working on
had been typical of the way their season had gone.
There had been so many wrecks and so many broken
parts that they had spent most of the sponsorship
money by the time they arrived at Darlington for the
"500" on Labor Day. Since then, they had been living
on purse money from secondary races for the last two
weeks. That meant they consumed far more cans of
Vienna sausages than they did hamburger steaks,
spent more nights stretched out in the tow car than
on real beds in motel rooms. Now, this blown engine
was threatening to have them hitchhiking back to

Chandler Cove if they didn't get it fixed and buttoned up in time to qualify the car. They would have to pool their pennies now to try to find enough gas money to even get started back home.

Joe Banker took each mechanical failure personally. No matter how much Jodell and Bubba tried to reassure him that it was merely "racing luck," he would insist on taking the blame.

"My motors don't break. There's no rhyme or reason for what's been happening. My motors don't break."

Finally, at least one thing went right. Once they had the engine apart, they found that the damage was exactly what they had expected and that they had bought the right parts they needed to fix it. An hour later they were putting everything back together and getting ready to wrestle the engine back into the car. Soon they would have to be ready to roll out for qualifying.

The last practice before qualifying was about to start. They prayed, quietly and out loud, that the motor would go back together right, that they could get it back in the car and tied down with a minimum of trouble, that it would actually crank when they got it reinstalled, that it wouldn't fly apart when it got gas. The clock was ticking!

The three of them were covered with mud, the recipe of dust and sweat, basted all over with oil and grease, and well cooked by the unrelenting sun. It had been a constant struggle to keep the flourlike dust out of the inside of the engine while they worked on it. They could only hope they had been successful. Motors didn't like grit in their innards.

"You cats look like y'all been wrasslin' in the hog pen," a familiar voice piped in from behind where they worked. It belonged to a tall, skinny man who was hurrying by, headed for his own car. Richard Petty slowed down long enough to peer over their shoulders at the task they were performing.

"We have," Joe offered. "Watch out or we'll throw a choke hold on you, too."

"No, thanks. Y'all need any help?"

Petty was serious. He would have willingly pitched in and grabbed a wrench if someone had handed him one. That was common among the racing crews. Someone would drop his own problems in a flash to help someone else, then they would try to knock off each other's fenders once they were out there on the track.

"I think we about got it now," Jodell said. "Much obliged though."

Petty grinned, wished them good luck, and was gone to get ready for his own qualifying run.

"Ease her on down, Bubba. Careful now!" Joe called as Baxter hoisted the engine back down onto its mounts. With Jodell on one side and Joe on the other, they carefully guided the motor into place in the hole in the front of the Ford.

"Whoa!" Joe suddenly cried out as he pushed on the engine, trying to help it settle into place. Pushed for time or not, this was no place to hurry and break something vital for which they didn't have a spare part.

"How's that right there?" Bubba called back, his huge muscles straining under the weight of the heavy engine.

"Drop it just another hair," Jodell said, poised to slip a bolt into the slot once the holes lined up.

They were still trying to get the engine back into place when Little Joe Weatherly ambled by, a soda in one hand and a paper-wrapped sandwich in the other. He was one of the most colorful drivers in Grand National, a prankster and partier with few peers. Jodell made a face at Joe. They certainly didn't have time today for any of Little Joe's foolishness.

"What you dirt daubers doing?"

"Looks like an ace race car driver like you could figure that out," Jodell snapped.

Weatherly ignored his irritation. He leaned against the Ford's fender and watched for a bit.

"I was about to stand here and eat this sandwich right in front of old Bubba just to watch him drool, but it looks like you boys got your hands full. Let me send several of my boys over here to help you."

For once, Weatherly was serious.

"Thanks, Little Joe, but looks like we about got it," Jodell said sheepishly. He was already regretting the way he had bitten at the man.

"Yeah, and if I tried to eat this thing in front of that big old buddy of yours, he'd probably swing that motor over here and mash me like a bug, wouldn't he?"

Little Joe winked and walked on, stopping and speaking rapidly to everyone he passed on the way. Somehow, he always managed to be competitive, though he spent far more time playing than he did getting prepared to race.

Then, before they even realized it, it was just over an hour before the start of qualifying, fifteen minutes before the end of practice. They had finally gotten the engine back together and inside the race car. Jodell crawled from beneath the car while Joe and Bubba were still tightening the last bolts. He pulled on his driving coveralls and climbed behind the wheel of the car. Bubba stood back, ready to give him the signal to try to crank her up once Joe had wrapped things up under the car.

Jodell squirmed impatiently, waiting, drumming his fingers on the steering wheel, pulling and adjusting on the seat and shoulder belts.

"Please start, Betty," he whispered. "Don't be contrary now."

Jodell had a superstitious habit of calling the car a woman's name, a different name for each race. Today, should she decide to run, she would be dubbed "Betty." She might be called far worse names if she proved to be contrary.

Finally, Joe came crawling out from beneath Betty and gave Bubba an unmistakable cranking motion. Bubba gave Jodell the same signal. All three men held their collective breath.

Jodell gave one last tug on the shoulder belt and reached over to punch the starter button. The starter growled, turned 'round and 'round for what seemed like minutes, then, suddenly, the engine caught fire, rumbling with the thousands of explosions captured inside its cylinders.

She lived! The engine was still alive. Now, was she healthy enough to survive the stress of full-throttle power?

Joe and Bubba dived back beneath the hood as Jodell revved the engine up and down. They checked everything quickly, looking for any visible fluid leaks. A loose hose clamp or stripped fitting or forgotten bolt somewhere and the motor could lose water or oil or compression and they would be sunk. But there was nothing leaking that they could see. And everything looked and sounded okay so far.

So far.

They closed the hood and pushed the car out of

the work area. Jodell shoved the shifter up into gear,
fed the motor some more gas, and accelerated out
onto the track to join those who were still getting in
their test laps.

He ran the car gently around the tight track for
several laps, listening to the motor for any strange
sounds, feeling for hesitations or burps, looking in the
mirror for any trailing smoke. Everything sounded,
felt, and looked okay. Maybe their luck was turning.
Just maybe.

Jodell steered the Ford back down into the infield,
toward the spot where he could see Bubba Baxter
towering over everyone like some giant gargoyle. He
brought the car to a quick stop but left the engine
running so Bubba could go underneath and Joe could
check things over from the topside.

No spurts. No smoke. No errors.

Joe flashed Jodell a grinning thumbs-up and waved
him back onto the track with a flourish and a bow.
Dr. Banker's patient was apparently all healed up.

Eight minutes left. That was all the practice they
would get. And in that eight minutes they needed to
get some feel for the car, to learn the nuances of the
track, pick acceleration and braking points along the
course, and do it all before qualifying started. Jodell
pushed the newly rebuilt engine hard now as he thundered off down into the first turn, but he still half
expected it to erupt in front of him, explode into
thousands of pieces and a spray of stinging oil.

"Betty, I might just as well blow you to hell and
back now as in the middle of the qualifying lap," he
told the dashboard almost apologetically, and then he
pushed even harder on the gas pedal.

The track still carried fifteen or twenty practicing
cars, and that made it hard for Jodell to run a clean,

unhindered lap. He really wanted to push the car, to see what she would do, to see how the track felt in each section, but he would have to make the most of what he had.

The setup, the way the car's suspension and tires were tweaked, seemed close to right-on, so far as he could tell. And that was lucky, since this was to be the first race run on this track since it had been paved back in the spring. The summer heat had apparently helped cure the asphalt, and that promised to make it fast. The tires would tend to stick to the surface, allowing the drivers to run even harder through the corners.

For Jodell Lee, this track was a slice of sugar-coated heaven. The paved surface reminded him of the tight, twisting back roads that cut through the foothills of the Smoky Mountains back home. Those were the same mountain roads where he had learned to drive, where he had run corn liquor for his grandfather. A fully loaded whiskey car, running flat-out on a spiraling black snake of a road, with a couple of revenuers hot on its tail! That's where Jodell Lee had learned many of the moves that he could put to such good use on a racetrack like this one. He felt as if he was at home. The only things missing were a sliver of a moon in a dark sky, a red revenuer light in his mirror, and the clink of 'shine jars bumping together in the back seat.

The car felt surprisingly fast, wonderfully fast, in the few laps he was able to run before the red flag ended the practice. Despite that, Jodell had made a mental list of the adjustments he wanted to make before they tried to qualify the car. As tight as the track was, they would need a good starting position if they wanted to quickly go to the front of the pack during the race. It would clearly be a problem trying to pass on this track. It would be much easier to win if he could start up front.

Now that it appeared they might actually be ready to qualify, Jodell began to get seriously worried. As he waited in line for his time to pull out and run his lap under the stopwatch, he thought he could hear all kinds of bad noises from the motor. Was that a miss he felt or just a gust of wind? Was something hissing, losing compression around some hastily set seal, or was it simply the wheezing of the carburetor in the old car that was lined up behind him? And when he rolled forward, he was dead sure he felt a tire out of round. Had they spent so much time worrying about the motor that they might have put a bum tire on the front end?

Then, before he even realized it, he was first in line and the official was waving him out onto the track. He swallowed hard, set his jaw, released the clutch, gave the motor a big swallow of gasoline, and pulled away, finally ready to try to shove the Ford race car around the track for the best possible lap he could get.

ALL WE NEED'S A FIRST

J odell missed church that Sunday morning. He usually managed to find preaching somewhere when they were on the road. He did it for two reasons, mainly because he had promised Grandma Lee he would, but partly because he felt better somehow if he did, as if he got a special blessing for having sat through a sermon and for singing along with the familiar hymns. Sometimes the little devotional some of the racers held before the drivers' meeting had to do. But today, he skipped that, too.

The Lord would understand that they had work to do on the setup of the car. The race wasn't until one in the afternoon, but there was going to be an early practice they could use to fine-tune some more. Jodell liked the feel of the track and knew that if he could just get a little more wheel time out there, they could

pick up a few other things that would help insure a
good run. They worked hard, trying to change the
right-side springs and adjust the camber on the tires
just a dab. Little Joe Weatherly had shared with them
a little of how he planned to set up. It seemed to
match what they all felt after the short practice time
the day before. All they had to do was to do it and
do it right.

Now, with Sunday morning here and the race's
start looming like a threat, Jodell was flat on his back,
studying the right front springs on the Ford. That's
when he noticed a new set of feet standing next to the
car. Female feet. He scooted out from beneath the
Ford and looked up into the beautiful, smiling face of
his wife, Catherine.

It was the most wonderful sight he had ever seen.

"Honey! What in the world are you doing here?"

He had talked with her the night before, at least all
the talking they could do for two quarters from the
pay phone in the infield. She had not mentioned making the three-hour drive over from Chandler Cove.
But he was delighted to see her. He quickly scrambled
to his feet, tried to dust himself off, and then gave her
a big hug and kiss.

"It was such a nice day when I got up this morning
and it's so rare that you are running this close to home
and you've been gone for almost—"

He hushed her with another kiss. This made it perfect! Catherine always seemed to bring them luck
when she watched them race. If there had not been
all kinds of problems, financial and logistical, he
would have had her right along with them on the road
all the time. But it was also the income from her job
at a lawyer's office in Chandler Cove that helped keep
them out there, trying to break into the big time. They

couldn't afford for her to miss work. And it would only have been fair for Bubba's wife to come along, too, and that would have had their little racing band rapidly growing into a traveling circus.

Jodell finally came up for air long enough to greet Catherine's brother, Johnny Holt, who was standing there making rude noises as they kissed, and the two other men he had recruited to help them crew the car during the race. Johnny was a regular and had become adept at making the quick pit stops they needed, and he somehow always managed to round up helpers and get them trained to perform their tasks quickly and efficiently, as if they were actually getting paid. They only received the satisfaction of helping a real, live race team from one of the worst seats in the house from which to watch a race.

"Hey, Jodell," Bubba called from the other side of the Ford. "Look who else's here!"

Someone had been squatting next to the big man, watching him adjust the springs on that side of the car.

Homer Williams, the Bubble Up tycoon, stood up and grinned across the hood at him.

Great! Jodell thought. That's all we need!

Jodell liked Williams. And he appreciated that the man had taken a great risk, signing on as the sponsor of a totally unproven race team. But here they were, struggling to make this race so they could keep the sponsor for another year, and he had shown up, ready to watch in person if they should blow the chance.

"Mr. Williams!" Jodell said, trying to act enthused. He stepped around the front of the car to offer his hand to the man. "It's great to see you!"

Jodell noticed then how dirty and greasy his own hand was. He quickly pulled it back and wiped it on the back of his overalls before sticking it toward Williams again.

"Jodell Bob Lee! My favorite race car driver in the world!" Williams didn't seem to mind the grease. For a man who was about to pull the rug right out from under them, he seemed especially chipper. "How in the world are you boys doing?"

"Well, fair to middlin', I guess. We got us a sixth-place finish the other day, but then we blew the motor Friday night and barely made thirty-eighth. That put us behind the eight ball here, but we got the motor rebuilt in time to qualify and make the race."

"Well, it looks like y'all did a pretty good job getting her pieced back together," Williams said, looking at the hood and tapping it confidently with the heel of his hand, as if he could actually tell the engine beneath it was sound and raring to run.

"We got her back together, and I guess we'll see in this next practice how she's working."

"You'll do just fine. I got all the confidence in the world in you boys. All you gotta do is go out there and beat all those other guys. We need us a win!"

Williams gave Jodell a broad wink. There was no mistaking the meaning behind it.

"Don't worry. I plan on running the wheels off of her. You know how I feel about second place."

"Yessir. That's the attitude. I got myself a good feeling about today. A real good feeling. Don't let me keep y'all from your work. Somebody promised to introduce me to Tiny Lund. I wanna see if he's as big a man as old Bubba here."

And with that, Williams gave them a wave and wandered off, disappearing in the swirling activity in the garage area. Jodell immediately lost his smile as he watched him walk away.

Homer Williams had made several trips to watch them race before, to Daytona, Darlington, and to the new tracks at Charlotte and Atlanta. But he had never shown up unannounced, nor had he yet made a trip to one of the smaller tracks. Until now, anyway. And he had certainly picked a dicey day for this surprise visit. Joe had joked before that Williams's presence seemed to be a jinx. Something bad happened to them just about every time he showed up. Jodell tended to agree.

"Catherine, what is he doing here?" Joe asked as he stuck his head out from underneath the front end of the car.

"I'm sorry, y'all." She knew how they felt about Williams, and how superstitious even levelheaded race crews could be. "I went by the office at the plant yesterday to give him an update on the last two Grand National races and we got to talking. When he found out we were thinking about driving down, he just insisted that he was coming and that we should ride with him. Me and Johnny. At least it saved us gas money, after all, and he did buy us breakfast."

"Well, thanks for nothing," Joe muttered, going on half under his breath about "sorry luck" and "bad omens."

Jodell had put his arm around Catherine again. She shrugged.

"What could I say? 'Uh uh, big boy? You're not going to watch the car you sponsor race'?"

She seemed on the verge of tears. He put his fingers to her lips.

"Let's think about it," Jodell said. "If we accidentally have a good showing today, this may actually work out for the best. I don't see how things could get any worse."

"Oh, they can get worse, all right," Joe said, now from back beneath the car. "You can total the car like you almost did in Charlotte. Heck of a way to break in a brand-new track. Or you could get caught up in a six-car pile-up like you managed to do in Atlanta when old Homer was watching."

"Bad things can happen anywhere, not just when our sponsor is watching us." Jodell knew he was trying to convince himself as much as he was Joe Banker. He turned to whisper to Catherine, "He's just irritable 'cause he hasn't had a chance to romance anybody lately."

"I'm gettin' sick and tired of all this negative talk," Bubba suddenly chimed in, his jaw out, as if spoiling for a fight. "I don't like losing, and I'm tired of all these guys who ain't us celebrating the wins. We got us a good car on a track that suits us to a tee and the best driver in Grand National racing and our 'Catherine good-luck charm' and I don't know what else it takes."

"All right, all right," Joe Banker conceded as he slid from beneath the car once more. "We're gonna win. And win big. And live happily ever after until death do us part. Now, y'all happy?" He didn't wait for anyone to answer. "Now, if y'all are through stroking one another, why don't somebody help me check the timing on this thing so we can go racing."

While Joe and Johnny went to work under the hood, Jodell and Bubba found work to do at the back of the car. As they toiled, Catherine told them about their trip over to the race in Homer Williams's big Cadillac. It had been her first time to ride in one.

"Closest I've come is riding along behind one at a funeral," she noted.

"You'll have yourself a big old Cadillac when we

make it big, Cath," he promised her sincerely. "Maybe one for every day of the week."

"Bicycle's fine with me as long as we're together," she said.

Jodell loved the sound of her voice. And he appreciated her interest in the life he had chosen.

Catherine actually enjoyed being at the racetrack with her husband. She had been there when Jodell ran his very first race, six years before, in a converted cornfield at the old Meyer's farm. Technically, that might have been their first date. She had helped them rebuild his grandfather's car that they had wrecked in that race, too, patiently fetching them tools, making them food, keeping the hot coffee poured when they worked late into the night. And along the way, she had seen the highs and lows of the career Jodell was trying to establish.

She didn't get to make many races anymore. There were simply too many of them and they were strung out at tracks all over the eastern United States. Their wedding the year before had been crowbarred in between the last local races at the end of the season and the start of the next Grand National run. The honeymoon had been a long weekend in Gatlinburg, and they had even cut that short to pick up some parts Joe needed from Knoxville. There had simply been too much work to do, getting the cars, engines, and equipment ready for Daytona and the start of the next season. He promised her he would make it up to her someday.

But she never complained, even when a week or more went by without Jodell's making it home, or even racing close enough to Chandler Cove for her to hitch a ride with Johnny to go watch. She had been a part of their racing from the beginning, after all.

She had known what she was in for. She had actually been the one who had helped get the Bubble Up sponsorship, trading her family's friendship with Homer Williams for an appointment for her and Jodell to make the pitch. It had been her carefully crafted business plan that had helped close the deal. She now helped as much as she could, keeping their finances and the business side of the team organized, submitting entry forms for races, getting the bills paid, managing what little money was left in the team bank account.

She enjoyed the business side almost as much as she liked watching her husband drive. But she was well aware of the dangers of what he did as well. Though she didn't dwell on them, she knew that what her husband did for a living was risky. Even she had seen at least one man killed at the racetrack. She took some small comfort that Jodell was an excellent driver, smart, solid, not prone to showboating or risk taking. And she also knew the boys built sturdy, safe race cars. As safe as they could be, anyway.

Catherine rarely talked with Jodell about the danger, though. She knew he was aware of the risks, too, but that anyone who drove tentatively could never win. No, she had decided early on to be supportive of him. And, at least so far, she had kept her worries to herself. She secretly hoped she could continue to do so, especially if there were others who might come along who would also depend on Jodell.

Bubba headed off in search of food while Jodell and Catherine sat for a few minutes alone on a stack of tires.

"How's everybody back home?" he asked.

"Fine, I suppose. Grandma Lee said to tell you she was praying for you to win. And if the Lord didn't

want you to win, that He would at least let you finish
second."

They laughed. His grandmother had been surprisingly supportive of his choice to race. It wasn't like
her at all. His grandfather, on the other hand, had
been dead set against it.

"Waste of a good car and gasoline," he had
growled the time or two the subject had come up.
The old man had figured cars and gas were better
suited for delivering the moonshine whiskey he
brewed in a deep cove up the mountain from their
house. And he knew his grandson had been blessed
with the ability to drive those cars. Blessed just as the
boy's daddy had been before he left for the war, never
to return. He also preached that the boy should use
that talent for something useful, necessary, not for
running ragged on some fool racetrack somewhere
with a bunch of other crazy yahoos.

But Grandpa Lee had died suddenly, shortly after
Jodell had begun to race on the sly, without his grandfather's knowledge or approval. The old man had
never gotten the opportunity to flatly forbid Jodell to
race.

Grandpa's death had led to a hard choice. As the
new head of the house, Jodell had to provide for himself and his grandmother, and he doubted he could
do that working the rocky hillside that could only, in
the broadest terms, be called a "farm." Somehow, the
limited success that they had had already had made
racing seem like an option, so the three of them had
made a pact and set out to conquer the world of fast
cars.

Then they had destroyed the only race car they had
in winning a sportsman race at Hickory, North Carolina, and it looked as if there was little hope. But one

of his grandfather's best whiskey customers had advanced them enough money to get started seriously. With bootlegger money, they had built a competitive car that didn't win but ran very well in the Labor Day race at Darlington, South Carolina, a race against the best in the game. And that showing, in turn, had led to their sponsorship agreement with Homer Williams and Bubble Up.

"I'm like Homer," Catherine said suddenly, showing her beautiful smile, looking deeply into Jodell's eyes. "I've got a good feeling about today, too."

He smiled back and gave a determined nod.

"Okay then. I guess it's up to me to bring her home."

He kissed her again and then watched her as she went off toward the grandstands to splurge for some sandwiches for lunch. He couldn't believe how much he loved her. And now, somehow, despite their ragged start, Jodell felt much better about their chances on this day.

Their run at the big time had so far been much like a typical race, with stops and starts, highs and lows. And right now they desperately needed one of those highs. They needed a first.

Needed it badly.

NOW OR NEVER

J odell sat there, strapped into the race car just like one of those astronauts they had been rocketing into space down in Florida lately. He could feel sweat running down both sides of his rib cage as he tightened his grip on the Ford's steering wheel. He caught a glimpse of his own eyes in the rearview mirror and startled himself.

"Lord. Look at that face, Judy," he mumbled, as much to the car as to himself. "That feller's one crazy so-and-so, ain't he."

The car seemed to shimmy as an answer, but it was really only Bubba, giving the front end one last shake to see how the setup felt to him. Jodell knew they had built a fast car, but there were others, at least a dozen, that were as quick or quicker. Richard Petty could fly. So could Little Joe Weatherly, Junior Johnson, Ned

Jarrett, Fireball Roberts, Buck Baker, and his boy, Buddy. There was another fast, young driver, too, a guy Jodell had run across a couple of times already named Cale Yarborough. He was a South Carolinian who had lied about his age and raced in the Southern 500 in Darlington before he turned eighteen. And even if those fellows had not been piloting a fast car, they each had the smarts and the grit to pull out a race on nothing more than sheer determination and driving skill.

Lee Petty had shown up at the drivers' meeting that morning. He had driven over from his home just south of Greensboro to watch his son race. Petty had run only a couple of races, then retired after almost getting himself killed at Daytona a few years before, but Richard had picked up right where his old man had left off.

The one Jodell really had to chase would be Tiny Lund, the driver who had won the Daytona 500 already this year. He was now sitting on the outside of the front row in a car that looked as if it was in motion, even when it was still sitting there waiting for the start. Fireball and Richard were in tandem behind him with the others stacked two-by-two back to where Jodell lined up in tenth position, on the outside row, directly in front of the Yarborough kid. Jodell had already seen the look on Cale's face in the mirror, too, and the sight was just as disconcerting to him as his own eyes in his mirror had been.

There was one other driver he had made a point of locating. Two rows in front of him sat the car of Dash Rockford, a continual pain in the side for Jodell Lee and most of the others. Jodell's first encounter with Rockford's aggressive driving had come during his first run at Darlington in the 500 on Labor Day in 1958, a brouhaha that had led to a fight in the pits afterwards and a series of run-ins and paint-trading episodes over the years since. Rockford seemed to take great delight in trying to shove Jodell into the wall, to send him spinning on the track, or in goading him into a fistfight any other place their paths happened to cross. But it wasn't only Jodell. He had his other favorite victims, too, and Lee took some pride in the fact that they all seemed to be the up-and-comers on the circuit. He supposed it was at least good company in which to find himself.

The sad thing, though, was that Rockford could probably have been a talented driver and usually showed up with a competitive car. Somehow, though, he had gotten the idea that it would help his image, with the press and sponsors as well as with the women, to acquire a bad boy, outlaw reputation. And, truth be told, his style had won him a certain cadre of loyal fans who seemed to be just as loud and obnoxious as their hero was belligerent and warlike. Most of the drivers simply considered him a troublemaker, a dangerous force on the track, and one other unpredictable hazard to dread, like an exploding engine or erupting tire.

Dash had already cost Jodell more than one victory with his rough driving antics. Jodell made a quick note of where Dash was in line because today, of all days, he couldn't afford any trouble from the guy. But if things followed true to form, he'd either have to knock him out of the way or get run over by him.

Jodell tried to clear his mind as he waited impatiently for the command to start the engine. He plotted yet again how he would work his way to the front, reviewing the same race strategy in his mind that he had mulled over all the night before and all day so far. Even during their brief lunch, when Catherine had been trying to catch him up on the news from back home. She had finally put down her sandwich and smiled at him.

"And the cow jumped over the moon," she had said.

He chewed on, staring blankly at her.

"Um hmmm," he had calmly agreed.

"You're driving this race already, aren't you?"

He blushed a deep crimson, then took her hand and apologized sincerely.

"I'm sorry, honey. I haven't seen you in so long and it's so wonderful to have you here and all, but I just can't quit thinking about getting up front and winning this race. Why do you put up with me?"

"Maybe because I love you. Ever considered that?"

"Yeah, but somehow, I still find it hard to believe."

"I knew before we got married that I'd have to share you with your mistresses. Just make sure it's always one that drinks gasoline and has four wheels."

She had made that face then, the one he loved so much, when she wrinkled up her nose as she made fun of him and her eyes sparkled and he knew without a doubt that she really did love him. He had wanted to reach across the blanket and grab her and hold her then, to tell her how much he loved her, how much he appreciated her support and understanding, but he couldn't.

First he had to take care of business. Soon as he won this race, down there in Victory Lane, he'd make certain he told her then.

But he had to shake it off now before the start-engines command came, get back on mental track, picturing his moves, plotting the strategy. Jodell Lee found it best to take a methodical approach to racing, trying to outsmart the others as much as outrace them. Most, like Junior Johnson, merely pressed the gas pedal to the floor and stood on it for enough laps to win. But Jodell firmly believed that strategy and preparation could often lead to a first place, even if the car was not quite as good as the others, the driver not up to par, or if bad luck played a part, as it often did.

"Gentlemen, start your engines!"

The words echoed through the static from the public address system, and the sizable crowd leapt to its feet in anticipation. Then, in unison, there was the deep-throated rumble of the herd of racing machines, shaking the ground into a mini-earthquake as they coughed and finally exploded to life.

Jodell felt his own motor wake up at his command, though he had no hope of actually hearing it over the din. Bubba reached through the open window and gave his belts one last check, making certain they were secure for the tenth time since they had rolled out for the start. He flashed Jodell the thumbs-up sign, then turned and hurried back toward their pit. Jodell glanced after him and immediately wished he hadn't. Joe and Johnny and the rest of the pit crew were there, all grins, decked out in their green Bubble Up uniforms. But so was Homer Williams, standing there on the wall with his own goofy grin pasted on. Somehow, it would have been better if he had been lost up there in the grandstand, anonymous among the rest of the crowd. Now, every time Jodell flew past, every time he wheeled in for a pit stop, he would be reminded of the sword that hung over him on a slender, slender thread.

Jodell shook his head to clear it of any more negative thoughts, pulled his goggles down over his eyes, and adjusted them tightly into place. He pushed the shifter up into first gear, waiting for the signal for the field to roll off. Then he went through his usual moves. He stretched his arms, tensed and relaxed his thighs, rolled his head about on his shoulders, all to relieve the tension he couldn't otherwise shake. Then he gazed off down into the first turn, trying to visualize how it would look and feel and smell when he stomped the gas as the field took the green flag to start the race. How it would be for him to surge forward and try to claim some positions right out of the chute before the others even realized what was happening.

The official with the red armband began to wave the mass of straining race cars off the line. The vehicles impatiently but dutifully rolled off after the pace car as it slowly circled the track, going maddeningly slowly. Jodell searched for his predetermined acceleration and deceleration points. He had to locate them all over again now that the grandstands were full. The cars made three circuits of the track, still holding back but grumbling about having to do so. Each time by, Jodell made a point of finding the flag stand and the man who was perched up there. He was cradling the green flag like a newborn baby as he showed them with his fingers how many more laps there were to go before they could free their dawdling engines and start the race in earnest.

Finally, rolling slowly down the backstretch and through the fourth turn, Jodell strained to find the flagman once more, to confirm that he now had the flag in hand. He tightened his grip on the wheel, gritted his teeth, and waited for the first hint that the green flag was about to wave.

Sure enough, the banner came up high over the

flagman's head, fluttering furiously as the lead cars rolled out of the fourth corner. Eager right feet were jammed down on accelerators, shoving them rudely to the floorboard. The roar that was painful enough already to listen to now swelled to an impossibly loud reverberating racket.

Like a powerful horse breaking from the gate, Tiny Lund got the jump on the pole sitter and beat him into the turn, assuming the lead with apparent ease. The rest of the field followed, bunched closely together like a herd of wild mustangs, jockeying for position, bumping and pushing.

Jodell was stuck on the outside of the track. He knew he would have a hard time making headway as long as he was boxed in by the inside line of slower cars and the driver in front of him, who seemed to be out on a pleasant Sunday drive. Jodell wished for a horn or a revenuer's siren so he could urge the slow-poke on or over, out of the way. He thought for an instant about going ahead and tapping him in the rear. But, with his luck, the guy would panic and lose it right there in front of him. And he would then take five or six trailing cars out of the race with him, all right here in the first half of the very first lap of a very long race.

Yarborough, coming up from behind, quickly slipped down into a gap in the inside line and made his way past. Jodell saw his chance and was able to nudge his wheel to the left, punch the accelerator a bit more, and tuck in behind him, following him past the slower car. Once on the inside line, he was quickly able to find his rhythm. The race car felt good beneath him as she hugged the inside line, gripping the track as if she had talons instead of tires.

Soon, the field started to string itself out around the

half-mile oval, with cars of like speed and drivers of like abilities finding each other. Junior Johnson had managed to take over the front spot after he and Lund had rubbed fenders for a few laps, bringing the people in the crowd to their feet, holding their breath, then exhaling with a frenzied scream when the pass had been completed. Tiny had finally relented and allowed Junior to go by. For a while, anyway. Lund preferred to be leading, but he, too, knew a race wasn't won on the first few laps.

Fireball Roberts and Little Joe Weatherly were having their own battle for fourth place, and the spectators had picked it up, too, waving and screaming for their favorite as they passed each section of the grandstand. The low banking of the turns was making for an abundance of beating and banging everywhere around the tight track.

Jodell was mired in a pack of cars farther back in the field. The Ford seemed eager enough to run, but the cars around him were slower, and he had been unable to find enough clear track to pass and break free of the others. Yarborough was still in front of him, seemingly running well, too, but he was also held captive by the pack of slower cars. Together, they would pick off a car here and there, making progress. But then Jodell realized that it was now Yarborough who was holding him back. Jodell gave him a couple of gentle taps on the rear bumper to let him know he was losing patience, to move aside and let the Ford eat some track.

Jodell fought to remain patient, but he could see that the leaders had continued to drive away from them. He gave Yarborough another nudge as they drove into a turn. The kid's car wiggled and seemed to break loose from the track, its rear end clearly on the verge of skewing wildly in one direction or the other. At that moment, Jodell could have tagged the vulnerable car again, sent it out of control, then driven through the hole where Yarborough had just been. Dash Rockford would certainly have played it that way. But instead, Jodell backed out of the throttle long enough to let the kid gather the car back up beneath him. And he did an admirable job of it, too. It was much too early in the race to run the risk of wrecking a fast car because of a little impatience.

Jodell, still grinding his teeth and pounding the steering wheel when he dared remove one hand, was forced to wait another couple of laps, biding his time. And sure enough, the kid finally slipped a little bit going into turn three, his car sliding upward on the track. Jodell pounced, pushing his Ford right on by through the center of the turn. The cars rubbed fenders slightly as Jodell scooted by, and they ran bumper to bumper as they raced down the track's short backstretch. Along the way, Yarborough managed to give him a good jolt in the rear end, a sure sign that he didn't appreciate getting passed. Jodell simply grinned and pulled away a few car lengths, looking for the next victim to put behind him.

Now the leaders were being held up by some slower traffic which they had already caught at the end of the field and were trying to lap, so Jodell spent the next twenty trips around the course trying to run them down, to gain serious ground on them. Fireball was up on the back end of Junior and was pushing him hard for the lead. Little Joe ran in third place, but he was having a particularly difficult time with some slower cars as the leaders pulled a dozen car lengths or so ahead of him.

By then, Jodell had caught up with Buck Baker and

was racing him hard, trying to take the sixth place away. It took some maneuvering, but he finally got around the veteran driver and set himself to run down the leaders. The car was working very well, and he had just outdueled one of the craftiest drivers in the sport.

He couldn't help it. He wondered what was about to go wrong. Would a tire blow? Would the engine start knocking and shuddering? Would one of the fool drivers in a slower car turn right into him and send him spinning just when it looked like things were finally going his way?

He swallowed hard, again forced the negative thoughts from his head, and tried to concentrate on what he could make happen. Not what might happen.

Now there was a stretch of clear track ahead of him, and that made it possible for him to run the car hard, to follow the line around the track that he wanted to run, not the one dictated by traffic. Within five laps, he drove right up onto the rear end of the fifth-place car. He hardly noticed how hot it was in the cockpit of the car, how dry his mouth was, how badly his arms ached from all the wrestling he was doing with the steering wheel as he tried to keep the car on the track at the speeds he was pushing. It seemed that all the bumps and vibrations from the track were being transmitted up through the tires, the axles, up the steering column, and directly into his arms and shoulders.

Inside the car, he inhaled the familiar perfume of blistered tire rubber, hot exhaust fumes, and burning oil. For Jodell, that was far better than the dust of the dirt tracks he had breathed so much of, but it still made it tough to get a good lungful of clean, refreshing air. He fought dizziness and tried to gulp down more air, tainted or not. The heat coming up from the exhaust beneath where he sat seemed to make the car's floorboard red-hot. It felt as if his feet were on fire through the sneakers he wore, and even the springs in his seat seemed to sear into his flesh where he sat on them.

Joe Banker was perched on a toolbox in the pits, timing the laps on his one extravagance, a double-faced Swiss stopwatch he'd bought in Daytona. Bubba Baxter stood with one foot on the wall and watched Jodell all the way around the track, never taking his eyes off the Ford. He liked to see how she looked running into and out of every turn, how she handled, how she reacted in the wind from other cars as Jodell passed. He was always looking for clues as to how he might tweak the car's setup.

Before they even realized it, they were almost sixty laps into the race. It had only been slowed once, a brief caution period after a minor spin in the first turn that damaged a couple of slower cars that had no chance anyway. The spin, with only a stalled car and no leaking fluids, had been cleared quickly. Less than five laps were run with the yellow flag waving. Once they got to racing again for a while, Joe checked his figures on a clipboard and yelled over to Bubba to be heard above the perpetual thunder of the race cars.

"We'll need to pit in another fifty laps. I don't know if the tires will hold up much past that."

"Awright! We'll be ready," Bubba hollered. He gave hand signals to Johnny and the others, indicating a stop in fifty laps, a four-tire change when Jodell came in.

"We could sure use another caution," Joe said.

Bubba read his lips as much as heard what he was saying.

"Yessir, we sure do. He can run with them guys up front if he can ever get up to them," Bubba offered. Joe nodded his agreement. He didn't say it but he was thinking that there were still too many slow cars out there, getting in everybody else's way. He would never wish for a wreck, but they could certainly use one to clear some of the rabble out of their way. Bubba seemed to read his mind. "A big old wreck might help us, but we don't want to get caught up in no wreck either."

Then he quit following the Ford, but only long enough to help Johnny Holt roll a couple of tires over by the wall to get ready.

A few minutes later their thoughts proved prophetic. Little Joe Weatherly was in the process of trying to pass the first car in a group of four lapped cars, but he wasn't getting around him as quickly as he wanted. He gave the car one bump, then a second, more powerful one. When the car didn't respond to the accepted signal that a faster car needed to get by, Weatherly simply cut the car off and motored on past. In the process, though, the slower driver panicked, oversteered, and spun, directly in front of the other three cars. The drivers, all inexperienced, piled into one another like dominoes, spinning, screeching, smoking, spraying fluids, and then finally came to a steaming stop, all crumpled together like a suddenly arranged junkyard, and virtually blocked the racetrack, collecting several other cars as they did.

Jodell Lee had been racing the fourth-place car, on the verge of moving around him, when they suddenly happened up on all the carnage on the track while it was still in motion. The car in front of him had no chance and clipped one of the whirling cars with his right front fender. That car went instantly sideways.

Jodell was following so tightly behind, he had no time to look for a way out, but merely relied on instinct to try to steer past. A lesser driver might have closed his eyes, left it to blind luck to get through, but not Jodell. He stayed true to his own reactions and somehow managed to thread a needle, to find a route through all the mess, through a hole that appeared to be only half the width of his car, and even then was still a moving escape passage.

Another couple of cars piled into the wreck before it was all over. Several of them appeared to be heavily damaged, unlikely to return to race any more this day. Bubba and Joe had their wish. The field was thinned considerably.

Pit stops were now in order. Jodell steered into the Ford's slot and took on tires and a full can of gasoline. After he had pulled back out into line behind the pace car, he could see that he was now in fourth place on the track, with Little Joe, Junior, and Fireball riding up there in front of him. He had raced these men before, knew them well from offtrack encounters, and was no longer in awe of them. But the thought that he was racing in such heady company still struck him hard. And so did the realization, once again, that he belonged here, with them.

Or even better, up there, ahead of them!

He checked his mirror as they slowly circled, waiting for the restart. There was a familiar face back there. It was Dash Rockford, who had settled in right there on Jodell's rear bumper, in fifth place. And he could even see the man's devilish grin as he suddenly drove up and bumped him hard in the rear end, backed off, then popped him again, even harder. He felt his neck pop with the impact.

"Judy, pay no attention to that maniac," he told

the Ford's windshield. "He's just trying to get our goat."

But Jodell could feel his blood pressure rising as he chafed with the slow speed under caution and in reaction to still more bumps in the rear end from the lunatic behind him. For certain, Rockford was actually only trying to make him lose his concentration, to cause him to make a bobble on the restart so he could scoot around him. And that only made Jodell more determined to get a good start of his own once the green flag waved again. If he didn't, if he hesitated or missed a gear, Rockford would likely run all over him, bulldoze him aside and be gone, leaving Jodell in the wall or the infield, licking his wounds.

He strained to concentrate, to ignore what he knew was bearing down on him from behind. He focused on the flag stand, honed in on the motion that would tell him the instant had come to stomp the accelerator and race once more. And he did just that.

It was a good jump, leaving Rockford behind, more intent on rattling Jodell Lee than in watching for the signal to resume racing. He and Little Joe Weatherly leapt ahead toward the first turn as if they had been shot from a two-barrel cannon. With a mostly clear track, Jodell was able to run right up on the rear end of Little Joe while, a couple of car lengths ahead, Fireball Roberts and Junior Johnson were battling side by side for the lead. Jodell could only imagine how the crowd must be enjoying this four-ring circus they were putting on. But he was too wrapped up in the middle of the dueling to give it more than a passing thought.

Little Joe raced hard into the third turn, not so much trying to pull away from Jodell as he was determined to run down Junior and Fireball. Jodell marveled again at how skilled a driver Weatherly was. He was as well known for his hijinks and all-night parties at every stop on the circuit as he was for his racing abilities, but the man could maneuver a stock car. No doubt about that!

And that's why it was so surprising to Jodell just then that Little Joe made a crucial bobble. Somehow, he steered a bit too hard into a turn and the car's rear end pushed out on him just a bit. He had to slow ever so slightly, and that left Jodell the best opening that he could ever hope for while racing with someone as good as Little Joe. He tucked the Ford's nose down to the inside and was past Weatherly's Mercury before he even had a chance to realize what had happened. Dash Rockford saw the same opening and followed Jodell to try to get past Weatherly as well.

By the time Dash had pulled alongside, Little Joe had been able to gather the car back up, and he had clearly decided that one car getting past at his expense was all he was going to tolerate. The two cars, the Mercury and Rockford's soot-black Ford, elbowed each other violently as they bumped along, side by side for most of a lap. But then Little Joe decided he had had enough. Or maybe he, too, had taken about all he intended to take from this jerk. With a quick twist of the steering wheel, he turned down hard into Rockford, pinching his right front fender and forcing him to lift his foot off the gas pedal or take both of them out. That allowed Little Joe to reclaim the fourth spot and sent Rockford falling back through the field, the crumpled fender rubbing against the racing tire, the car trailing a cloud of blue smoke behind it. Dash would now have to pit and bang the metal away from the tire before he could resume racing or wrecking someone.

Jodell was hardly aware of the battle behind him.

He had his sights lined up on the two lead cars. The Ford of Fireball Roberts and the Chevy of Junior Johnson ran together, in line, nose to tail. Jodell suspected that the tight racing they had been doing for the last twenty laps or so had almost certainly heated up their tires. The fact that Junior had fallen back behind Roberts and was suddenly content to run there for a while further confirmed it. Now would be the best opportunity to pass that he was likely to get.

He picked his spot and easily slid up past Junior, then nosed his way between him and the rear of Fireball's car, making it three cars running in line, well ahead of the rest of them. Junior was clearly miffed that someone had had the audacity to pick him off that easily and kept pressuring Jodell, even as he went to work on trying to get around Fireball and take over first place.

Circling quickly, they suddenly came up on the lapped car driven by another one of the stars of stock car racing, Freddy Lorenzen, as he pulled back onto the track from a stop in the pits. His "28" Ford had been one of the faster cars all day but had started overheating, sending him into the pits often to try to cool down the radiator. Lorenzen had just managed to get back up to speed when the three lead cars came barreling around. Fireball tried to take his own Ford, the "22" car, first high and then low to get around Lorenzen, but overheating or not, Lorenzen's car was simply too powerful to get past so easily.

Jodell could have predicted the next move, and he quickly decided to take advantage of it when it came. He knew that both Roberts and Lorenzen were driving cars owned by the Holman-Moody team, and Freddy was too many laps down to have any hope of winning the race.

Jodell watched for a signal he was certain was going to come. And then, there it was.

Lorenzen gave an ever-so-slight wave of his left hand, indicating to Roberts to go by on the inside as they headed into the second turn. Lorenzen suddenly moved slightly higher through the corner, allowing his teammate to get past, and was set to slide right back down and cut off Jodell as soon as his buddy was clear. Jodell yelped when he saw the wave and jumped on the accelerator as they roared out of the corner. Jodell planted himself firmly on the rear bumper of Fireball and powered right on past Lorenzen himself, forcing the "28" to drop back in line behind them and in front of Junior Johnson.

Bubba watched with a practiced eye as Jodell circled the track. Joe stood on a toolbox, clicking and checking his stopwatches, confirming what Bubba was seeing. Try as he might, Jodell could not manage to get by Roberts. The pit stops came and went along with two more short cautions demanded by minor get-togethers among the also-rans, but the two leaders stayed locked together, Fireball and Jodell, dueling, scuffling, scrapping, running hard. Little Joe, Junior, and some of the others would close up after the yellow flag periods but then fall back when the serious laps started again after each restart.

"What are his times?" Bubba yelled, even though he could see that Jodell was only a few feet off the rear bumper of Fireball's car.

"Still the same. You see anything?"

"Yep. Fireball is startin' to push in the center of the corners but not enough for Joe Dee to get by."

"I don't know. We may not get by him. He's strong!" Joe studied the watches again. The drivers were running a blistering pace.

"Just watch. He ain't set up as good as we are. He'll heat them tires up again with Jodell pushing him. Jodell will get by!"

Joe hoped the big man was right and not just being overoptimistic. Maybe they could get their first win. It had been a long enough time coming. He caught himself crossing his fingers and that made it hard to work the watches.

"Well, we got thirty more to go. Let's don't be counting our first-place money yet. Anything can happen." Joe didn't want to jinx their chances by admitting out loud that they actually had a chance. He clicked the watches again as the two lead cars flashed by in front of him. "Fireball's strong as two-day-old coffee!"

Meanwhile, back out on the track, Fireball and Jodell were approaching some slower lapped cars, including some that were still running in the top ten. And just ahead were two drivers who were running in seventh and eighth place, locked in their own private battle. One of them was Dash Rockford, and he and the eighth-place car had been swapping fenders and paint for the last dozen or so laps. Roberts closed in quickly on the duel and made a move to clear both cars before they came up on the next turn.

Fireball, with Jodell hitched to his bumper, pulled in tight on the rear car. The driver had wisely dropped in behind Rockford when he saw the leaders in his mirror. As Fireball took a run on the two cars on the front straightaway, he got inside the eighth-place car, then got a fender alongside Rockford as they approached the first turn. But suddenly, Dash chopped down hard on him, trying to cut off the assault no matter what the consequences. Jodell wasn't surprised at all by the foolhardy move. He impulsively feathered the throttle to give himself room to avoid whatever was about to happen directly in front of him.

Fireball held his line, not giving an inch. Rockford was more accustomed to drivers bending, giving way when he made such bold, reckless maneuvers. Fireball Roberts had just called his bluff, assuming any sane driver would steer away and let the faster car go on past. Dash Rockford was nowhere near a sane race car driver.

The driver's-side door of Rockford's black Chevrolet smashed hard into the front right corner of Fireball's Ford. The cars kissed hard, the metal crumpling. Fireball made the only move he could. He stomped the gas and literally pushed Rockford out of the way. The black Chevy veered high through the second turn and rammed hard head-on into the outside rail.

Somehow, Jodell had already been able to visualize exactly what was about to happen, where the geometry of the collision would send each vehicle. He went the way his intuition told him to go and was able to steer clear of the mess. For once, he was not caught up in someone else's wreck through no fault of his own. Maybe he had seen enough of such collisions at close hand that he had finally learned how to weave through them.

Dash Rockford pulled away from the wall and limped back to the pits, the right front wheel not turning at all, the fender pushed solidly back on the tire, and with something thick and black pouring from beneath the car. Fireball surely had damage, too, but he still led going down the backstretch because everyone else had braked to avoid Rockford's wrecked car. It was clear, though, that the front end of Roberts's car had been knocked out of line. Whether it was enough to slow him remained to be seen. Jodell got back up to speed and scrambled to catch up. Within the lap, before the yellow flag could hold him back, he was once again firmly attached to Fireball's rear bumper.

During the caution, while the crews spread something in the oil slick Dash Rockford had left, Jodell could only sit nervously behind the Ford's wheel and think of all the things that could go wrong between here and the checkered flag. He tried to ignore the sweat that poured down his face, and tried not to dwell on every single knock, ping, and rattle from the car. He tried to stay focused in on the bumper of Fireball's Ford, directly in front of him. He'd been looking at the same spot of black paint on the bumper for the last eighty or so laps.

Finally, they were ready to run again. And Jodell knew it was time to get the job done.

As he raced down in front of the grandstand, he glanced over to see the towering figure of Bubba Baxter holding the signboard with a big number "15" written on it.

Fifteen laps to go. Seven and a half miles. Their destiny could be played out over the next fifteen short laps.

For Jodell Bob Lee, it was now or never. Time to take care of business, to see if he actually did have what it took to make it on this level. He had long since determined that second place was not for him. If he couldn't win the game, he didn't see the point in playing. As the cars resumed racing speed and rolled quickly down into the first turn, Jodell kept his eye focused on the black spot on Fireball's rear bumper.

Fireball struggled to hold his position through the corner. His Ford wanted to go off on its own tangent, to drift high in the corner, but Roberts knew that if he allowed the car to ease up on the track at all, Jodell Lee would pounce like a hungry cat. It must have taken all the strength he could muster to simply hold the car in a line through the turn. The tires were screaming, whining, as he held the wheel tightly, with plenty of engine to run but an out-of-whack front end trying to shove the car in the wrong direction. He could see the Ford of Jodell Lee parked solidly on his rear bumper. That's when it must have occurred to Roberts that it was only a matter of time before the blue Ford rolled right on past and that there would be little he could do about it but move over and wave.

From Jodell's perspective, Roberts was merely impeding his progress to the front of the field. He knew that now was the time to get on with the race, on with their assault on big-time stock car racing. And that if he didn't, he would soon have to race Little Joe Weatherly, who was going to close the quarter-lap gap between them. If that happened, he would have his hands full for sure.

Off the corner, he finally reached out to take what was his, what should rightfully be theirs. He dove to the inside of Fireball Roberts's crippled car.

Jodell raced Fireball side by side down the back straightaway. Roberts raced him cleanly, doing all in his power to hold his car low on the track. But try as he might, the "22" car kicked upward, and Jodell pulled ahead coming out of the third turn. Once he had cleared Roberts, Jodell was gone. Now all he had to do was stay clear of all the lapped cars and pray to God that the Ford held together for a few more minutes.

Up in the stands, Catherine Lee couldn't remember the last time she had breathed. Maybe not since the last pit stop. Certainly not the entire time her husband had raced hard with Fireball Roberts. And her heart had not stopped racing since Jodell had ducked through the multicar wreck, and then again when he had jumped past a careening Dash Rockford. He seemed almost indestructible out there, charmed. Maybe they were finally, thankfully, destined to win. But she knew better than to start celebrating yet. She had actually been present a few times when it looked as if they would get their initial win, had listened to others on the radio, only to see or hear something happen to head them off yet again.

She had been there, scoring the race, when he had been running near the front in the first contest at the big track at Daytona, had even led several laps. But that time, a small part gave way and knocked them out for good. Now every lapped car Jodell came upon was another latent obstacle to their realizing their dreams. She squinted, almost closed her eyes, but then ultimately had to watch until he had safely cleared another potential disaster.

Bubba Baxter wore a broad grin as he stood confidently in his spot by the wall. He had tried to tell everyone who would listen that they could take this race, and now they were about to do just that thing. Three more laps. As long as he kept his eyes on the Ford race car he had helped build, so long as he followed him all the way around, there was no way Jodell was going to lose this race. He crossed his arms in dismissal of all the rest of them. This one was won!

Joe Banker timed every lap. He allowed himself a slight smile. The interval between Jodell and Little Joe Weatherly, now back in second place after taking over from Roberts, had continued to grow by a couple of tenths of a second per lap. There were only a few lapped cars that he had to get around in the last two circuits.

Two laps!

Jodell certainly wasn't celebrating yet in the stifling cockpit of the Ford. He was still concentrating intently on hitting his marks, on driving smoothly through the corners, on allowing plenty of room when he whirled past the slower cars. He knew one moment's inattention could be disastrous, one slight burp in the engine a hint of a major malfunction that could snatch the victory away when it seemed so close to being in his grasp.

He started to pray, first asking forgiveness for missing church that morning. And asking that Joe's engine would hold together this time. And that they could somehow remain humble in the face of such long-delayed success.

Then, as if in answer to at least some of his prayers, as he came out of the fourth turn, Jodell could see the white flag in the flagman's hand. And he realized the flagman was showing it to him!

One lap!

The last lap rolled by as if in some kind of weird slow-motion sequence on the big movie screen at the Foothill Theater back in Chandler Cove. He caught up with a couple of lapped cars that were racing side by side for position, jockeying for place money. A quick glance in the mirror confirmed that there was no one close behind, so he eased up and gave the two cars plenty of room to make their run to the finish. His heart seemed to be beating in time with the pistons in the Ford's powerful engine as he rolled off the final turn and pointed the nose of the car toward the checkered flag, waving like a mirage in the distance.

Jodell didn't actually see the flag flying overhead as

he flew beneath the stand. His eyes had already filled with tears.

Homer Williams had been somewhere in the pits, studying the carcass of a wrecked race car, when someone recognized him from the Ford's pits.

"Hey, ain't you the sponsor of that car of Bob Lee's?"

"Yes. My company is. Bubble Up soda," he answered proudly.

"You're about to win the race, you know."

Williams's eyes grew big and he hustled back to the pits. But the area was deserted. Joe, Bubba, Johnny, and the rest of the crew were nowhere to be seen, so he followed the crowd. He assumed the race had ended already because most of the constant roar of the engines had suddenly ceased and now he could clearly hear the cheers of the crowd reverberating around the grandstand.

Williams stopped suddenly, a panic spreading through him. The big Bubble Up sign and all the cases of soda he had brought over from the plant, just in case they won, were still in the trunk of his Caddie. And the car was parked outside the gates of the track. But then he remembered the extra case of Bubble Up he had brought in for the crew, the one they had hardly had time to touch in the frenzy of the race. It still waited underneath a tarp next to the tool chest. He grabbed it, lifted it to his shoulder in a move he had first learned while working in the distribution warehouse as a kid, and trotted off to wherever everyone else had gone.

Jodell was actually finishing his victory lap just then. It was still hard for him to believe he had finally won a race against the best there was. Then he had his own burst of panic. Something awful had just occurred to him. He didn't know the way to Victory Lane!

Catherine was getting strange looks from all the people around her in the grandstand. She was still jumping, squealing, and hugging everybody who would stand still. Several of the other drivers' wives finally grabbed her and pointed her toward Victory Lane after congratulating her. They seemed genuinely excited, sharing her enthusiasm. Some of them remembered their own first victories, and if their husbands couldn't take the race, they were glad to see a popular driver like Jodell get his initial win. As Catherine made her way to where she could see the car parked amid a mob of people, she couldn't help but notice that the crowd was still cheering—for her husband, for the race he and the others had put on.

Jodell pulled up to the start/finish line. People were everywhere and he was worried he might run over someone, but they parted and made way for him as he steered through the throng. Finally, he pulled to a stop, shut off the engine, and began trying to unbuckle the restraining belts. They finally popped loose, but when he tried to climb out the window, he fell back, exhausted, his strength sapped by the heat and from wrestling with the steering wheel for the last several hours. The people who were swarming all around the car were urging him to come on out and claim his trophy, but he suddenly felt too weak to move. He slumped back down in the seat for a second to try to catch his breath, to find the strength to climb out of the car.

Suddenly a pair of giant hands reached in through the open window and grabbed him under his arms. The next thing he knew he was being hoisted out through the open window and set down on his feet by a grinning Bubba Baxter. And before he could get his balance, Jodell was wrapped up in a massive bear hug that threatened to smother him and leave him with some broken ribs. When Bubba finally let him go, Joe Banker stepped in to give him a slap on the back and a big wink.

"I just appreciate you not breaking my motor again," he said, grinning, then he slapped him on the back again.

"We won! We won!" Bubba kept screaming hoarsely, over and over, as he alternately hugged Jodell, Joe, Johnny, and pure strangers who happened to be standing too close by.

"Praise the Lord. What a ride! What a ride!" Jodell yelled as he tried to get his breath.

Finally, he took a leap up onto the hood of the Ford and acknowledged the continuing cheers from the huge crowd that seemed to still be growing. He was doing an impromptu jig when he spotted Catherine trying to make her way across the track to where he stood triumphantly. He immediately jumped down off the hood and pushed his way over to her, swept her up into his arms, and gave her a deep kiss. She hung on to his neck as he swung her around and carried her back to the car, then sat her down and kissed her once again. She didn't seem to mind the sweat and grease and tire dust that covered his face and driving uniform.

"Jodell Bob Lee, Grand National winner!" she sang, savoring the sound of the words as they rolled off her tongue. Then she looked deeply into his eyes and told him, "I am so proud of you, honey."

The checkered flag and the race trophy were produced from somewhere, and the track photographer tried to pose everyone. That's when Homer Williams came running up with the case of Bubble Up and set it up on the roof of the car. He was beaming, clearly pleased, and he joined in with all the hugging and backslapping that was going on. Finally, the presentation of the trophy was made, followed by a kiss from the beauty queen. The track announcer interviewed Jodell over the public address system though later Jodell could not remember a single thing he had told the crowd, even though he had secretly practiced his winning words a hundred times. Words he had rehearsed working alone beneath a race car, when bringing up the rear of the field in a struggling car, driving along lonely highways between tracks at odd hours of the night while the others slept.

Suddenly, someone grabbed one of the bottles of Bubble Up and started shaking it, then sprayed it everywhere. Before anyone knew what was happening, bottles were open and were spewing all over the place. Jodell looked as if he had been dipped in a vat of Bubble Up, his long, black hair soaked and wild, but he never lost his grin. The crowd milling around the car pulled back from the soda bath, but they set up another round of cheers as Jodell and the crew danced in the shower. In the mist of green spray, newspaper photographers were snapping away, and the photos would run on the sports pages of newspapers all over the South the next day. The bottles of soda would show up clearly.

The celebration went on for a while, but Joe left the others long enough to watch while the race officials tore the car down for the postrace inspection. He couldn't relax and truly savor the win until he was sure it was official, that the car had passed the checklist and the victory had been certified. Finally, a good two hours after the race had been completed, one of the officials smiled and signaled to him that the car had passed. At that point, Joe Banker knew for sure that no matter what else might happen, they had won a major stock car race. He jogged back to join the party, to give the news about the passed inspection, and to see if maybe some of the ladies would like to meet the chief mechanic of a winning race team.

The party by now had moved back to the pits and to the tow car, where everyone was just beginning to reluctantly reload the tools and parts. It seemed none of them was in a hurry to leave this place of their triumph. Many of the drivers stopped by and offered their sincere congratulations on the first of what they all said would be many wins. Even a disappointed Fireball Roberts came by to shake Jodell's hand, to slap Joe and Bubba on their backs.

"That was a good race you drove, man," Fireball told Jodell as he offered his hand.

"Thanks. I thought my car was maybe a tick faster but I just couldn't get a good run at you."

"Well, I know you could have pushed me out of the way, but you didn't. Thanks for running me clean. That's the way to win a race. Driving hard but driving clean."

"Speaking of which, that was a tough bit of luck you had with Rockford."

A dark cloud seemed to cross Fireball's face, but then he grinned.

"I guess it was just my turn. That idiot has wrecked just about everybody else but me."

"Still, I hate it for you. He sure got me good a time or two, and I knew what kind of snake he could be."

"I was just on my way over there to pay the old boy a visit, maybe have a little prayer meetin' with him," Fireball said. "That is, if he hasn't done slunk off to that hole he crawled out of. But hey, don't let any of that take away from your first win, Jodell. You'll get plenty more. And I intend to do all I can to keep you from it!"

Fireball was still smiling as he walked away, but his stride had a purpose about it. He seemed fully intent on straightening out Mr. Dash Rockford.

As the others sat talking, reliving the race, Jodell quietly rose, walked over to the trunk of the tow car, and pried open a crate in the trunk. He pulled from it a half-gallon Mason jar that was nearly full of a clear liquid. It was a sample of his grandfather's corn liquor. For a moment, he flashed back to the many dark nights when he and Papa Lee had worked the still, high up on the mountain above the farmhouse. To the runs he had made through the mountains, trying to stay a step ahead of the revenuers, who would have put them out of business if given the chance. But he had won that battle night after night, races that were just as crucial in their own way as the one this afternoon had been. Now, this jar of his grandpa's 'shine was the only thing he had to show for those times.

Not much of a trophy, he thought. He glanced at the race trophy he had just been presented, still wrapped in the checkered flag that had flown over his victory. He decided he liked the flag-draped one better anyhow.

"Boys! You too, Cath," Jodell yelled, showing them the jar full of moonshine. "Me and Papa Lee made this years ago. I believe he would think it was appropriate for us to use it for a little toast to winning big-time."

Jodell screwed the lid off the jar and took a sip of the fiery liquid, then passed it in turn to Bubba, Joe, and the others. They all solemnly took their turn at the jar, including Homer Williams, who was still hanging around, savoring the win. Catherine even took a tiny taste, tried not to make a face, then smiled as she passed the jar on to the next person in line.

That's when Little Joe Weatherly came wandering up as if he might have been attracted by the scent of a little white whiskey on the breeze.

"Jodell, I hope you appreciate me letting you win your first race today," he said, his face as serious as a preacher's. "Even though it was clear to everybody that I had the fastest car out there."

Jodell laughed out loud. The couple of drops of Grandpa Lee's blend had left him with a warm glow already. He was in the perfect mood to spar with the little man.

"Fastest car? Last thing I remember was catching a glimpse of you every once in a while in my rearview mirror. Least, I think it was you. You was so far back there I had trouble making out the number."

"Well, I hate to say it, but I was feeling sorry for you 'cause you ain't never won one, so I decided that I would let you get a taste of what it's like." Then he seemed to finally notice the jar making the rounds. "And speaking of a taste . . ." He smacked his lips as he accepted the fruit jar, tried a swig of the home brew, then nodded appreciatively. "That's some mighty fine Kool-Aid, Jodell. Now, I got to get along so I can get ready to win another race next week, but I wanted you to know how proud we all are of you. I'm looking forward to running you in the ground for many years to come, old buddy."

But he didn't leave. Even as he was saying his good-byes, he sat back on the tow trailer and helped finish off the whiskey, doing most of the finishing himself, all the while telling stories of his past exploits on and off the track.

Jodell, Joe, and Bubba set to work loading all the things that had to be loaded, but they listened to Little Joe talk, too. He was a walking history of the sport, and they never failed to learn something when he was around, or to be entertained by him. If they could get past all the bluster and embellishment, that is.

As he worked and listened, Jodell couldn't believe how wonderful he felt despite the soreness and fatigue. And it wasn't merely the liquor and the win that had done it. Nor the continual parade of autograph seekers who stopped by to tap him on the shoulder.

He finally felt a part of all that was racing, as if he had been baptized by the victory. And he was proud to know that people like Weatherly and Turner and Roberts and Petty and Johnson were as much his friends as they were his rivals on the track. It was a tight-knit fraternity, but he was now a full-fledged member of it in good standing.

He had had his long initiation, but he was finally one of them. And he couldn't wait for the next chance to prove to them all that he and his crew actually belonged in their lodge, that his race that day was no fluke.

Just before he finally stood to leave, Little Joe held up the final few drops of whiskey in the jar and made his own toast.

"Here's to a long, long, long time of me and you runnin' against each other, buddy. And may you live long enough to someday beat me again!"

Then he drained the jar and ceremoniously licked the rim.

SAVORING VICTORY

Late that night, the three-car victory procession noisily made its way back toward Chandler Cove. They were blowing their horns at sleeping cows and horses, waving wildly, and blinking their headlights at every car they met, letting the closed-up stores and deserted crossroads towns know a real, live stock car champion was passing through. The intoxicating buzz of their first victory had rendered all of them half drunk, mostly delirious.

Homer Williams led the way in his big Cadillac. He usually jokingly called the car "the White Hearse," but it was far from a somber vehicle this trip. Joe Banker, Bubba Baxter, and Johnny Holt rode along with him, the car's deep-voiced radio cranked up painfully loud. They were tapping into a case of ice-cold beer somebody had given them as congratulations for winning the race.

Jodell and Catherine followed closely behind in the tow car. Except for the race car following along obediently behind, they were truly by themselves for the first time in a while. Jodell didn't mind driving or begrudge the boys the good time they were having up there ahead of them. He knew Homer didn't drink anything stronger than Bubble Up and would remain sober. And he knew, too, that they had all worked awfully hard for the better part of five years to accomplish what they had finally achieved on this day.

Or, in reality, had achieved yesterday. It was already past midnight, into Monday morning. The farmhouses they passed were dark, the people sleeping inside them only a few hours away from rising for the first workday of the week.

"Reckon any of these folks know who's passing them by?" Jodell asked Catherine.

"No, but I bet they think it's either the Second Coming or the circus parade coming through." She laughed.

One of the men in the Caddy was, at that moment, leaning out the right side of the car, tossing a beer bottle at an innocent road sign, screeching like a banshee all the while. The four men had told and retold one another the story of their first big-time win, embellishing the tale to the point that soon it was a fact that they had led the race from the get-go and had won it going away. And they were now the greatest stock car race team to have ever graced a track. By the time they made the final run into Chandler Cove, showing up for all the races next year was only a formality, and they might just as well send the championship trophy on down to East Tennessee right now and get it over with.

Homer Williams pulled into the closed-up gas station in the middle of Chandler Cove to let Joe, Bubba, and Johnny climb out. But he crawled out to hug them all once more, to shake Jodell's hand.

"Boys, next time you're in town between races, I'm gonna take all of y'all out to Sadie's Roadhouse for the biggest steak you can imagine."

"I don't know, Homer. I can imagine a mighty big hunk of cow," Bubba said wistfully, doing just that as he blissfully licked his lips.

"Son, if you can eat two of Sadie's big T-bones then I will buy you two. If it takes three of 'em to fill you up, then we will make it three. I want you to keep your strength up. What do you think about that?"

"I think you better not wave raw meat in front of a hungry bear," Jodell interrupted, laughing as he stepped into the glow cast by the Caddy's headlights.

"Besides," Joe Banker interjected, "if you buy Bubba a steak every time we win a race from now on, you gonna go broke or they'll run out of cows!"

They laughed, slapped each other on their backs some more, and finally said their good-nights. All of them seemed reluctant to leave the mutual admiration society they had just formed but it was late and getting later. Johnny crawled into his own car, parked in the shadows of the service station's shop building, while Jodell, Catherine, Bubba, and Joe climbed back into the Ford and headed for Grandma's house. Bubba and Joe had left their own cars behind the barn-shop there and a freshly made bed would be waiting upstairs for Jodell and Cath. Homer Williams, silhouetted in the Cadillac's headlights, was still waving happily at them as they drove away.

According to the deejay on the radio, it was after two in the morning when they pulled into the driveway to the farm. Even from the main highway they could see immediately that all the lights were blazing throughout Grandma's house.

"Something's up," Jodell said quietly. Grandma Lee never burned an unnecessary light. The last time Jodell had returned home in the wee hours to a brightly lit house had been the night Grandpa Lee had died. He shivered slightly and pulled Catherine closer as a dull dread swept over him.

"Why's Joyce here?" Bubba asked, his nose against the glass of the Ford's window. His wife's car was parked beneath the big walnut tree, near the freshly dug foundation of the house Jodell and Catherine had started building above the barn. Other cars were parked about, too.

Then they could see a crowd of people on the front porch of Grandma's house, but they hardly seemed to be in the mood for a wake. There was Grandma and Joyce and a crew of other smiling, familiar faces, waving, whooping, and hollering as Joe steered the old Ford and its tow to a stop in the yard. As they all spilled from the car, the crowd rushed to meet them and there was the unmistakable sound of fiddles and a banjo and a mandolin cranking up a mountain hoedown.

The victory party was now officially off and running!

They were still playing, dancing, laughing, and singing when the sun peeked over the brow of Chandler Mountain. Inside, Grandma Lee got busy with her giant iron skillets, cooking a massive breakfast for the assemblage. Over eggs and sausage and flapjacks, Jodell retold for the hundredth time how he had come from behind to win the previous day's race, adding a firsthand viewpoint to how everyone in the house had heard it described on the radio.

For a little while, then, he forgot how bone tired he was, how numbed his brain had become, maybe as much from the constant praise he was hearing as from the gnawing fatigue. When his head finally hit the pillow, it was nearly lunchtime. He pulled Catherine close to him, but he was dead to the world before he could even tell her again how much he loved her.

FOLLOW-UP ACT

Their excitement had hardly subsided at all by the time they met Homer Williams at Sadie's for the victory dinner he had promised them. It had been a busy week already. Still operating on race-winning adrenaline, Jodell, Joe, and Bubba had spent most of the week in the shop getting the cars ready for the next run of three contests. They would race at Martinsville, Virginia; at Moyock, North Carolina, just south of Norfolk; then come back to North Wilkesboro, all in the course of a week. They would get to spend one night at home after the Moyock race since North Wilkesboro was only a couple of hours across the mountains from Chandler Cove in North Carolina.

Jodell was already waking up nights in a sweat, though, worrying about the last race of the trio, the one that would be so close to home. Unfortunately, someone had let slip that a flock of family and friends would be driving over for the race. Homer Williams was planning on bringing a busload of his best customers as well to show off Jodell and the car that Bubble Up sponsored.

During the dinner at the steakhouse, Williams talked excitedly about what a great opportunity it would be to be able to bring some of his key accounts to see the Bubble Up car run and win.

"Y'all are going to win, aren't you, Jodell?" he asked between bites of steak.

Everyone else nodded animatedly and assured him loudly that they would do that very thing. Jodell only smiled and said, "We'll do our dead level best."

Bubba Baxter had wanted to order two steaks to start with, but Jodell had kept him from it. However, the big man did claim one full bucket of peanuts on the table as his very own and left all the rest of them, all six of them, the other bucket.

Joyce and Catherine sat together talking at one end of the table, while the rest of them discussed cars, racing setups, and tracks. Homer listened attentively, still in awe at being so close to serious racing. He even threw in a comment or two here and there, and Jodell, Joe, and the rest accepted his thoughts gracefully, humoring him.

"I do feel good about Martinsville," Jodell said. "It's a lot like the track we won on this week. Same surface, and the turns are almost identical, just a tad tighter, and the straightaways are a hair longer."

"I don't think we'll have to change the setup we got under the car a whit," Bubba agreed through a mouthful of biscuit.

"What do you mean by 'setup,' boys?" Homer asked.

Joe and Bubba were only too glad to explain all the details that went into getting the car's suspension, tires, and other elements properly aligned to make it handle well on different types of tracks in varying racing conditions. Homer ate it all up as surely as he did his rare steak and home fries. He loved all the racing talk. Even though he'd sponsored the car for several years now, he had never seemed to have the time he wanted to actually roll up his sleeves and get involved at the track. He lived for the weekly calls from Catherine in which she would update him on how the boys had done at that week's race. She could give him far more detail than he could get from the newspaper or from the description on the radio if he was lucky enough to be able to hear a broadcast. This first win had him primed, ready to try to squeeze more racing into his schedule.

As they attacked the thick steaks, mountain of potatoes, and endless supply of homemade biscuits, Joe and Johnny talked about their plans for rebuilding the Ford's engine. Joe was of the opinion that they had been lucky to even finish, let alone win the last race, considering the motor they had cobbled together out there in the dust and dirt of the infield just in time to qualify.

While the rest of the crew began literally talking the engine apart, lining up salt and pepper shakers to show where everything would go, Jodell and Homer Williams finally got around to talking business. Jodell had known it would be inevitable that they did. He had heard through the grapevine that business was suffering lately over at the bottling plant. He needed some firm idea of what the plans were for next year's sponsorship. And tonight, still flush from their first win, while they all hovered over rare slabs of beef and all the fixings, it seemed like the best time to run that torturous lap. To see what they actually had under the hood, so to speak.

There were plans that had to be made since they intended running in all the next season's events, including a painfully expensive trip way out to Riverside, California, early in the year. If Bubble Up money was not going to be there for them, they either had to find someone else to bankroll them or risk being left sitting inert on the starting line while everyone else left them in their dust.

Bubba Baxter had facetiously suggested they rob a bank. Jodell Lee wasn't totally ruling it out. He was that desperate to keep running, to keep winning.

When Homer paused to chew a big bite of steak, Jodell saw a narrow opening in the conversation and he dived in, like splitting two cars on the track.

"So how are things in the soft drink business, Homer?"

Williams chewed deliberately and swallowed before replying.

"Jodell, to be honest with you, they are getting mighty tough. We're running into more and more competition every day. It's not like the old days, when I could sell all I could bottle." He took a big swig of his iced tea, then winked. "I got to tell you, though. That win last week gave us a good bump in sales. I got to the plant Monday, there was folks actually calling us up on the telephone, wanting to take more cases of soda. Been a while since that's happened, I'll tell you!"

"You don't say," Jodell said in amazement. It was still hard for him to believe that people would actually buy more soda simply because a country boy with a particular logo on the side of a car had won a stock car race. He was tickled they did, but he was amazed, too.

"Folks love to go with a winner, Jodell. Even the board members were in a good mood for a change yesterday when I showed them the orders."

"Well, I'm glad we finally did our part," Jodell mumbled humbly, then put down his fork and tapped Williams on the shoulder sincerely. "You've been mighty good to us, Homer. We would have never gotten this far without all the help you've given us."

"That's the purpose of this little business relationship of ours, Mr. Lee. We want to help you race to win, and we can only hope that you help us sell a lot of soda along the way. That's why we do it. Aw, I'll admit I like hanging around the races and being in the pits, getting in the way and all. I sincerely like all the folks I'm meeting at the tracks. But you better believe that if we don't move some bottles of pop, we got to go do something else with that money to make sure we do."

"And we know we can do a better job for you and Bubble Up if we win. And believe me, we intend to win some more."

Jodell stabbed a French fry with his fork for emphasis, dipped it in ketchup, and popped it into his mouth. He listened to Joe talking about timing settings and Joyce Baxter describing some friend's precious new baby, and waited for Williams to bring up the inescapable.

"Jodell, let's talk about next year," Homer finally said.

Those were the words, all right, but Jodell wasn't sure he wanted to hear the next sentence. Would it be: "Jodell we love you and the boys, but we can't afford to sponsor you next year?" Or, "Sorry, but we got to cut way back on what we can give you?" He could only nod, chew, and wait to hear for himself.

"Jodell, I want to be honest with you," Williams started. He even set his fork down beside his plate and wiped his mouth with his napkin. This was going to be serious. "Times at the plant are starting to get tough, but I think I can see things picking up by the middle of next year. Summer's our best time anyway. The truth is, much as I hate it, I can't promise you all of next year. But I can at least agree to advance you enough money to get y'all through the middle of the year."

Jodell realized he had been holding his breath, as if he had just steered through a tight stretch on the track. It wasn't all he could have hoped for. But, thank God, they weren't dead in the water. They could start the year! Then, if they won, it might be much easier for Homer Williams to help them finish it.

"We appreciate that, Homer," Jodell said, as calmly as he could manage. He really wanted to let out a whoop and dance Homer around the table a time or two. "I can understand your position, as poor as we've been running. But you can bet that now that we've got our first taste of a win, we sure don't want to go back down."

"No, let me finish. This has nothing to do with how y'all been running. You showed last week the reasons why we sponsored you in the first place. It's just that the business is not what we need it to be at the moment to keep spending this much money on advertising in this manner. One of our board members owns a radio station and can't understand why we don't put the money in commercial spots. Or on some of the new television shows like the big boys do. They just don't see the push we get out of being all over that blue Ford out there, circling the track in front of thousands of thirsty race fans."

"Well, we intend to have your name all over Victory Lane everywhere we go from now on. We're aware that we've got a tough follow-up act to what we did this week. But you've got to know how much I hate anything from second on back."

"I know. I know. Now, that's enough talk about business. We came all the way out here to celebrate. Let's have a toast! To the first of many more victories!"

Glasses were raised and they all toasted their bright collective futures. Catherine smiled at Jodell from the other end of the table. She must have been able to tell from the look on his face that the conversation with Williams had, at least, not gone badly. He tipped his glass in her direction and smiled back at her.

"To the greatest race team in the business!" Joe Banker cried, and they all clinked iced tea glasses and drank deeply.

"To the best wrench and the best setup man and the best pit crew man in racing," Homer Williams shouted, nodding toward Joe and Bubba and Johnny. They all bawled their agreement.

"To the best couple of wives any racers could ever want . . . Joyce and Catherine!" Bubba roared. They all whooped as the women turned crimson.

"To the best stock car driver on the planet, Jodell Bob Lee!" Johnny Holt yelled, and most of the other diners in Sadie's joined in with the salute.

Jodell could only blush and grin. Then he caught Bubba trying to order another steak from the waitress. He cuffed the big man on the shoulder and waved her off. If Bubble Up money was going to be tight, he was going to start saving it right then and there! Bubba scowled at him, then sat back and used a piece of biscuit to sop up the remaining juice from the first huge slab of meat.

REALITY

I t didn't take cold, brutal reality long to assert itself. Jodell qualified well at Martinsville, and for a wonderful moment, he even thought he might have gotten the pole. But then Junior Johnson toured the track in a blistering qualifying lap. Joe Weatherly was chasing his second straight championship, and he qualified well, too, and then along came several others who made Jodell's lap look slow in comparison.

From that point onward, they found themselves behind the curve for the rest of the weekend. They were tantalizingly close to being very fast, but they couldn't quite seem to get the car set up like Jodell wanted it. They wrestled with the right-side suspension and the front-end geometry, trying to dial it in exactly right. But it took them until the very last practice before they finally got it correct. At last Jodell was finally one of the fastest cars on the track, and just in time for the race. Again, after starts and stops, they thought they were in good shape for the contest.

Then, the race started well, with Jodell immediately making a run for the front of the field. By the thirtieth lap he was in fourth place, pushing the third-place car of Little Joe Weatherly hard, angling for the position. Little Joe dipped down to the inside to pass a slower car while Jodell tucked in tight on his rear bumper to follow him past. But then, before he could even react, the slower car got loose, lost traction, and clipped Jodell as he tried to slip by. That sent him spinning 'round and 'round in a sickening twirl.

Somehow, Jodell got the car straightened out without hitting anything, and spun it back around, amazingly heading in the right direction. He gunned the engine disgustedly and spun off, ignoring the appreciation of the wildly cheering crowd, and tried to catch up with the back of the field.

He hated it back there, bringing up the rear, knowing he had to make up all that hard-won ground all over again. He despised the view of nothing but butt ends of race cars, the taste of their tire grit in his teeth, the smell of their exhausts fouling his nostrils. Hated it!

As the green flag waved again, Jodell took off like a man possessed. He ran even harder than before, pushing himself and the Ford lap after lap, driving as deeply as he dared into the corners, aggressively jumping on the gas again well before the others thought it prudent. And it worked. He steadily made his way back toward the top ten.

With a hundred laps to go, it looked as if he might salvage a good finish yet. Driving down into the first turn, Jodell tried to steer inside a slower car, then outbrake him to the corner. He set his line and hit the brakes hard. He knew instantly, in a sickening moment, that something was seriously wrong.

The brake pedal went all the way to the floorboard, and the car, seemingly with a mind of its own, sailed full speed toward the outer wall of the track. In that fraction of a second, Jodell had to react or collide headforemost with the immovable retaining wall. Somehow, he managed to at once climb off the gas, find the clutch and gearshift, and steer into some semblance of a controlled slide, then shift down and ease off on the clutch to regain dominance over the car. Amazingly, he merely kissed the wall gently and bounced back down, but not enough to get in the way of all the other cars that now whizzed past below him.

Of course, with no brakes, all hopes for a good finish had evaporated. He limped home a distant thirtieth, many laps off the pace. Freddy Lorenzen claimed the win. Little Joe Weatherly drove his Bud Moore car home in third place, three laps down. Another young driver, David Pearson, took his Cotton Owens Ford to fourth place. Richard Petty rounded out the top five in his number "43" Plymouth.

Things didn't get much better in the swamp in far eastern North Carolina. The locals called the tight quarter-mile dirt track in Moyock "the Dog Track Speedway." Jodell had even more colorful names for it before they left the place behind.

"Three hundred laps around in that dirt is gonna make for one long evening," Joe observed. "Hope you brung plenty of temper, Joe Dee, 'cause I expect it's gonna be in short supply directly."

Jodell wasn't looking forward to the short dirt track. The more he ran on the newly paved speedways, the more he felt that he was in his element on asphalt.

And the less comfortable he felt spinning and spewing in the dirt.

One of the first things Jodell did when they pulled into the makeshift garage area was look to see if Dash Rockford had shown up for the race. This was the perfect track for Rockford's rough driving style, and there wouldn't be a fender intact by midnight if he was going to be in the race this night. That is, unless someone politely put the fool into the wall before he could do any serious damage to anyone else. Luckily, he seemed to be nowhere near.

The tight track and the quality of the competition made qualifying tough. The best Jodell could do was seventeenth out of the twenty-five or so cars that made the race. And that was despite the fact that several of the others broke loose on their own qualifying laps, a couple of them almost losing it altogether.

"What's the problem, Joe Dee?" Joe asked him as he pulled in from the disappointing qualifying run.

"The track's slick as ice," Jodell reported. "The groove's worn down so much it's like polished marble out there. And then, you get too high and it's bye-bye time with all that loose dirt up there on the high side."

Jodell knew that with the short, tight corners, it would be hard not to get caught up too high on the track, skating out of control. Spins would be commonplace.

And the race was exactly as he expected it to be. The traffic on the tight track was jammed together, nobody able to get out of anyone else's way. Within forty laps, Jodell had the leaders parked right on his rear bumper, trying to pass him while he was boxed in by weaker cars that he couldn't get enough clear track to work around. It wasn't long before Jodell started using the "chrome horn," a nudge with the car's bumper, to try to move people out of the way.

And it worked. The tactic helped clear him a path around the slower cars but it certainly didn't win him any new friends out on the track. Then, everyone else was doing it as well.

Even then, because of cautions and spins, he continued to fall farther and farther behind. To add insult to injury, every time Little Joe Weatherly came up behind him, ready to zoom past and put him another lap down, he gave Jodell a bone-jarring *whap* in the rear first. Jodell could only grip the wheel tighter and try to drive a little harder. But he knew that the harder he drove, the slower he would go because he kept breaking the car loose in the dirt, losing traction, spinning his wheels in the corners.

Ned Jarrett fought fiercely with Little Joe over the last few laps of the race, to the great delight of the sizable crowd that was there to watch them. When the checkered flag finally fell, he'd beaten Little Joe to the line for the victory, but it kept the Virginian on track for his championship. Jodell took little pleasure in his friend's finish. Once again, he had eaten far too much of his opponents' dust to be happy about much of anything else.

Jodell was a mess when he climbed out through the open window of the race car. He looked as if someone had dumped a big sack of flour all over him, completely covered with powdery dust except for the area around his eyes where the goggles had shielded them. He slammed his helmet down on top of the race car and tried to slap the dust off himself and his racing uniform, but that only resulted in a coughing and sneezing fit, and in disgust, he gave a swift kick to the Ford's left-front wheel.

Bubba pulled up his wagon then, loaded with equipment to carry it back to the trailer. Joe and Johnny were close behind but they wisely waited a moment before speaking while Jodell finished his coughing spasms and danced around a bit on his now-throbbing foot.

Joe finally dared to get close enough to hand Jodell a wet towel.

"Tough race, Cuz."

"Dammit, Joe. Them slow cars were all over the track in my way. I don't think I got a clean run at anybody all night long."

"I know."

"What difference does it make if we got a fast car if we can't get around all the slow ones? Dammit, Joe! I can't tell you how frustrating it is!"

"Here," Bubba said, passing him a cold bottle of Bubble Up.

He took the offered soda and held the icy, damp glass against the side of his face before he finally took a long swig. Then he wiped his face with the towel as he slowly slid down next to the dust-caked race car. His muscles still twitched spasmodically from wrestling with the steering wheel, and the bottle of pop seemed to weigh as much as an anvil. He could only imagine what a sorry, used-up sight he must make, sitting there dejectedly after losing yet another dismal race that he had been certain he had the car and the driving skills to win easily.

Just then, a man approached the car timidly, accompanied by a boy who appeared to be about ten years old. The boy clutched a souvenir program in one hand and a ballpoint pen in the other. Jodell didn't pay them much attention, assuming they only wanted to check the car's number through the dust

or the name scripted over the driver's window, to see
if it might belong to someone famous, a Petty or a
Baker or a Flock or somebody else who was a winner.

"Will you autograph my son's program?" the man
finally asked haltingly. The boy swallowed hard and
stepped closer, then bashfully shoved the program and
pen toward Jodell. "Please."

At first, Jodell didn't realize the man was talking to
him. He took another big draw on the soda, then
comprehended that the boy was holding the program
out to him to sign.

Why, he thought, would someone want my autograph after the miserable race I ran tonight?

"Please?" the boy asked.

"Sure," Jodell mumbled, a little embarrassed that
the kid had had to ask again. "Be glad to."

He took the offered program and neatly signed his
name on the cover. As an afterthought, he added his
car's number beneath his signature. The kid stood
there wide-eyed as Jodell signed.

"Thank you, Mr. Lee!" the boy sang excitedly,
carefully clutching the freshly signed program to his
chest so as not to smear the fresh ink.

"You sure done a good job in that race a couple
of weeks back, Mr. Lee." The daddy grinned. "I listened to the whole thing on the radio."

"Yeah, we had a good car that day," Jodell said,
beaming and reliving for a moment the glory of being
in the winner's circle that day.

Suddenly, he didn't feel quite so tired and dirty. He
stood up as tall and straight as he could and leaned
back against the side of the race car. With a sudden
impulsive flourish, he lifted the boy and set him down
inside the car, behind the wheel in the driver's seat,
and he pointed out the steering wheel, the gearshift,

the instruments. The daddy merely stood back with a huge grin on his face.

And then he was interrupted over and over again by others who wanted him to sign autographs. Jodell stood there patiently, taking time to talk to each person, to answer all the questions.

"We got to load this car up, son," Bubba finally said as he gently picked the kid up out of the driver's seat.

Jodell walked the boy out of the way as Bubba climbed back into the race car and started it up. The kid's mouth fell open when the loud, powerful engine roared back to life.

Jodell stood there a while longer, signing more programs, answering questions, talking away with people who seemed genuinely interested in him and what he did and what he had to say. It was clear that one visit to Victory Lane had led to more attention than the previous five years of driving combined had garnered. And it was clear, too, that it could become addictive.

Nearby, Richard Petty's crew was loading up his Plymouth while Richard himself stood by, patiently signing autographs for the dozen or so fans who formed a circle around him. Jodell marveled at how at ease he was with the fans. He moved in beside Petty and congratulated him on his good finish.

"Richard, how do you do it? You got to be as dog tired as I am but you stay so patient with all of these people."

"Jodell, you got to treat 'em like they're your kin. When these cats quit coming around wanting your autograph, you'll know you're washed up. You better remember, too, that they are the ones who pay the money to buy the tickets to come see you and me ride around out there. They quit spending their hard-earned paydays, we don't got a show for too much longer."

"You're right, Richard. I'm not used to all the attention, I guess."

"You win you a couple of more races and those cats won't leave you alone. Learn to enjoy it." He smiled his trademark wide grin and signed his big, round signature on the cast on a little boy's broken arm that had been thrust his way.

Jodell thought more about what Richard had said as he helped the rest of them pack up the equipment. Petty would still be standing there, signing and talking, even when the rest of them had stowed their gear, trailered their cars, and pulled away from the track. The attention of the race fans was only one other thing Jodell had learned to love about this sport. And as with everything else about the game, it was miles better, tons sweeter, if he won.

And like so many times before when he had ended a disappointing day, the frustration had galvanized his resolve to excel, steeled his conviction to be the very best that he could be at this racing thing.

And he vowed to start doing just that with the very next race, even if he killed himself doing it.

HARD LICK

The crowd for the North Wilkesboro race the following Sunday showed up typically early, determined to not miss a minute of the day's show. The track, tucked neatly into the mountains of northwestern North Carolina, was unique. The course actually ran downhill into the first turn and then climbed uphill again through the backstretch and toward the third and fourth turns. And fans could be found spread out everywhere around the property.

Jodell's prerace nervousness was reaching its maximum. Joe Banker finally slapped him on the shoulder as he paced for the hundredth time past where he was working on the engine, muttering to himself.

"Cuz, you tight as a banjo string. You don't calm down, you gonna snap."

"I don't know what we got to be nervous about,"

Jodell said sarcastically. "We got our sponsor and a whole covey of his best customers up here to see us run, and all we've been able to do this week so far is putter around out there like we been driving Grandpa's old tractor. In reverse. Uphill!"

"Well, you are giving me one big case of the heebie-jeebies with all that pacing and talking to yourself you been doing all morning. And you're downright scaring the bejesus out of the boys over yonder."

He nodded toward where Williams, his customers, and the rest of the race crew were having a picnic on a big blanket behind the pit area. Homer and his folks were clearly in awe of their surroundings, the cars, the name drivers, the rapidly filling stands that surrounded them. But Bubba and Johnny and their two friends from Chandler Cove, Clifford and Randy, who had driven over to help them crew the race, were watching Jodell as if they fully expected him to explode at any moment.

Despite the previous night's party, they had all been up early, anxious to get to the track so they could get things set up before Williams and his bunch got there. Joe and Bubba had impressed on everyone the importance of getting everything done so they would have a few minutes to spend with the people who paid most of the bills. But Jodell was having a hard time with the concept. He usually only had to focus on race preparations before the start, getting the car ready, reviewing the course over and over in his mind until he could have driven it blindfolded.

This whole sponsorship thing had turned into quite a quandary. He knew that he had to keep the sponsor happy, to show off for the people he was bringing to the race. But Jodell also knew that if he didn't maintain focus on the task at hand, winning, then it could easily turn into another long, frustrating day. And enough of those kinds of races and no amount of smiling and greeting would keep the Bubble Up money coming in.

There was more, too. Grandma Lee had showed up for the race, riding over with Catherine and Joyce. She had never seen Jodell drive, had never seen a real, live, loud, stock car race. She was holding her ears already, merely from the car or two in the pits that had periodically fired their engines to test something.

"Lord, Jodell Bob! I ain't seen so many folks in one place at one time in my life," she said when he hugged her. "I reckon they ought to be at church, though."

"I'm sure they'll go next week, Grandma," he offered.

"Well, you just be careful out there and don't drive too fast."

"I won't."

Joe Banker stood behind their grandmother where she couldn't see him, a mock scowl on his face, then winked at Jodell.

"Don't worry about that, Grandma. Jodell Bob's driving real slow lately."

Jodell looked about for a handy tool to throw at his cousin, but Homer stepped up then to begin introducing the people he had brought all the way to North Wilkesboro to meet a real, honest-to-goodness stock car driver. And then more familiar faces from Chandler Cove came by, all to pound Jodell on the back, to wish him luck, to express their sincere belief that he would win the day's race by a mile and a half. It had taken the first win to convince even these homefolks that he was a serious driver. And now, just that quickly, they were convinced that he would almost certainly be the season champion soon.

Jodell was a full fifty laps into the race before he had his mind in sync with what was happening with the car and the track. Thank heavens he apparently had one of the faster cars out there or he would have been lapped before the crowd got good and settled in their seats. By the first pit stop, he had worked his way up to eleventh. And all the soda peddlers, the folks from back home, Grandma Lee, and the rest of the group completely faded from his head. He concentrated on nothing but the car, the slight uphill-and-downhill track, and how rapidly he could get to the front of the field. Jodell stood on the Ford's accelerator and steered toward the leaders.

And it was a smooth, steady march to the front, the way it happened sometimes in his fondest dreams. High, low, or in between, wherever he needed to go to pass a car that blocked his way, he placed the nose of his Ford there and drove right on past.

Back in the pits, Joe could see the results on his stopwatch every lap, and the leader board in the center of the infield confirmed it. Jodell was consistently running a tenth of a second or so faster than the leaders. At that rate, it wouldn't take long to catch and pass them.

Then, one hundred and fifty laps into the contest, Jodell and the Ford were on the rear bumper of the race leader, "Fast Freddy" Lorenzen, tapping him gently in the butt to let him know someone faster had arrived. High on the track, low into the corners, with fenders rubbing and sideways glances exchanged between the drivers, they fought for the coveted top spot as if every lap was the last trip around. The duel continued lap after lap until finally, with teeth gritted and hands gripping the steering wheel as if they were part of the assembly, Jodell slipped past Lorenzen and claimed what was rightfully his: the lead.

He traded the lead for most of the next 250 laps or so. Only jammed-up slower traffic or an occasional messy wreck or pit stops took away the point for a bit, but he never fell out of the top five. And even then, he made his way back to race for the number-one position.

With fifty laps to go, Jodell found himself back in third after the last round of pit stops, but once more he was closing in on the leaders, ready to again show them the way to the checkered flag. The traffic on the track was now a serious concern. Many of the slower cars were wrestling with each other for position money and were not so willing to slow and move out of the way as the lead cars came up on them from behind.

That forced Jodell to drive harder and harder into the corners as he diced with the also-rans. The laps were still winding down, though, and the Ford felt stronger than ever.

Nothing could keep him from the lead. Nothing.

He had just reclaimed second place and was about to give the lead car a "hello" tap once more as he drove the Ford hard, steering down into the first turn.

Boom!

Jodell Lee had never before actually heard a grenade explode, but that had to be the way one sounded. And it had detonated directly beneath the right front fender of his automobile. The Ford instantly took its own line, directly toward the railing that guarded the first turn.

The impact with the guardrail was quick, direct, head-on, and hard, and a race car that had been hurtling forward a split second ago was instantly stopped dead still. Inside, though, Jodell Lee kept rushing forward, but only for a fraction of an inch or so. The shoulder belts caught him, knocking the wind out of him, while his head snapped forward wickedly.

Catherine was watching Jodell all the way, just as she always did. She clearly saw the right front tire explode, the puff of blue smoke, the shards of rubber being flung outward from the wheel well, and she watched as the car turned abruptly toward the outside of the track. She stood, hands to her mouth, as it came to a stop there, smashed into the rail, steam already billowing from its crumpled front end. And she held her breath as other cars whipped past his, some having to steer quickly downward to avoid piling into him. Then she watched, waiting to see him climb out the window.

Back inside the car, smoke, dust, and steam were everywhere, like some deep, multicolored mist. Jodell tried to suck in a breath but it was as if the only available air was noxious, not breathable at all. As he choked, grunted, tried to force his diaphragm to work, he realized that he was having a familiar feeling. Once, in a high school football game, some huge defensive lineman had crashed through his blockers and whacked him from the blind side as he set to pass the ball downfield. He knew there was no reason to fight it. The ability to breathe that he had so taken for granted would return in its own good time. He could only hope that was before he was stone cold dead.

When he was finally able to take in a small gulp of air, he coughed and sputtered, then tried to breathe more deeply. Someone, for some reason, was shoving a hot, sharp knife into his right rib cage and giving it a twist each time his chest heaved and tried to inhale.

Fire.

Somehow, the thought of fire had suddenly entered his head. But he had seen no flames yet. He tried to remember how long it had been since the last pit stop, how much gas might still be on board. And how big a fire that might make if there was a leak, a spark.

That's when he sensed some urgency in getting out of the car. Jodell wrestled with his shoulder belts to try to free himself. He could already feel the deep bruises they had left in his skin when they had bitten him on impact with the wall. But they had done their job. He was still inside, not flying through the air. He unsnapped the belts and slumped back in his seat, then started to climb out of the car.

He had no strength. No matter how strongly he willed himself to move, he simply couldn't. He slumped back down in the seat, hoping a few more gulps would give him the power, the energy he needed to get out.

Suddenly several pairs of hands reached through the open window, grabbed him, and jerked him outside. They set him upright on the asphalt. He tried to stand by himself but his knees buckled beneath him. Two of the safety crew members grabbed him, one on each side, and walked him down the track to the infield.

Feebly, he waved a hand to the crowd. They erupted into a wild cheer, congratulating him on his emergence from the demolished car.

Finally breathing better, he limped over to where their equipment was set up and eased down to a seat on one of the toolboxes. He noticed then that the race had been resumed and realized dejectedly that he was not in it.

Bubba was there then, having run full speed from

the pits. He produced a damp towel from an ice chest and draped it over Jodell's sore neck.

"You look like you took a nap in a cement mixer, Jodell," the big man said, trying to manage a grin, but there was worry in his eyes.

"I feel like somebody's been using me as a punching bag, Big 'Un." He hardly had the air to spit out the sentence, and it still hurt to breathe.

"Tire blowed, huh?" Bubba asked as he wrapped more ice in another towel.

"Yep. Right front. I don't think that railing gave an inch. I've never stopped so sudden in my life and I've been in a lot of wrecks in a race car." He couldn't decide whether he needed the new towel on his ribs or his right knee that was already beginning to swell. "That tire exploded and she was in the fence before I could even find the brake pedal. Hell, before I could even *think* about finding the brake pedal!"

"Jodell, what have I told you about trying to use our pretty race car like a bulldozer?" Joe Banker called as he ran up and kneeled down next to his cousin. He, too, had a worried expression on his face.

"How is the car?" Jodell wheezed.

"Johnny and Clifford are riding back with it on the wrecker. I'd say she's about half as long as she was fifteen minutes ago. You ever seen a June bug hit a windshield at sixty miles an hour on a hot summer day? That's kinda like what our pretty race car looks like now."

Jodell glanced wearily over at Joe.

"You think we can get her together enough to run a few more laps?"

"You mean today?"

Jodell winced in pain, then nodded. Joe laughed.

"If they'll let us pull her around the track behind

the wrecker, maybe so. 'Sides, I can't see you driving much of anything for a little bit."

Catherine and Joyce had been sitting high in the stands with Grandma Lee. The old woman had been having the time of her life, drinking in all the noise, the people, the spectacle of her first stock car race. She tried to ask a continual skein of questions over the rumble of the race cars but soon gave up, then Joyce's and Catherine's excitement became contagious once her grandson was leading the race. The demure grandmother had sat there, her hands folded neatly in her lap, watching wide-eyed as Jodell circled the track time and again.

"You girls love this," she had said, smiling broadly, during one of the caution periods when the din had subsided enough for them to talk.

"Yes, ma'am, we do," Catherine replied.

"There's something special about sharing something your man loves to do so much. I never had that with Grandpa Lee. Squirrel hunting and whiskey making was about all he really enjoyed, and I didn't take much interest in either."

The girls laughed out loud at the image of the old woman with a squirrel gun or standing over a vat of steaming sour mash. She joined right in with them.

Then, minutes later, the fun was over. Catherine was standing there, tangled up with Joyce and Grandma Lee, watching impatiently for any signs of life from inside the smoking, motionless race car.

"He's okay," Grandma reassured calmly. "I done sent up enough prayers to the Lord to keep him safe for a long, long time. He's okay."

Then Catherine had seen the safety crews pull him out, and he stood, wobbly yet, and gave the little wave to the crowd. Only then did she breathe. And only then did she notice a tear creeping down each cheek. She quickly wiped them away before anyone else could notice. She owed it to Jodell not to let any of the fans see his wife crying over her husband's having a little tangle with a guardrail.

Joyce volunteered to sit there with Grandma while Catherine climbed down to the fence, ready to go through and across the track the instant the race was over.

Jodell and his blown tire had brought out the last caution flag of the day. Fifteen minutes later, Marvin Panch had beaten Freddy Lorenzen to the finish line and the race that should have been Jodell Lee's was over.

And Jodell was still hurting, not only from the sudden end to his great run but in at least a dozen spots all over his body. Joe fetched the track doctor to come look his driver over while Bubba kept the cold towels coming.

"I reckon he'll live," the doctor reported after poking and prodding and holding up various numbers of fingers for Jodell to count. "You got some bruised ribs and a banged-up knee, and I suspect you'll have a headache for a few days. Aspirin and cold towels. That's all I can recommend. And not running into immovable objects, of course."

"I generally try not to," Jodell said weakly, leaning back against a light pole.

"Just be glad she didn't catch on fire," the doctor said. "Not much I can do if you burn up in one of those things."

The race car was much sicker than her driver was. The wrecker had deposited what was left of her next to their trailer, and most of the crew walked around and around the cadaver, trying to decide what they would have to do to even get the thing back to Chandler Cove.

The gates to the infield were finally opened, and fans began pouring in to get close to their favorite drivers. Catherine was one of the first across the track. She came running at full gallop, collapsed next to where Jodell sat, and threw her arms around him. He let out a deep, involuntary groan but tried to return the embrace.

"Sorry, honey. That hurts just a little bit."

"Are you okay?"

"Battered and beaten, but nothing is broken. I'll be an old sore-tail for a few days, but I can live with that if you can."

"You scared me to death when you hit that wall so hard."

"I've told you not to worry, baby. Me and Joe and Bubba build one mighty tough race car."

"Still . . ."

Catherine nodded, but she continued to hold on to him as tightly as she dared. Several other drivers and crew came by to check on him and to look at the race car. Even Little Joe Weatherly stopped by and squatted down next to them.

"I believe it would be worth it to me to run headlong into a guardrail if I could have as pretty a girl as that making over me." He winked at Jodell. "Blow a tire or did you just decide to steer into the wall so nobody could see how much faster I was than you?"

"Did you even run today, Little Joe? I don't remember seeing you after I took the lead." Jodell tried to laugh, but it hurt too badly. He took a deep breath and felt the sharp pain again where the shoulder belts had cut into him. "It was a hard lick. Those shoulder belts bruised me up pretty bad."

"That's why I hate to wear the blame things. A lap belt is all I ever need."

"Little Joe, a wreck like this is a perfect example of why you need to be wearing a shoulder belt," Jodell fussed, but he immediately felt odd, trying to give advice to this veteran, this proven champion.

"I hear you," Little Joe said, smiling. "But I got the kind of belt you need. A good, strong belt of Canadian Club oughta make you feel fine in a little bit."

"I'll think about it," Jodell said, waving him off.

Joyce and Grandma Lee soon joined them, and along came Homer Williams and the group of customers and a pack of fans, all concerned about Jodell Lee and his health.

"Y'all about to smother me!" Jodell finally yelled. He sent them all off to get some food ready for another picnic while the crew began loading the trailer. He had just finished signing yet another autograph when he heard a gruff, gravelly voice from behind him.

"I just seen me one mighty fine race car driver today." The voice was familiar somehow. "Just as fine a driver as I knew he would be."

The old man wore a long, black coat, its collar turned up. He was woefully out of place on this hot, dusty day.

"Augustus!"

He spun around and hobbled over to give the old man a bear hug. Augustus Smith. Gus had been one of his grandfather's best customers. And he had been the bootlegger who had advanced Jodell the money to buy his first serious race car, the one he had taken to Darlington for their first real race. Without Smith's confidence and money, there was some doubt about whether the Ford would ever have run its first big-time race, much less won one.

"You tagged that wall pretty good. You all right?"

"I'm fine, Gus. How are you? I've been meaning to drive over and see you, but I just don't have much spare time these days."

"Don't you worry none about coming to see old Gus. You keep doing what you're doing and make me and your grandpa proud, God rest his soul. I even did a little jig in the parlor when you won that race the other week. I was mighty proud, mighty proud as I listened to you cross the finish line."

"Well, I sure didn't look like a winner today."

"You looked pretty darn good to win the thing till that tire blowed all to pieces on you."

The old man seemed almost ghostly with his white hair and beard and the long, black coat. Jodell shifted his weight off the bum knee and eased back down onto the toolbox.

"Tell you the truth, I do feel like I been dragged behind a runaway mule across most of Chandler County. I got to admit, Gus, that sometimes I think about quitting when it gets as frustrating as it has been this week. When ain't nothing going right and we tear up the car and I hurt all over."

"Well, I have a bit of medicine here that just might help you feel better." Gus grinned, then dug deep down into a pocket of his coat to pull out a small Mason jar. "When I saw how hard you smacked that rail, I figured you might need this, so I went by the car on the way over here and picked it up."

"Gus, I think you might be onto something."

He took the offered jar and inspected the couple of inches or so of familiar amber liquid inside. Then he took a sip of the home brew and felt its warmth spread all through his abdomen. Sure enough, the aches seemed to ease immediately, as if he had been given a shot of morphine.

"Your grandpap could have saved the world with that stuff," Augustus proclaimed with a grin, then seemed to shift gears. "Son, I hope you know how proud we all are of you and what you've gone out and done with next to nothing. Don't let a setback like this 'un get you down. If it was all that easy, everybody would be a champeen.

"That's what I come here to tell you. They's a whole passel of folks that you don't even know that's pulling for you. Folks that won't ever have a chance to run a race or win a trophy or even get off a farm or out of a factory long enough to see one in person like I done today. But you quit, you're quittin' on them in addition to yourself. Just remember that. All right?"

Jodell started to nod, to let the old man know how much he appreciated his words. But just then he spotted Catherine and Grandma and the others coming from across the infield with a blanket and sandwiches. He stood carefully to motion them over so they could meet Augustus Smith, so he could explain to them all who he was and how important he had been to their racing dreams.

But when he turned around, the old man was gone as surely as if he had never been there.

The next few races seemed to go by in a blur. Junior Johnson won at Charlotte, while Richard Petty claimed the races before and after. Jodell and the crew couldn't complain about their showing at Charlotte or the other races. Except about not finishing first in any of them, anyway. They had impressive runs in all three, with a superb run at Charlotte, in which they had been a real threat to actually win the race. He ran with the leaders all day before the motor developed a hiccup and they faded at the end. The Ford at anything less than full strength was no match for Junior Johnson's engine that day.

The close-but-no-cigar finish actually left Jodell jubilant. He was confident he had found the fastest way around the track. It promised better things for the race in May of the next year.

By the time they got to the Occoneechee speedway in Hillsboro, North Carolina, for the race at the end of October, the brutal schedule had finally and completely caught up with them. They were dog tired from the traveling, the under-car work, the pressure to always be on the top of their form when the green flag fell several times a week. And they were especially thankful they had decided to pass on the race all the way out in Riverside, California, at the end of the year. They would make that trip the following year for the early-season race now that they were assured of the sponsor money from Homer Williams. After Occoneechee, they would compete at Concord, near Charlotte, in two weeks, then take some time off to begin getting ready to make a serious run for the 1964 season.

They desperately needed to build a couple of new cars. Both the vehicles they had been running were worn out. The car wrecked at North Wilkesboro still lay in a pile in the shop back home like a crushed and discarded beer can. They were finishing the season in the car they preferred to run on dirt tracks, and it had definitely seen its better days. The only good car they had left was the one they had run at Charlotte, and there were serious changes Jodell wanted to make on it before they could rely on it to be their third car.

They had a buyer for the wrecked machine if they could get it put back together enough so it looked like a race car again. With their finances squeezed tight and the sponsor money only certain for half a year, they had to cash in anything they could. And win every race they entered. A first-place purse at Occoneechee, then Concord, would warm up an otherwise cold winter.

Thirty or so cars sat on the starting grid at the nine-tenths-of-a-mile dirt oval, all with the same intentions and aspirations as Jodell Lee. He was mad at himself already for sliding wide during qualifying and thus having to start in fifteenth position. Once again, he had one of the fastest cars on the track, but his impatience had cost him a better starting position.

It was a big race for Little Joe Weatherly, a chance to clinch his second straight season championship.

When the green flag fell, the cars set off a massive dust storm. The laps were fast for a dirt track, and Jodell drove the car for all it was worth, sliding practically all the way through the long, sweeping turns. It was clear early that Joe Weatherly was the class of the field, though, with only Bob Welborn able to push him at all.

With the choking dust quickly clogging radiators and air breathers, and with the hail of small stones kicked up off the track, the field was soon whittled down by mechanical and tire troubles. There were also numerous spinouts in the thick, tan fog as drivers simply lost their way.

Jodell was no exception. He got tagged several times by slower cars and had no hope of a good finish. His frustration on dirt continued. When Little Joe took the checkered flag for the win, Jodell was laps down and fuming, mad as much at himself as at the other drivers who couldn't keep their cars headed straight.

"I don't know whether to kick my own butt or look up some of the yahoos that ran all over me and kick theirs!" Jodell groaned as he climbed out of the car. "Either way, somebody needs his butt kicked!"

"Hey, don't sweat it, Cuz," Joe cautioned. "These sand traps ain't for us and you know it. And they are hell on the car. Look at this thing." He pointed to the steaming radiator of their race car and the dirt that caked the grill.

"Joe, I've been run over, run around, and spun out until I just can't stand it anymore," Jodell spat.

"Wait till we get to the big tracks next year. Then we'll show them," Bubba chimed in. "These dirt dens are going the way of the dodo bird anyway, 'least for big-time racing."

He shook his head sadly as he popped the hood and inspected the mess underneath. Jodell kicked a toolbox in frustration, jammed his hands into his pockets, and stood beside Bubba looking at the dust-choked engine. Joe joined them, standing there for a moment before he put his arm around his driver's shoulders and talked quietly to him.

"Jodell, all you need to do is calm down and think about the race. You win by picking your spots and making your moves with your head, not your foot. You drive with a lead foot and you'll wind up like some of the others who jump out front but then break their cars. Drive smart, like you used to."

"You're right, but I despise running in the back of the pack when I know I have a car that can run at the front."

"Well, you can't run up front if you're getting spun out back there in the traffic. It's like Grandma Lee always says: 'Patience is a virtue.' "

Jodell nodded. His cousin was right, of course. In his eagerness to win, he was making the very mistakes that were costing them victories in the long run.

Still deep in thought, Jodell stepped over to where Weatherly's victory soiree was already well under way. The enthusiasm was infectious, and he was immediately in a better mood. The party threatened to be legendary. Weatherly had perfected partying long ago, and twenty-five trips to Victory Lane over the years had given him plenty of practice in pitching a whale of a celebration.

"Where's them other convicts you run with?" Little Joe asked when he spied Jodell.

"They're loading up."

"I know you keep 'em busy, 'Tennessee,' but I don't want 'em to miss our victory party we're about to pitch."

"They'll be along directly. I just wanted to congratulate you, Little Joe. That was one heck of a race you ran today. Better yet, one hell of a season."

"Hey, I appreciate it. You know what I always say: 'Flat-out and belly-to-the-ground.'" Then the man suddenly turned uncharacteristically serious. He must have sensed Jodell's mood. "You know, Lee. Every time I win one of these damned things, I want to win the next one that much more. It's like a good drink of whiskey or a beautiful woman. You can't have too much of a good thing. But no matter how bad you burn to win, you got to be smart. You can only do so much. You got to let the track, the race, the competition come to you. You start pushing it, forcing it, and it'll come back to bite you like a mad dog. That's the hardest thing you have to learn about this game. You get that down, Lee, and there ain't no telling what you can do out there."

With that, Weatherly was swept away by his jubilant crew to continue the party back at the motel. It was good advice—and it echoed what Joe Banker had just told him.

Little Joe Weatherly was at the peak of his career. The way things were going, he would have a good shot at winning his third championship in a row in

'64, and he was sure having a ton of fun doing it.

Jodell watched him and his entourage until they were out of sight. Then he gritted his teeth hard, spun on his heels, and went on back to help Joe and Bubba load up and get ready for the next race.

I t was midway through a late-November afternoon, and Jodell and Bubba were hard at work
in the shop that now claimed all of Grandpa Lee's
giant old barn. Except for a couple of cow stalls where
race cars and parts of dead race cars now rested, there
was little inside the old rough-plank building to sug-
gest that it had ever been anything else but a shop for
working on such vehicles. The two men were busily
welding together the roll cage on one of the two new
cars they were building for the '64 season. This would
be the car they would tow out to California, to Riverside, an hour or two east of Los Angeles. And it was
the one they were planning on Jodell's driving to a
win in that first race of the year.

"Reckon what's taking Joe so long fetching them

parts?" Bubba asked, his voice muffled by his welding mask.

"Better question is 'Reckon what her name is?'" Jodell answered.

Joe Banker was supposed to be finishing up rebuilding the motor for the car, but he had disappeared a couple of hours before, making a quick trip to Chandler Cove that had turned into an all-afternoon sojourn.

"Maybe he had to go on to Kingsport to get them piston rings."

"And maybe I'm the president of the United States," Jodell groused, and grabbed a new, firmer grip with both hands on the metal bar they were working on, as if he was actually choking his tardy cousin.

The last few weeks had zoomed by. They had run one or the other of the older cars in a few races here and there, all at smaller tracks within a few hours' driving time from home, looking strictly for first-place money. They had won several, and the money was going into what Joe had dubbed their "California kitty." If they weren't competing in a race or driving to or from one, they were almost always in the barn shop performing surgery on the new cars. They had hardly noticed the cold, gray weather that seemed to have settled in for the winter, or the first Christmas decorations that had already gone up on front porches up and down the highway to town. Most evenings, Grandma had to bring them plates of food for their dinner when they simply forgot to come up to the house to eat.

When she got home from work each day, Catherine would come out and work on the books in the little office she had set up in the room where Grandpa had once kept the harness for his mules. Or she and Joyce would stand by, watching over their husbands as they worked, simply to be near them.

"Well, Mr. Kennedy, if you'll hold that bar still then maybe I can tack it down," Bubba grinned. He often fussed at Jodell for being so all-fired serious all the time. They had plenty of time to get the car ready for California and maybe enjoy a little Thanksgiving and Christmas, too.

Now, as he fired up the torch again, he was glad to hear that Jodell was at least humming along with a song that was playing on the radio. They had the radio set up on a shelf in the shop, tuned today to the country station out of Kingsport. Before long, both men were singing out loud with another familiar song, singing horribly off-key but with plenty of enthusiasm.

They had welded in several of the side roll bars, Jodell measuring them, cutting them, then holding them in place while Bubba hit the junctions with the torch. Finally, while Bubba made the welds solid, Jodell would cut and bend the next bar. They were so intent on the job at hand they hardly noticed the music on the radio had stopped abruptly and that a serious-toned announcer was talking. They could barely hear the words anyway over the hissing of the welding torch.

"Wait, Bubba. You hear what they're saying?"

"Huh? Hear what?" He cut the flame and raised his mask over his head. The torch fell silent, and then they could hear the news announcer clearly.

". . . and we repeat, the word out of Dallas, Texas, is that shots have been fired at the motorcade and President Kennedy has apparently been wounded."

The two men stood in stunned silence staring at the

radio. The monotone voice continued with the update as Jodell stepped over and turned up the volume while Bubba stood stark still, the torch in his right hand spitting softly as the last of the flame died away.

". . . and reports are that the president has been taken to Parkland Hospital, where his condition is not known at this time . . ."

Jodell slid down to sit on the dirt floor, leaning back against the race car. He idly wiped his sweating face with the rag from the back pocket of his jeans as he listened intently. Bubba numbly eased down to rest on the rear seat they had removed from the car and had leaned against the back wall of the barn. Before they had even had time to absorb the initial blow of shocking news, the hammer fell again.

". . . and this has just come over the Associated Press wire, folks. The president of the United States has died. Just after one this afternoon, President Kennedy was pronounced dead . . ."

Jodell suddenly needed air. He wasn't surprised at all to see that a gray sky had claimed the afternoon sun, that a cold wind had begun to blow down the mountain from the north. He walked across the yard to Grandma's house and found her inside, crying softly as she rocked gently in her favorite chair. On the television set, her usual programs had been swept away by a sad-eyed newsman clutching his ear while someone talked to him about what was going on in Dallas. He, in turn, dutifully relayed it to those watching.

"It'll be all right, 'Ma."

"He was so young. So young and so alive," she said. The television now flashed photos of the president with his wife and children on a sailboat somewhere, film of them all playing football on the White

House lawn. "And those poor babies have lost their daddy."

"I know," he said, and then seemed to suddenly run out of words for her.

"Jodell, it seems like it's always the good ones who die young. The ones with babies that'll need their papas." She paused and gave him a strange look, one he had never seen on her face before. "Just like your daddy."

He stared at her. She never talked about his father. He'd heard more about him from family and friends than he ever had from Grandma or Papa Lee. It seemed like a subject too painful for them to discuss.

Now she was watching intently as the shocking news played out on the blinking screen, as raptly attentive as she ever was to her daytime stories or the television preachers.

"I better get back and help Bubba," Jodell said softly.

When he stepped back inside the shop, he found Bubba welding away furiously on the roll bars they had placed earlier, working as if he had to have the job finished before the day was done. The radio was off, the only sound in the room the insistent hissing and popping of the torch. Jodell walked to the workbench, picked up the bar he had most recently cut, and carried it over to the pipe bender to start working it into shape.

The two of them worked for a while in silence, until Bubba finished with the joints, raised the welding helmet, took a wire brush, and began buffing the rough seams.

"Whatta ya think, Joe Dee?"

"They look good to me."

"They won't be cracking, I don't expect."

"Good and sturdy." He tugged on the bar to confirm it. "Look, let's call it a day. My heart ain't in it no more."

"How about something to drink?" Bubba asked, motioning toward the cooler in the corner.

"Okay."

They sat in virtual silence, sipping their drinks, until Jodell switched the radio back on. There was little for them to say, not even when Catherine and Joyce showed up together after work, red-eyed and subdued. The half-built race car sat just as they had left it, with the torch and tools still scattered all about.

But then, as Jodell talked quietly with Catherine and Joyce about the day's events, Bubba suddenly stood and walked back over to the car. He picked up the torch, turning it over slowly in his hand, studying it as if he had never seen one before. Then he reached for the welding helmet and pulled it back onto his crew-cut head.

"Sometimes, y'all, there ain't nothing to do but go back to work."

And that's exactly what the big man did.

Slowly, Jodell stood and walked over to join him. So did Joyce, then Catherine, handing them tools as they needed them, holding a piece in place while it was fastened down.

Sometimes, no matter what had happened, the best thing to do was simply to go back to work.

He slept through most of the flight to Los Angeles. Jo-dell Lee had always been able to sleep about anywhere he could stretch out his long legs, and the first-class seats on the 737 were downright luxurious compared to some places he had napped. Certainly compared to the backseat of the old Ford tow car they had once owned. Rusty Wallace and many of the others flew their own planes now. Bobby Allison had started it all way back when. Alan Kulwicki had died in his. But Jodell Lee didn't mind letting someone else do the driving sometimes.

He had been in Nashville, doing a promotional appearance on the Nashville Network and taking part in a satellite hookup interview with sportswriters all over the country. It must have taken more out of him than he had realized, because he had still been sleeping when the plane touched down at LAX four hours after leaving Nashville. The businessman next to him had given him a gentle nudge as the plane taxied up to the gate. Then he had asked Jodell for an autograph.

"I saw you that time at Talladega when you and Marty Robbins got together at the end of the race," the man said. "That was some kind of a wreck!"

They always seemed to remember the crashes more readily than they did the wins.

He walked stiffly through the terminal to the rental car counter, his aches and pains aggravated by the close quarters in the airplane. He made a promise to himself that he would not turn down any of his sponsors' offers to have someone pick him up next time he came this way. One of the clerks at the counter recognized him, so he had to sign autographs for everyone there, including several customers. So did the shuttle bus driver, who had once shaken his hand after a race at Sears Point and actually believed Jodell when he assured the man that he remembered. It took the better part of an hour for him to get his car and be on his way.

It was a typically pleasant Southern California day as he pulled out onto the 405, heading toward the intersection with the Santa Monica Freeway. He relaxed behind the wheel. Something about being in this place seemed to always bring a strange calm over him. As he steered through surprisingly light traffic, he found his mind wandering, swiped by a thousand trespassing memories.

As the freeway finally bisected the far eastern outskirts of the sprawling city, he could at last see through the smog the mountains that ringed the Los Angeles basin. He had always been struck by the contrast in scenery between the mountains here and those back home in East Tennessee. That, of course, wasn't the only difference between these disparate places.

The car almost seemed to be driving itself as it took the exit off the freeway. The streets looked familiar to him somehow, even though construction was going on everywhere he looked. He was still daydreaming as he drew closer to where the road was supposed to be that led to the sparkling new speedway at Fontana.

Suddenly he slammed on the brakes and pulled the car to the side of the road next to a huge, dust-covered lot. The car behind him swerved, the driver honked his horn, and the vehicle angrily peeled away.

Jodell was shivering, bathed in an abrupt cold sweat. His hand was shaking as he reached to flip off the air-conditioning.

He could feel his heart pounding in his chest as he looked around, trying to get his bearings, to figure why he had screeched to a halt here at this eerie place. Where was he? Certainly not in Fontana at the beautiful new raceway.

Suddenly, as if someone had opened the floodgates, it all came pouring back to him in a rush. This dusty lot? It was all that was left of the old Riverside raceway. He was sitting near what had been the main entrance, but development had gobbled up much of the property.

He climbed out of the car and stepped through a gap in the chain-link fence. Bulldozers had shoved aside most of what had once been the track, but he was still awash with the familiarity of the place, with the memories of all he had seen the first time he had come to this place over thirty years before.

A housing development had eaten up the land where one of the turns had been, and a shopping center owned a couple more of the turns where some of the grandstands had been. Then he heard something. He cocked his head sideways and listened harder. Maybe it was only the Santa Ana winds, but he could swear he could hear the roar of the engines as they lined up for the start of the race.

And he didn't even have to close his eyes to see Little Joe Weatherly's car coming at him out of the shimmering dust at ninety miles per hour, sweeping out of the far S-shaped turn. And there was a big smile on Little Joe's face as he rumbled past, stomping the gas hard to put another lap on some poor, unfortunate driver, racing for glory.

Over there, beyond the pile of dusty rubble, was where the garage had been. It was probably only a construction shed obscured by the smog, but he thought he could actually see the building next to where he held Catherine close to him minutes before their first race here. It was the spot where she had smiled up at him as he held her close, basking in the still-new glow of the wonderful news she had brought with her all the way from Chandler Cove on her first airplane ride, her first trip west of the Mississippi.

The vivid memories almost overwhelmed Jodell as he stood there in the ruins of the speedway. He felt dizzy, as if in some kind of a trance, and he had no idea how long he might have stayed there. He had not even noticed when the tears had finally come.

What an old fool! Passersby must have been shaking their heads at the sight of the gray-haired old man standing out there in the middle of the dusty, windswept, vacant lot, twisting slowly as he followed ghost cars zooming around a phantom racetrack.

He had no idea how he finally got back to the car and then drove on to the speedway at Fontana. But when Jodell first stepped into the shade of the garage,

Bubba Baxter took one look at his ashen face and knew at once why he had run late getting to the track this day.

"I stopped there, too, Joe Dee. Yesterday. I don't know why, but I just wandered right into the place and had to get out and walk around. You know what? I thought I heard the cars again, the way they roared around those turns. And don't laugh. I could have sworn I saw Little Joe's car coming right at me out of all that dust and smog."

Jodell could only smile. Maybe he had not gone totally loco after all.

Someone else had seen the ghosts, too.

THROUGH THE S-TURNS

The highway finally found the edge of the mountains and dropped off the edge as if it were the
lip of a table. The three men in the cab of the
truck had been mesmerized by the limitless miles, the
numbing distance they had ridden, the hypnotic hum
of the tires on the pavement for the past three and a
half days. But the sudden drop-off, the view out ahead
of them, jarred them into instant consciousness.

"Lord, that's a pretty sight," Bubba Baxter said as
he steered the truck over the edge and down the backside of the San Bernardinos.

"What's that blue out yonder?" Joe Banker asked.
It looked as if the sky had fallen below the horizon
way off in the distance, beyond the dusty tan of the
dirt and scrub brush directly below them.

"Why, that's the Pacific Ocean, boys," Jodell answered.

He stared hard at the bluish haze, a slight smile on his lips. He had looked forward to his first sight of the sea that had swallowed up his father's submarine during the war. Somehow, being here, viewing the big water, made him feel a little bit closer to a man he had not seen since he was a child. And somewhere, out there in that big basin that had suddenly opened up before them, his mother likely lived. Dazed, distraught, she had left home soon after they had gotten the news about his father. They had received letters, a few postcards, a phone call or two from her for a while, but then nothing.

Jodell had thought about the odds of running into her out here, what it might be like to see her again. Maybe, against all odds, she would see his name in the sports pages and come to see him. Or maybe she was long since dead.

The brakes on the truck squealed and complained as Bubba eased down the twisting mountain road. The trailer that held the shiny new race car under its tarp grunted and groaned and threatened to break loose and pass them if they didn't hurry to the track.

But nobody wanted to get there any quicker than Joe, Bubba, and Jodell. It had been eighteen hours of driving a day since they had pulled out of Chandler Cove in the midst of a light snowfall and into the maw of a cold wind. Along the way, they had seen countryside they had only glimpsed before in the western movies Bubba loved so much. The vast, deflated plains had especially been a revelation for the mountain natives.

"This place is flat as a flitter!" Joe observed.

Then, when they had stopped for gas near Amarillo, Bubba had had trouble even keeping his balance when he crawled from the truck. The lack of hills, the brisk wind, almost blew him over.

"I can't help it!" he growled when the other two laughed at him. "This place is so danged flat it makes me swimmy-headed."

Then when they had finally wound down the mountainside, they noticed that even the air in Southern California looked and smelled differently than it did in East Tennessee. That the houses and stores looked foreign to them.

"Boys, I ain't sure we're on the same planet anymore," Joe noted. But then he noticed the uniform good looks of every woman they saw and instantly revised his opinion of this strange place. "But we may have accidentally ended up in heaven."

Joe went to check them into the motel while Bubba stepped back to inspect the truck and trailer. Jodell simply leaned back against the truck and soaked up the warm afternoon sun.

"Everything okay, Bub?"

"Just checking the tie-downs after all the winding we did coming down that mountain."

The big man suddenly stopped and sniffed like a bluetick hound catching the scent of rabbit. He lived for three things: food; the race car; and his wife, Joyce. They had not eaten since a hurried breakfast early that morning, and with the car apparently okay, Joyce safely back at home two thousand miles away, food was suddenly his only priority. A delicious aroma was drifting across the motel parking lot from a burger place nearby, and it had caught Jodell's attention, too.

"Let's stow our bags and we can eat. Then I want to go see that track. We better check on Joe, too. He might have found him a beach bunny already."

Never mind the beach was sixty miles west. Joe had been gone a long time. And sure enough, when Jodell walked into the small motel office, he found Joe conversing with a young blond woman behind the desk. She was certainly beauty-queen-quality.

"Whatever he's telling you is a lie, ma'am," Jodell said seriously as he walked up.

She looked at him with big, blue eyes.

"You mean he's not the chief mechanic of the best race team there is?" she asked.

"Oh. That part's the gospel."

"I just love race cars," she cooed. "And I love the way you boys talk, too. Say something else for me, Joe."

Jodell took the offered key from Joe and went back out to help Bubba bring in their bags and to go get something to eat. It appeared Joe would not be accompanying them to their first dinner in California. They were going to share one room until Catherine and Joyce flew out later in the week. It would be their first airplane ride, and neither of them had been any farther west than Oak Ridge in their lives. All of them hoped to make this trip a vacation of sorts before they dived headlong into the new racing season.

All except Jodell Lee, of course. He refused to think or talk about anything else but the race.

They got their first look at the Riverside track early the next morning. Their body still in another time zone, they were up before four and at the track before the gates opened. But finally they were in the pits, rolling the race car down off the trailer, setting up their space while most of the other competitors were still rolling in.

They heard Little Joe Weatherly long before they saw him, jabbering away merrily, not a care in the world, as he worked his way among the rows of race cars. They gave him only a quick wave as they hurried to get things ready.

The Pettys were setting up nearby, and not far away were Ned Jarrett, Freddy Lorenzen, and Marvin Panch, along with some other familiar faces. There were some new ones, too, drivers from the West Coast eager to try their cars and driving skills against the boys from down south.

Finally, there was the first tentative rumbling of the engines as more of the cars were backed off their trailers, or as crews made their initial adjustments. Then the inspection line was set up, and there was a steady stream of race cars being pushed along for the obligatory probing from the officials.

Jodell Lee was getting more and more fidgety. He was eager to shove the new car through inspection and get her out on the track. He'd never laid eyes on a road course, much less run on one. But behind his trepidation there was considerable confidence. From what he had heard, the winding, twisting track would be similar to the mountain roads back home. The same ones he had driven so many times he could probably navigate them at high speed with his eyes closed. But this time he wouldn't be toting a load of glass jars full of white corn liquor.

Joe had instructed him to simply pretend the driver on his tail was a revenuer intent on confiscating his grandfather's whiskey and sending Jodell up the river. Jodell conceded he might do that very thing. He was most eager, though, to get the new car out there, to put her through her paces, to push her, test her, demand more of her than they had been able to do back home. Except for a quick run or two up the highway in front of the shop, the car had never actually been driven.

One by one the cars cleared inspection and began to line up for the start of the day's first practice session. As they had waited, Jodell had sparred back and forth with Little Joe Weatherly, who had been lined up right behind him. He had to listen to the man brag about how he would almost certainly repeat once more as champion, how many sponsors wanted to throw money at him, how many women were asking him to marry them. But he also got a complete rundown on the track from the man.

"Now, watch the esses. Those three turns are tight. To go fast, you have to hit them just right. If you don't, you'll get left behind and it's hard to catch up here," Weatherly had said. He used his hands to show the way to lunge into the S-turns exactly right in order to hurl through them the fastest way possible. "So you have to hit them just so, then feather it a hair, jerk the wheel just so, and then stand on it as you clear the last part of the turn.

"Like I told you, you gotta be delicate and precise if you want to be quick. Now, you could drive like old Bub does that truck of yours, but I don't expect y'all will be winning no races on this coiled-up snake of a racetrack. No sir. All you'll get is bit."

Jodell stepped to the other side of the car, where Bubba lay on his back, once again checking the front suspension.

"What you looking at now, Bubba?"

"Aw, nothing in particular. This is new to me, Joe Dee. Having the car turning both ways on this track ain't like anything I've ever seen before. It's making me about as dizzy as that flat land and all them tumbleweeds did."

"You checked everything a hundred times before we left Chandler Cove, and you were under there last night in the parking lot working on her till way past dark."

Bubba slid from beneath the car.

"I just want to make sure everything is right and that she's safe and fast."

"She will be. Joe's got us a good motor. You got her set up the best you could, and we can tweak on her some more over the next few days. She'll be plenty fast. Let's get me strapped in and see what kind of mood the old girl's in today."

"Where the heck is Joe? He set the jets on the carbs and then disappeared like a ghost."

"I hope he's doing something with all the equipment. But I think he's in love again. I saw that girl from the motel out here this morning."

Jodell swung his long legs in through the open driver's-side window, then scrunched down into the seat and began to fasten the belts. Bubba reached in to make sure the lap and shoulder belts were cinched up tightly. The sudden left and right turns on this track would sling a driver all over the cockpit if he wasn't well tied down.

Directly behind him, Little Joe Weatherly climbed into his number 8 Mercury. He paid much less attention to his own belts, leaving them loose so they wouldn't bite into his flesh in the twists and spirals of Riverside. In his mirrors, Jodell could see someone lean in the window of Weatherly's car and make some kind of a joke. Little Joe cackled loudly enough that Jodell could actually hear his infectious laughter from inside his own car.

Sometimes he wished he could be as carefree as

Little Joe was. All the man did was win. Win and have a good time.

Jodell's engine kicked in with a welcomed throaty roar. Jodell was convinced that something important might have vibrated off on the long trip out. That the engine would never run right again. But now he felt that confident feeling come over him, the one he always got when he first fired the engine up at a track and felt its considerable harnessed power vibrating up to him through the car's chassis. At least there, on the starting line for practice, he could just as well be a winner as an also-ran. But he knew, with the car they had built, with his confidence in his own driving ability, they had a better chance than most.

He pulled the shifter down into first, eased out on the clutch, and gunned the engine as he pulled out onto the track. He had hardly reached the first turn before Little Joe went flying past him as if propelled by a jet engine. Jodell was tempted to follow him closely, to learn the track from him, but he suspected it would be prudent to learn at his own pace. For the first lap, he restrained the urge to speed, taking it easy, allowing anybody and everybody to go by as he assayed the track and where the car would need to be positioned to hit each corner just right. He could tell already that the tips Little Joe had shared with him were on the money, especially through the esses.

On the second lap, he was harder into the gas and flying into the corners. The tires screamed in protest as he flung the race car back and forth through bend after bend. Uphill and down, left and right, 'round and 'round he went, loving every twist and elevation, feeling as at home as he ever had on a racetrack.

He was tempted to stay out until he ran out of gas. But finally, after a dozen laps, he brought the Ford back to the pits, to a waiting Bubba and Joe. He shut the engine off as Bubba handed him a canteen full of water and Joe put aside his stopwatches and clipboard and went for the hood. Bubba leaned down by the window.

"How did she feel?"

"Like she was made to run on this highway."

"That's what I like to hear!" The big man wore a broad grin.

"Just like the roads back home. Except there ain't no holler on one side and Caney Creek on the other. All I need is a government agent on my tail and I would have this race in the bag."

"What do we need to do to make her better?"

That's what made the three of them such a good team. None of them were ever satisfied.

"We need to change the rear springs. Old Katie here tends to want to sail through some of the bumps. We probably need to put in a little stiffer set."

Bubba didn't say a word. He nodded and headed for the box where he kept the assortment of springs they'd brought.

While Bubba jacked up the rear end to change the springs, Joe and Jodell huddled over the clipboard.

"How's my motor?"

"Plenty of power. Sounded real good. Minded me when I told her what to do."

"Good oil pressure?"

"Pressure is good, and the water temp was right where it was supposed to be."

Jodell used his ever-present rag from his back pocket to wipe his face, swigged another gulp of water from the canteen, then crawled right up under the car to help Bubba change the springs.

As they worked, they listened to the odd sound the

car's engines made on this track. They sounded more like the hum of a swarm of angry bees instead of the normal freight train roar at most tracks. With the vast winding road course coiled out across flat, dusty terrain, the engine noise was more a steady buzz than a deafening roar captured by hills and grandstands clustered around an oval track. And even that was broken occasionally by the metallic grinding sound when a gear was missed on a shift.

The spring change finished, Jodell pulled the car back out onto the track to see if they had helped or hurt things. He stomped down on the gas and headed off toward the first of the esses. He sailed smoothly through them, heading for the tight right-hand bend. He feathered the gas, kicked in the clutch, downshifted, set his line, and was smoothly out the other side. Once through, he stomped the gas again and headed down the short straightaway toward where another tight right-hand curve waited for him at the end.

He downshifted again, stomped on the brakes, and felt the car shake slightly as she tried to wheel-hop beneath him. He cut the steering wheel sharply, yanked the shifter down into second, and then jammed the gas pedal down hard to the floor. He feathered the gas through the gentle left-hand curve before roaring off down the long straightaway.

He could feel the speed build as he raced down the long straightaway. The engine hummed happily as he flew down into the tight 180-degree turn that awaited him at its end. As he drew close, he eased off on the gas and jumped hard on the brakes. The car began to wheel-hop once again as he guided her out toward the wall, then cut down toward the inside in the center of the corner.

The car then swung out wide as he jerked the shifter down into a lower gear. He was careful not to break her loose as she came off the turn. Once he felt the back end safely under him, he set sail past the pit road, took the easy left-hander, then headed back up toward the esses once again. He hit them at speed this time, hitting his marks perfectly, and raced through them.

This time, Jodell ran another seven or eight laps, gaining a much better feel for the car and the track. The rear wheels were still trying to hop on him in spots, and he made a mental note to adjust the brakes before he went back out. He came up on the number 8 Mercury of Little Joe Weatherly, and this time he felt comfortable following him around for a couple of laps. He watched the line the Mercury ran, studying how Weatherly approached each corner.

Joe Banker was standing on a platform where he could get a decent view of most of the track. He kept clicking on his stopwatches and writing down the times they revealed on his clipboard. Jodell's speeds were getting better and better since he had pulled in behind Little Joe. As he watched those two, he also kept an eye on the Wood brothers car number 121, piloted by a local racer named Dan Gurney. The stopwatches confirmed that he, too, was flying around the track.

Jodell dropped off the rear of Little Joe's Mercury as he hit the 180 at the end of the long straightaway, then eased through the corner, staying low coming out before dropping down the pit road. He cut the engine and paused a second to catch his breath before he unsnapped the shoulder belts and climbed out the window. He unfastened the strap on his driving helmet and set the helmet on the roof of the race car next to where his name was painted over the window.

Joe came running up, smiling, his stopwatches flapping wildly around his neck.

"Those last laps were great, Cuz!"

"Yeah, I thought I had the fast way around here figured out, but then I got in behind Little Joe and found a better way."

"What about the car?"

"We need to adjust the brakes. I'm getting some wheel-hop with the rear tires when I get in the brakes real hard."

"Got it," Bubba said, and dashed to the toolboxes to grab a couple of wrenches.

Bubba was dead tired late that afternoon, bushed from all the heavy work he'd done on the car. Jodell was hot and tired, too, but reinvigorated by the knowledge that Catherine and Joyce were supposed to arrive at the airport in Los Angeles at seven-thirty that evening. By the time they got back to the hotel, Jodell and Bubba only had time to grab a quick shower, borrow a car, and head out to the airport.

Jodell had not talked with Catherine in two days. She had not been feeling well, but had gone to see the doctor before they left so the bug she had picked up wouldn't ruin the trip for her.

Bubba dozed in the car most of the way to the airport, but Jodell woke him up long enough to see the Hollywood sign on the ridge above the city.

"I'd hate to have to paint that thing" was all he said, then he was snoring again.

The Constellation had come in twenty minutes early after catching a tailwind out of Dallas. As they waited with their bags on the curb in front of the terminal, Catherine and Joyce tried not to act too much like tourists. But they couldn't believe how warm it was, or that they were actually all the way out there, on the other side of the country from Chandler Cove. Even tired as they were from the all-day trip, they were still excited to be there, eager to take in the sights, but most excited about being with their husbands.

As Jodell pulled into the airport entrance, Bubba wet his finger to slick back a wayward strand of hair. He shuffled nervously in his seat as Jodell circled with the drive and eased around to the front of the terminal. He slid the sedan up beside the two women and shut off the engine, but they were busy talking, looking about at all the hubbub of the busy airport, and obviously didn't recognize the car.

"You girls wanna be in the movies?" Jodell finally shouted to them.

They both jumped, then ran to the welcome embraces of their respective husbands. Jodell kissed Catherine deeply, then finally held her away from him so he could get a good look at her, as if she might have changed drastically in some way in only four days.

"I love you, honey," he said, and kissed her again before he suddenly remembered she had not felt well. He looked hard at her again and felt her face for fever with his hand. "How do you feel? Are you okay?"

She had an odd look on her face, seemed on the verge of saying something, then quickly appeared to change her mind and merely smiled and embraced him again, even harder, then kissed him once more.

She didn't get around to answering his questions just then.

The girls chattered away, anxious to share every detail of the plane trip with them, the things they had seen out the Constellation's windows as they crossed the big mountains.

"I can't believe we were in Tennessee this morning and in California tonight," Joyce was saying as Bubba and Jodell loaded up their suitcases in the borrowed car's trunk.

"Yeah, y'all were traveling in style," Bubba agreed.

"You oughta try spending three days in the same truck cab with Bubba and Joe." Jodell laughed. "Between Joe's snoring and Bubba's stomach growling I almost rode back there in the race car."

"By the way, speaking of food, I believe I could go for . . ."

"We better get him in the car and find him some

burgers or he might start gnawing on one of them suitcases!"

Their first stop was at a drive-in restaurant a few blocks from the terminal, a place with waitresses on roller skates who brought the food right out to the car. They ate cheeseburgers, fries, and milk shakes from a tray that had been hung on their door. Meanwhile, the women recounted every moment of their flight.

Then they drove up the freeway and meandered slowly through the streets of Beverly Hills, taking in the unbelievable homes, trying to figure out from a map they had bought which ones belonged to movie stars. They explored the fairyland until it got too dark to see much beyond the massive gates of the mansions.

Jodell gave Catherine a long sideways look when she asked him to stop at another drive-in for a sandwich, but he pulled over anyway. The cheeseburger near the airport would have usually done her for two days.

"All this traveling must have made me hungry," she explained.

"Me, too," Bubba joined in. "I'll take two. And a chili dog."

Then, with the windows down and the warm air rushing in, they drove through the bright lights of the Sunset Strip and into Hollywood. It was past eight o'clock by then, but the streets were full, cars everywhere, people on the sidewalks, a crowd around the theater where the stars' footprints were immortalized in cement. Bubba was on a mission to try to see John Wayne, so they all helped him scan the folks on the swarming sidewalks for a glimpse of the man as the thick traffic crawled along. Jodell, though, caught himself looking for someone else, for a slightly familiar face, a pair of eyes he might recognize amid the sea of strangers.

"I don't reckon none of these folks have to get up in the morning and go to work," Bubba observed. "It's mighty near bedtime where I come from."

Somehow, they managed to wind their way up into the hills to the twisting, winding Mulholland Drive and to the deserted overlook directly above the Hollywood Bowl. They left the car and walked to the edge of the rocks to look out at the carpet of lights that seemed to stretch away as far as they could see, winking mischievously at them, at the full moon overhead in a brilliantly clear sky. And at the Hollywood Freeway, to their left, a steady stream of taillights working their way toward downtown.

"Look at that!" Catherine said, pointing out across the valley and pulling Jodell closer to her. "I could never have imagined a view like this existed anywhere."

"It's a far cry from what you can see off the mountaintops back home for sure," Jodell offered as he returned her hug and eased her down onto a bench. "I didn't know there could be so many people living in one place."

Joyce had grabbed Bubba's hand and dragged him off to a secluded part of the overlook.

"We'll be back in a minute. I want to show Bubba something," she had said with a wink toward Catherine.

Neither Jodell nor Catherine minded being left alone. The warm breeze and sea of lights had put them both in a romantic mood. As soon as the other couple disappeared down a narrow trail, he leaned down and kissed his wife again, this time deeper and more passionately.

"I missed you, honey. I am so glad you are here with me."

"I missed you, too, Jodell. I've been excited all day just knowing we were going to be able to spend a few days out here together. Even if I do have to share you with Joe and Bubba and the race car."

"That's the only thing I don't like about racing. Having to be away from you."

"I know."

There it was again. That odd look on her face in the faint light, as if she was holding in a secret that wanted to get out but didn't know how.

"Maybe this weather will help you get over that bug anyway."

She pulled away, stood, and took a step or two away from him, then turned suddenly and kneeled at his knees, taking his hands in hers. She looked him in the eyes and smiled, and the moonlight caught what must have been a tear rolling down each cheek. Jodell caught his breath.

"I went to the doctor like I told you I would. I didn't have the flu after all."

Jodell felt himself go dizzy, saw the lights in the valley begin to swim and swirl behind her.

"But what . . ."

"We're going to have a baby, Jodell. You're going to be a daddy."

He stood suddenly, almost knocking her over, then reached to pull her up next to him, to hold her close, to wrap her in his arms as if he would never let her go.

"Oh, Cath! That's wonderful!"

"Are you sure, honey? I didn't know . . ."

"Lord, yes! It's the most wonderful thing in the world!"

"I didn't know, with the racing and all, and the new season, and all the traveling . . ."

"Wheeeeyeeee . . ." he squealed, his yelp echoing off the hills around them.

Bubba came scrambling back up the path to see what in the world was happening. His flattop was slightly askew, and even in the dim light, there appeared to be lipstick smeared all over his face.

"What in the world? I thought some critter was attacking y'all."

Jodell let out another yell, grabbed the big man, and began dancing around in the dust of the overlook. Catherine could only laugh out loud at the silly scene.

"You'll never believe it," Jodell sang. "Never in a million years!"

"What?" Bubba asked, pulling away from his loony friend. Jodell kept right on dancing by himself, raising a little dust cloud at his feet as he did.

"I'm having a baby! I mean, Catherine and I are. Aw, Catherine is. Can you believe that? I'm gonna be a daddy!"

"A daddy! Wheeeeyeee!" Bubba's screech matched Jodell's in both volume and duration. He grabbed Jodell and danced with him again, this time leading the jitterbug. Next, the big man grabbed Catherine and gave her an embrace, waltzed with Jodell some more, then hugged Joyce before he suddenly thought of something. "Hey! Little Joe's having a party tonight. We gotta get out there and tell everybody they've really got something to celebrate this time."

Jodell ended up letting Bubba and Joyce go on to Little Joe's continuous gala, where they were all expected. He knew Catherine was tired from the flight and he certainly didn't want to leave her alone. He knew Bub would spread the news just fine without him. He still tingled, still found it hard to breathe as he lay beside her and held her hand to his face, idly kissing her fingers.

"I was serious, Jodell," she said finally. "I didn't know how you might take the news."

"I've got to be the happiest man in the world," he said simply.

"But I know how serious you are about racing, Jodell. I wouldn't want this to slow you down." He stroked her arm, kissed her cheek. He wasn't sure what she meant, though. How could being a daddy slow him down any? "Bringing a new life into the world is a serious thing."

"I know, Cath."

She turned and kissed him on the lips.

"I just don't want you worrying out there, Jodell. Worrying about the responsibility. About what would happen to me and the baby if something happens to you. I know what you've always said about how you can't drive scared or race tentatively or you'll get in trouble for sure. That would be the worst thing."

"Honey, if anything this is only going to make me race harder. I'll have to do even better. For you and the baby."

He meant what he was saying, and he loved the feeling her news had set loose in his heart. He loved her so much, already loved the new life that was growing in her. But he had to admit to himself that there was a slight twinge of something else there inside him, too. Something odd besides the pride, the love.

He couldn't quite decide what it was, but he quickly shoved it aside, pulled his wife close to him, and held her as tightly as he dared.

CONCENTRATION

They made it to the track early the next morning. Even Joe, Bubba, and Joyce dragged in before the gates opened, obviously the victims of too many Canadian Club toasts the night before at the Weatherly party.

"We had to celebrate Jodell's and Catherine's good news," Joe Banker whispered, holding the top of his head with his hand as if it might fly off if he didn't. "And take up the slack with y'all not being there and all. Now, if y'all would quit breathing so loud, I'd sure appreciate it." He scowled at a grove of trees that held a flock of happily singing birds. "And find out how to turn them birds off, too. Ooooh."

Joyce Baxter could hardly keep her eyes open in the bright California sun winking at them from the distant mountains.

"I don't see how you boys can race all day and go to Little Joe's parties all night, too," she moaned. "I think I'm fixing to die."

"Well, we're sure sorry we missed all the festivities," Jodell said, winking at Catherine, then instantly turning serious. "Let's see if Joe and Bubba can quit dragtailing around long enough to help me qualify this car on the pole."

Catherine and Joyce went off to meet up with some of the other drivers' and crew members' wives with whom they had become friendly. They called themselves "the Perfume Pit Crew" and they had themselves a leisurely day planned, most of it in the warm sun somewhere, maybe a picnic in one of the turns, but always within sight of what Jodell and his crew and the rest of their husbands were doing. Catherine never tired of seeing Jodell race, whether it was practice, qualifying, or the main event. Since she'd been with him from his very first race, their first "date," she had loved all the excitement that went with the sport.

Joyce Baxter had been a casual race fan before she met Bubba at one of Little Joe's parties before one of the Darlington races. Now, she too was neck-deep in racing and all that went with it. And she never strayed far from her husband whenever she had an opportunity to be at the track with him.

Finally, Jodell, Joe, and Bubba stood in the inspection line waiting for the car to be cleared for qualifying. After a shock absorber change that morning, they'd run well in the last morning practice. Very well. Jodell was beginning to feel comfortable on the twisting, winding track, and that was translated into good results each time Joe had clicked the buttons on the stopwatches that almost always hung from his neck.

Jodell's circuits continued to get faster and faster as he found different spots and moves that shaved fractions of seconds out of the time it took to navigate the meandering course. Now, he couldn't wait until he could get out there and do a lap that actually counted for something.

They slowly pushed the car ahead a spot at a time as each car in front of them cleared the short qualifying inspection. It was a chance for Jodell to catch his breath before the Ford would be pushed on to pit road. From then on, he would have to concentrate, to bear down and get the best starting spot they could muster.

Bubba wasn't relaxing, though. All the way up to where the inspectors waited, and then the entire way out to the end of pit road, where they would line up with the cars waiting to qualify, he kept thinking of things he wanted to check, to eyeball, to tweak an infinitesimal amount to make them as good as he could make them. Joe and Jodell talked strategy as they waited in the warm sunshine, mostly saying the same things over and over to each other. But it helped to stave off the inevitable nervousness and helped Jodell concentrate on the task at hand.

Finally, ahead of them, the first car rolled off the line to start its run for the pole, then the next, and qualifying was under way. They were four cars away from the head of the line when Jodell swung his long legs in through the open driver's-side window. He settled in the seat and started buckling up the lap and shoulder belts, then retrieved his helmet from the floorboard and fastened the chin strap. Once he had the bindings tight, he wiggled about in the seat, making sure that the belts would not let him slip around inside them. A road course track like Riverside could bounce a driver around inside his car like a pinball if he wasn't gussied up and tied down securely.

Bubba finished checking the air pressure in the tires yet again, then he stood to poke his head into the window and check the belts for himself. Joe watched the official at the head of the line, waiting for him to signal when they needed to move up.

Jodell worked to clear his mind of everything but the track itself and how he would beat it. Hard as it was, he worked to completely block out the wonderful news from the night before. Every driver he had met so far today had shaken his hand or slapped him on the back, congratulated him, kidded him about manufacturing his own little pit crew. He grinned when he thought of how earlier that morning Joe Weatherly had handed him a greasy, gnarled old knob off a gear-shift lever.

"Jodell, here's a little present for you, a teething ring for that young 'un," he had said in mock seriousness.

Jodell shook his head again to clear it, then visualized the way he would attack every turn, how the car would likely react, and where his marks were to brake, to shift up and down. He rested one hand casually on the steering wheel, and the other gripped the diagonal roll bar. But he was growing impatient. He had never liked the waiting, and especially the down time just before a chance to go out on the track and do something to win a race.

Simple fact: Jodell Bob Lee hated to sit still for very long.

Catherine and Joyce and some of the others in the Perfume Pit Crew had found themselves a nice spot near the S-turns. It allowed them to see much of the rest of the track, too. They spread their blankets and dealt out a huge picnic lunch. Joyce had had Bubba pack over a cooler filled with Bubble Up and crushed ice. The girls settled in to munch on the sandwiches, work on their tans, and watch for the first of the qualifying cars to pull out onto the course.

"Sure a lot warmer than it is back in Chandler Cove," Joyce observed.

"Where?" Catherine deadpanned.

"Chandler Cove."

"Where?"

The girls giggled. This place did seem a million miles from the tiny town in the foothills of the Smoky Mountains. A place where a quick call home to Catherine's mother had confirmed that a couple of inches of snow had fallen since they had flown out the day before.

"Joyce, here comes the first car," one of the other girls reported.

Sure enough, the PA announcer was naming the driver of the initial qualifying car, and they could hear the far-off reverberation of a race car engine. They listened to its whine as it came to speed, as it quickly grew closer, then watched the car go flying past them and off towards the far turn. Before long, it roared past again, this time pushing for its actual qualifying lap. And then, here came the next hopeful, straining to do better than the first as well as all those that would follow.

"Where is Jodell?" Joyce asked.

"I think somewhere toward the front. He ought to be coming out shortly."

"He looked fast in that last practice. I saw Bubba hopping up and down in the pits so that's a good sign."

"He looked about as fast as anybody, except maybe that Gurney fellow."

The clamor of the next car as it thundered past drowned out their conversation. They watched it until it disappeared around the far corner, the noise of its motor dying to a distant buzz as the car hit the far side of the track. The sound wavered eerily as the car tracked down the long back straightaway, heading into the tight 180 that lurked at its end.

Jodell sat one car back on pit road, impatiently waiting his turn to go out and take the qualifying lap. Had he been sitting here an hour? Two? It certainly seemed like it. The car beyond his hood finally got waved out onto the track, and Jodell watched as it pulled away, feeling his own vehicle being pushed up a spot by Joe, Bubba, and a couple of members of the team directly behind them. When the car came by to take the green flag on the start of its qualifying lap, Jodell reached over and hit the switches that fired up his own engine. The powerful roar of the motor was like the best rock and roll song he had ever heard.

"Let's show them, Gracie," he said, and thumped the dash, revving the engine as he waited for the signal for him to roll off the line. The other car on the track finally flashed by to finish his qualifying lap and the official waved Jodell out. He eased off on the clutch and kicked down on the gas. The car leapt forward as the power in the motor transferred itself to the drivetrain.

He rolled off the pit road and pointed the Ford's nose up toward the esses. He worked the gears and the brakes smoothly as he rolled around through the sharp right-hand twist and down the short straight. Next he pumped the brakes, kicked in the clutch, and hauled down on the shifter, simultaneously turning the wheel sharply as he got back into the gas through the left-hander. Then he was onto the long straightaway toward the 180 at the end. Once through the corner, he flashed by the pits, where he could just get a glimpse of Bubba standing in his preferred perch right up by the wall.

Joyce had caught sight of him first when he had gunned the Ford out of the pits. The low rumble of the car's powerful motor could clearly be heard from where they rested on the blankets.

"Here he comes!" she said, pointing and punching Catherine.

The car had built up considerable speed as it came roaring past them. The Bubble Up logo against the blue backdrop of the car's paint job shimmered in the bright sunshine, and Catherine was so close she could almost read her husband's name written above the door.

"Go! Go! Go!" Catherine yelled, waving her hand over her head like she was twirling a lariat, trying to lasso her husband's race car as it rumbled past. She loved watching Jodell drive, took great pleasure in knowing how much he loved racing and that he was getting a chance to actually do it for a living.

The two women stood and waited until Jodell zoomed past again, this time for the qualification run. They jumped and waved him past, screaming all the time, urging him on.

"Oh, he looked fast, Cath!" Joyce yelled as the car flew off into the distance. "He's top ten. I just feel it!"

"He'll be fast," Catherine declared, but she was still crossing her fingers, folding her arms across her chest the way she always did when Jodell ran a qualifying lap. He kidded her about her superstitions, but he had plenty of his own that he hated to admit. Most of the drivers did. Little Joe Weatherly, for example, would not drive a car with the color green anywhere on it, nor would he have anything to do with the number 13.

Jodell hammered the throttle as he took the flag starting his qualifying run. He took the left at the end of the pits and ran hard up toward the esses. He hit them smoothly and flew down toward the right-hander. Hard on the brakes again, he pumped them once, then twice, before cutting low in the turn and roaring out the other side. The car felt good under him. The engine sang a beautiful song. He could feel his heart pounding in his chest.

And then, for some reason, he thought of Catherine watching him from out there beyond the esses. She would probably be standing, screaming, her fingers and arms crossed the way she always did. But this time, she had his child in her womb. The child he would be responsible for raising, for feeding, for providing everything he or she needed. That is, so long as nothing happened to him out there on the track to keep him from it.

Then, suddenly, he realized that he had kept the gas pedal down too long, and the next corner came up on him much faster than he was expecting. That made him a tad late in slowing, forcing him to have to stand harder on the brakes than he wanted to. He went deeper into the corner than he would have liked, losing a couple of tenths of a second when he was forced to stay in the brakes a little longer than he should have. But he had to in order to keep the car from sliding off the track coming out of the corner. As he exited the turn he instinctively knew that his shot at a top-five starting position was likely gone and there was certainly no chance now for the pole. He felt his stomach drop in disappointment.

Down the long straight he forced himself to forget his bobble, to concentrate harder so he didn't drive too hard into the final turn. Losing concentration, overdriving, had already cost him several spots, and he had to hit the corner perfectly if he was to salvage a decent starting spot at all. He expertly worked the gears and brakes at the end of the straight shoot.

He loved this track! For a moment, he had to remind himself that he was at the racetrack in Southern California and not on some mountain road back home with a government agent on his tail.

Around to the checkered flag he went, crossing under it at full throttle. He stayed in the gas until he was well past the start/finish line. As the car slowed, he finally allowed himself to show emotion. He grunted and banged his fist down hard on the steering wheel, knowing he had blown a chance for a top-five start, if not the pole position itself, simply by an instant's inattention.

Back to the pits, he shut off the motor and coasted to a stop. While the car was still moving, though, he jerked the belts loose and flung his helmet angrily onto the car's floorboard, then sat there steaming for a full minute. Bubba was there to help him when he finally climbed out.

"Dang it!" Jodell spat, kicking the ground.

"What's wrong, Joe Dee? That was a heck of a run," Bubba said, perplexed at the outburst.

"It was okay, but I overdrove into one of the corners and it's gonna cost us. I knew better, but . . ."

He gave the poor, innocent dust another good, solid kick.

Joe walked up then, smiling. He knew what he had seen in the hands of his stopwatches. Compared to what the others yet to qualify had done in practice, they seemed to be in good shape.

"What's the problem?" Joe asked as he assayed the look on his cousin's face. "That was a fine run."

"He don't like the way he went through one of the corners," Bubba said, shaking his head. It was not like Jodell to throw a fit like this. Not like him at all.

The driver sat down on the ground and leaned back against the side of his car, still muttering under his breath to himself. Joe and Bubba kept out of his way, getting busy looking at tire wear and timing and anything else they could think of until he cooled off.

Meanwhile, Fireball Roberts rolled out for his run, then so did Joe Weatherly, Ned Jarrett, Dan Gurney, Junior Johnson, Richard Petty, and all the others. It didn't help Jodell's feelings at all when they ultimately found that they had qualified eleventh, just a mite out of the top ten. The tenths of a second he had frittered away could have won them several positions at the start of the race.

Too many people depended on him not to have lapses like that one. And at least one more would soon. No way could he afford such stupid mistakes.

Finally, he stood, looked into the waning California sun, and set his jaw. The way to make sure his child had all he or she would need was for him to do the job he had chosen to do. And for him to do it the right way. Losing his attention the way he had was a sure way to lose a race, to get himself badly hurt, or to have even worse things happen. Things he didn't even want to consider.

No, the best thing he could do for his unborn child, for the child's mother he loved so much, was to take care of business, to keep his head in the race.

And to win.

Yes, and to win.

GETTING READY TO RUN

Race day at last! Jodell and Catherine were up early, neither of them able to sleep past six even though it was still dark outside. Catherine said her body was still on Chandler Cove time. Jodell simply couldn't sleep and was already steering, accelerating, braking in his head. They found a café open for breakfast a short walk away and weren't surprised at all to see Bubba and Joyce just taking a table when they got there.

"We was gonna let y'all sleep in," Bubba said.

"We were gonna do the same for you," Catherine explained.

"No Joe, huh?" Jodell asked.

"Naw. I think he had a date with that girl from the motel. They were going to party with Little Joe and

Lord knows where else," Bubba answered from behind a menu.

The eggs and toast made them all feel better. So did the ride in the truck through the golden California morning to the track at Riverside, all four of them crammed into the cab. There was already a steady stream of cars heading that way, too, their drivers and occupants clearly in a festive mood. And it was obvious also that there would be a huge crowd to watch the event that day.

Jodell had stopped talking altogether by the time they got to the drivers' entrance at the track. That wasn't unusual. He often got quiet and tried to think only of the race that he was about to drive. But he seemed to have switched off earlier and more completely than usual this morning.

They found a carnival atmosphere at the track. Flags and banners flew everywhere, vendors selling souvenirs and food were lined up on every thoroughfare, and the crowd was already gathering. Unlike a conventional speedway with its oval track and surrounding stacks of main grandstands, here people were literally everywhere, swarming all over the speedway property, staking out the better viewing spots. Lawn chairs, blankets, and ice chests were all over as the fans settled in for the duration. The ticket booths had lines snaking away in serpentine columns as race fans queued up to buy their tickets. So did the rest rooms. The parking lots had already begun to fog up with dust, and the sunlight glinted off thousands of cars' windshields, lined up like dominoes as far as the eye could see.

Down in the pit area the crews were already stirring, buzzing like a hive of bees all over their gleaming machines. There were people milling about everywhere around the race cars and in the pit stalls. Mechanics checked and adjusted their sleek race cars in the garage. Crewmen worked feverishly in their pit stalls, arranging tools and parts like scrub nurses preparing for surgery. Others worked, sweating already, stacking tires, filling dump cans with gasoline, sweeping dust from underfoot so no one would slip during a crucial stop.

Joe showed up shortly, his hair slightly misarranged but otherwise none the worse for the all-nighter. He and Bubba went over one more time what they wanted to do on the day's pit stops and which one of the pickup crew would do what and when.

"You sure they know what to do, Bub?" Joe asked.

"Sure as I can be. We went over everything yesterday and they've crewed before, so we ought to be okay."

Jodell stayed out by the truck with Catherine for a long time after the others had gone on inside. He talked quietly with her, avoiding the subject of the day's race completely.

Catherine listened to him as he talked about the weather, the mountains, the odd characters he had spotted in the crowd. But she could sense a vague uneasiness about him and the race. It seemed he was avoiding going back inside until the last minute. For the first time that she could remember, he was leaving all the prerace preparation so far to Joe and Bubba.

Then finally he quit talking, and they sat there quietly on the tail of the truck, holding hands. At last, with little more than an hour to go before the start of the race, it was Catherine who had to leave. She was due to meet Joyce at the scoring stand. Reluctantly, Jodell helped her down off the truck and hugged her tightly once more. Then he gave her a long, lingering kiss, as if he was leaving her for a long, long time instead of merely the duration of a stock car race. It left her breathless.

She walked off toward the scoring stand wondering what had gotten into him. He never acted this way before a race. It was so unusual for him.

As she walked away, he stood and watched her until she disappeared into the growing crowd. Only then did he make his way back toward the pits and the job he had to do.

He walked past the other pits and the familiar cars and faces of the race teams that worked there. He by now considered most of them family, as close to him as many of his own relatives back in Tennessee. They shared so much, bounding from race to race, trying to make a go of full-time racing, competing viciously on the track, but for the most part and with a few exceptions, they were fast friends the rest of the time. Some saw him, waved, yelled a "Good luck" his way. Others were simply too busy getting ready to try to beat his brains out on the track. He shook his head and smiled at the thought of that irony.

Bubba and the boys had already pushed the new Ford car out to its place on the line by the time he got there. Joe walked up with his clipboard and motioned Jodell to join him under the umbrella shading the pit area a few stalls away.

"Let's plan our stops for every hundred miles. If we get some cautions we'll play it by ear," Joe suggested.

"Sounds good. Bubba shown the boys what they need to do on the stops?"

"Yeah, they'll be okay. Bubba's gonna jack and they'll change the tires and gas. They seem to be pretty good."

"Okay. I wish this thing would hurry up and get started. I hate getting to the track early, then having to wait and wait and wait for the darn race to start."

"Now, don't be getting a case of nerves on me. They can't run races on 'Jodell time,' you know. Besides, we have to have a good run today to pay for this trip, so we need you to think about what you're doing. This little trip west has cost us a fortune already and we ain't even fed Bubba on the way home yet."

"I'm not getting nerves. I just want to get this race done."

"Why? I thought you liked this track. You said the other day that it was just like driving whiskey runs on the roads back home."

"That's what I mean. You never knew what might happen on those runs. Always dangerous. Always."

"Hey, racing is always dangerous, too. I figured you knew that going in! Clear your head and get focused," Joe said sharply. "We have a race to win."

"All right, I'll be okay," Jodell said with a crooked grin and a wave of his hand.

But he couldn't shake the odd, uneasy feeling that had dogged him all morning. He stood next to the car as Bubba finished up yet another all-over inspection and came up for air. The big man was already soaked in sweat.

"Relax, Bubba. You gonna wear out the stems on them tires if you put a gauge on them one more time."

"Aw, Joe Dee. You of all people oughta know that you can't check things too much. Something breaks or comes loose because I didn't check it and then you wreck up, you gonna come looking for me, right?"

"Yeah, but you're making me nervous. That's all."

"What's wrong with you today? You're wound tighter than a high-C fiddle string."

"Nothing's wrong with me. I always get a little nervous before the start of a race."

"No, you don't either. That's what's bothering me and Banker. You've looked danger in the face since you was old enough to start driving that old moonshine car of your granddaddy's. I ain't never seen you nervous when it comes to driving a car," Bubba said, the concern obvious on his dirt-streaked face.

"Okay, suit yourself. I'm a nervous wreck." He managed his best grin and gave the big man a sharp cuff on the shoulder. "Let's look things over one more time."

And the two of them went back beneath the hood of the car.

He found himself as comfortable a seat as possible on an old piece of the concrete retaining wall where it had been broken and twisted. It had probably been rudely bulldozed over when they had cleared the acreage for whatever strip mall or housing tract they would eventually throw up here. He sat there in the middle of the dusty, weed-strewn lot for the better part of an hour, not even considering moving out of the hot sun or brisk, chapping wind. He had no trouble at all ignoring the constant stream of cars zipping past on the busy highway at the far end of the wide expanse of dust and rubble.

Busily, hurriedly on their way to someplace vitally important, their drivers likely did not notice the silver-haired old man, dressed in his dark jeans, black polo shirt, and sunglasses. Far as they were concerned, he might simply have been another pile of debris, another slab of graffiti-scored concrete out there.

Something mystical had drawn him back here to this place for the second day in a row. He had been there that afternoon at the two-mile-long speedway in Fontana, watching the beginning of the last practice, when the notion had suddenly hit him. He should have been concentrating on how his car and driver were doing out there on the new track, how they would try to win the race on Sunday, but instead, his mind kept wandering back to the moonscape which had, at one time, been a storied racetrack.

But then, without saying a word to any of the crew, he had set his radio headset down on the top of the rolling toolbox and had marched purposely out of the fenced-in garage area to where the rental car was parked. Bubba Baxter had seen him go. He didn't try to stop him. He knew where his friend was headed.

He had signed a few autographs along the way, mostly out of habit, but the next thing he knew, the car had been driving itself along the freeway and had somehow found its way back to the old razed track. It had parked itself at the edge of the demolished speedway and the old man had stepped out into the midst of the spinning dust devils and shimmering mirages.

He had been sitting on the broken retaining wall for over an hour before he finally realized why he had come back there; he wanted to be among the ghosts again.

There it was, drifting on the dusty wind. It might have been only the whistling of the breeze, but it sounded to him like the tinny voice of the loudspeakers calling his name and car number. And almost masked by the drone of traffic on the highway was the roar of the race crowd, cheering, screaming. And if he stared hard enough at the heat-rippled haze, he could almost make out a bleacher full of fans, a swirl of color way over there in the dense smog that had rolled in during the last few minutes from greater Los Angeles. And the line of traffic on the distant roadway merged into a line of strung-out race cars, all shined up and polished, resplendent in their gaudy paint.

Suddenly, from somewhere in the distance, the buzz of an engine grew stronger, as if one of the cars was actually approaching at speed. It might only have been an airplane on approach to the airport, but it certainly sounded like the engine of a stock Mercury, ready to race. Startled, he turned quickly to the spot where he reckoned turn two had once been, fully expecting to see the flash of a stock car quickly heading his way. He strained to see it, tried hard to pick it out of the wind-blown dust. He could now hear it clearly, the engine's pitch changed with a shift of gears, as it grew louder and louder.

Then, all of a sudden, he heard the grinding squeal of brakes, the solid smack of metal against metal as a heavy automobile slammed into a retaining wall.

A cold sweat covered him as the concussion of the collision faded to an echo and the old man tried to decide if he had actually heard anything at all. Or was it only the wind playing tricks on him? Or maybe it was his mind that was playing the tricks.

Then, far away, there was the sound of a man's voice. A rapid-fire, staccato voice with a broad Virginia drawl attached. The words were so indistinct, so quick, that he could not actually understand what was being said at first. If only he had not lost so much of his hearing, long since erased by the loud engines he had ridden behind for so long. He cocked his head to one side and thought, for an instant, that he could see a wisp of smoke in the direction from which the wreck sounds had come.

A sickening feeling swept over him. And suddenly, the voice became clear as could be. Jodell started to speak, to answer, then realized that the words were not aimed at him. But the voice was so distinct that he fully expected to see Little Joe Weatherly come hopping over toward him out of the swirling sand, goading him, inviting him to that night's party.

As Little Joe talked, he could also hear other voices joining in, those of Fireball Roberts and Curtis Turner and Tiny Lund and Neil Bonnett as well. He was surprised he recognized them so easily since it had been so long since he'd last heard them. They were clearly involved in a friendly but heated discussion about who was the best driver. Not "had been" but who "was now" the best.

The old driver was hardly aware that big tears were plowing furrows through the powdery dust on each of his cheeks.

Finally, when the voices had ultimately been washed out by the gusting wind, the old driver stood and walked for a while through the weeds and rubble that had claimed what was left of the old speedway. He eventually found himself where turn six had once been. He kicked the crusty dirt with the toe of his boot, then looked up at the burning yellow sky overhead.

Somewhere up there, they were still racing. He grinned broadly.

Down here, so was he.

J odell zipped up his racing suit and strode over to the car, still stretching and stifling a yawn. He was always one of the first gladiators to climb into his chariot on race day, and there was a good reason. In the sanctuary of the cockpit, he could begin to focus on the race ahead with most of the distractions left outside. He would finally be able to relax inside the car, the one place on the planet where he still felt most comfortable.

Dozens of different thoughts kept spinning through his mind this day, though, spinning around his head like pesky hornets. One by one he fought them off and began to focus in on the task at hand: winning this, the first race of a critical season in their racing venture. He never considered the possibility of having to quit. That was not an option. But a win would certainly make the whole picture a hell of a lot brighter!

As the minutes clicked off toward the start, Bubba finally came out from underneath the car, satisfied that everything was as ready to go as it would ever be. Joe was busy in the pit making sure everything was in place for the first stop. All along the line, the other drivers had now started making their way to their respective race cars as well.

"Hey, Bubba, can you hand me something to drink?" Jodell asked, wiping his face with the rag he always kept in his pocket. He didn't want to drink too much. It would be hours before he could take a bathroom break.

"Here you go!" Bubba handed him a small paper cup of ice water. "You want a wet rag?"

"Naw, it's not very hot in here. Not like Daytona or Darlington, for sure. I think I'll be fine."

"You sure?" Bubba asked, holding up the dripping rag.

"Yeah. Let's just get this thing going so we can win it and go home."

"Suits me. You need help buckling in?"

"I can get it. Can you clean this window off? I'm getting a little glare on it."

Bubba stepped away to get a rag and something to clean the windshield with while Jodell started strapping himself in. He was reaching for his goggles when he felt someone reach in and unsnap one of the shoulder belts. Jodell twisted around to see Little Joe Weatherly leaning in his window.

"Damn it, Little Joe! Now ain't the time to be horsin' around."

"Here, I brought you something."

With that, he dumped a paper bag full of peanuts

from the concession stand onto the floorboard of Jodell's Ford.

"Stop that, you superstitious so-and-so! You know
I don't believe in all that hocus-pocus stuff of yours."

Weatherly had a fairly believable look of hurt on
his face.

"I'm just casting a good luck spell on you, that's
all."

"Jinxin' me is more like it. Weren't you the one
who took flight number thirteen out here? Didn't I
hear you groaning about that yesterday?"

"Yeah, well, them peanuts are going to bring you
good luck." Then he broke out in an evil grin. "And
you'll need it to stay within sight of me today."

"You just watch yourself out there, old man. I don't
want my wind to blow you right off the track every
time I pass you."

With that, Weatherly winked, pulled out of the car,
thumped Jodell affectionately on the side of his helmet, and then he was gone.

The call for the drivers to come to their cars
screeched over the loudspeakers. Jodell watched in the
rearview mirror as Little Joe climbed into the driver's
seat of the red-and-black Mercury. He could feel the
peanuts crunching underneath his feet on the floorboard. He started to try to scoop the stupid things out
so they wouldn't annoy him through the entire race,
but there was no time now. Besides, he'd have to un-
fasten the belts he had just spent all that time getting
tightened just right.

Damned old fool Weatherly! Why couldn't he be
serious for once?

Aw, to heck with him, he thought, then sat there
and focused in on the start of the race. He plotted in

his mind where he wanted to go when the green flag fell and whom he wanted to follow.

"Gentlemen, start your engines!"

All along the line of cars, the engines began to rumble to life, their amalgamated revving a solid wall of thunder that spread over the entire expanse of the complex. The huge cheer from the crowd added to the cacophony as they all rose to their feet, screaming, waving their arms, their caps, anything they could find to flutter.

Jodell pushed the starter button and felt the starter turn the engine over, saw the gauges all line up normally as the RPMs rose in response to his goosing of the throttle. He stretched out his arms one last time, then gripped the steering wheel tightly, more than ready to go. Kicking in the clutch once again, he reached over and shifted the car up into first gear, anxious for the signal to come that would tell them to begin to roll off.

The crowd's excitement level was reaching a crescendo, the spectators lining the viewing areas around the track pressing tightly up against the double fence that separated them from the cement retaining walls or piles of tires that ran around much of the track. All around the long circuit, they strained to catch first sight of the cars as they took their pace laps around the twisting 2.6-mile course.

The officials at the head of the line finally started waving the cars off the line and out onto the track. Jodell Lee pulled the shifter down into neutral before shoving it back up into first, then eased out on the clutch. The throbbing power of the motor vibrated throughout the race car like the stomping of a herd of horses itching to be cut loose from their corral.

Over in the scoring stand, Catherine watched the

cars move off. She bowed her head quickly and said a short prayer that God would bring Jodell home safely. She was worried about Jodell, and especially after the strange way he had acted before the race. It had seemed almost as if he had not wanted to leave her. She wondered if he might have had some kind of bad premonition that spooked him. Or if the news about the baby had distracted him. She could only pray that he didn't let anything . . . anything at all . . . take his focus from the car and the track and the race.

Once the cars began moving, Jodell cleared his mind once more and zeroed in on winning this race. With the distractions of all the prerace activities gone, he could concentrate on getting up front and staying there. As they rolled along slowly behind the pace car, he reached up and pulled his goggles down over his face, tightened his jaws, and intensified his grip on the wheel.

The Ford felt good under him. The engine sang a sweet song each time he goosed the gas, and the front end felt good and tight as he swung the wheel back and forth. If nothing broke and the brakes held, he was confident he would be a contender when the end came.

The pace car sped up a bit on the second parade lap, allowing the cars trailing behind to build up some heat in their engines and tires. Jodell watched his own water and oil temperatures climb into the normal range. As they snaked past the pits, he could see Bubba holding up their signboard with a big "OK?" scrawled on it. Jodell gave him a thumbs-up out the window and got a tip of the signboard as acknowledgment.

The cars came back around again, coming out of the 180-degree turn toward the pits. Just then, he felt a tap on his bumper as the car behind him pulled up tight on his rear in anticipation of the start. Likewise, he had pulled up close as he dared on the car in front of him. And then he spotted the green flag going upward in the starter's hand, and next waving figure eights high over his head. Jodell stomped on the gas and raced off happily toward the esses, ready to seek the point as quickly as his motor, the track and the traffic would let him.

He jumped down to the inside immediately and powered past the car in front of him, outbraking him as the first corner came up. Through the esses he ripped and cut, trying to claim another spot just as easily. As he braked hard to take the sharp righthander, he bumped the car in front and had to get out of the gas for a moment so the driver could regain control. If he hadn't, if he had been bullheaded about it, as some would have been, both cars would have likely spun off into the sandy soil of the infield, their day over for all practical purposes.

The car on his tail, a Plymouth, closed right up on the Ford's back bumper. The driver was able to get up along his outside, but Jodell managed to hold his preferred line and made it out of the corner first. As they hit the short left-hander and then went out onto the long straightaway, the power of Joe Banker's motor allowed him to put more distance on the Plymouth, leaving him behind for the moment.

The laps started to click off as the cars twisted and wound their way through the various turns on the track. Jodell picked off another car on the second lap, moving up another spot, the experience he had on the track now paying off as he felt more comfortable racing on it than at any time so far. He felt himself falling into a smooth, consistent driving style, and he knew Joe's stopwatches would confirm that his lap times would be more constant. That, Jodell figured, would be the way to win at Riverside.

Joe was, indeed, making that very observation. The front cars were quite fast, but Jodell seemed to be holding his own, so far not gaining much on them but not losing ground either. His times were consistent with what they had run in practice. That was a good sign that the track was coming to him. Joe scribbled down the time for the first two laps into the appropriate boxes on his clipboard. Unlike most of the tracks they ran, it took a long time to make one lap of this circuit, so he actually had time to catch his breath, to study the lengthening column of numbers between each pass by.

Bubba Baxter watched appreciatively as the cars swung back and forth around the snaky course. Sometimes he almost wished he could be a simple paying spectator, enjoying without prejudice watching the skill of the drivers and the strength of their well-prepared machines. But in the end, he much preferred doing exactly what he was doing at that moment: being in the middle of the action, intently watching his own car for signs of adjustments they might need to make after a hundred miles of competition, and studying with equal intensity the other cars out there for any signs of weakness they might be able to exploit.

And that's when he spotted something. When Little Joe Weatherly's number 8 Mercury went by, only a couple of cars behind Jodell's Ford, he thought he caught a whiff of smoke. Sure enough, he could make out a little smoke at the car's rear end as he followed it all the way to the left turn beyond the end of pit road where the track went uphill toward the esses.

Maybe it was only tire smoke, he thought. But his

nose was trained better than that. It was likely something more serious. He'd watch it and tell Joe Banker about it the next chance he got.

Jodell tore his way through the esses confidently now, pumping the brakes hard as the front end set, then yanking the shifter down into second as he dived low through the corner. He was quickly out the other side then, accelerating toward the next turn, shoving the gearbox up into third, then yanking it down into fourth gear for speed. But almost immediately, he had to be hard on the brakes again to set up for the next turn, then back in the gas for the long straightaway, and back down once more for the 180-degree turn at the end. Finally, he crossed the start/finish line again, putting another tally mark under another lap on the scoring sheets.

Bubba watched Little Joe's car even more intently the next time by. No doubt about it. This time he was sure he saw smoke coming out from under the Merc's rear end. He wondered if Weatherly or his crew knew it. It didn't appear that the car was spilling oil, so it had to be coming from the rear end or the transmission.

Somewhere in the esses or the first part of the long straightaway, Weatherly's car suddenly slowed. Jodell happened to check his mirror and could see Little Joe wrestling with the gearshift, trying to force it, but then he pulled away quickly and lost sight of the Mercury.

Just then, farther back, one of the slower cars suddenly lost control and a pack of trailing vehicles piled into him before they could swerve away. It had been close racing back there anyway, so before anyone could blink, a whole assemblage of pushing, shoving race cars joined the melee, strewing parts and dead cars about, effectively blocking the track. It took the officials only a few seconds to throw the red flag, stopping the race entirely until they could get the killed race cars hauled out of the way. Soon, all the cars that were still running were parked along the straightaway in a straight line to await the restart.

Little Joe came coasting into the pit lane with the engine idling okay, but the car was clearly not under power. He didn't even slow but instead took the red-and-black Mercury directly back to the garage. Bud Moore, the car's owner, and the rest of his crew swarmed underneath looking for the trouble. Curious, Bubba edged close enough to see if he could tell what was wrong.

"Transmission. She's all to pieces," someone reported dejectedly.

The crew had had high hopes of repeating their championship one more time and had planned on getting the run started with a win here on the West Coast. Now, at least for the first race in the new year, those hopes appeared dead.

The crew members began crawling slowly from beneath the race car, knowing the car was done for. At the same time, Little Joe was squirming out the window.

"What y'all doing?" he asked, wide-eyed, once he hit the ground.

"That transmission is done torn to shreds; she's going nowhere," Moore reported, shaking his head and waving for the boys to push the car towards the trailer.

"Well, shoot, Bud. If that one won't go, then have them put another one in!"

"Do what . . . we can't . . . ?"

"The damn race is red-flagged, in case y'all ain't

noticed. If we hurry, we may not lose any ground a'tall," Little Joe declared.

Somebody hustled back to get a transmission while the crew worked feverishly on pulling the broken red-hot one out from under the car. Little Joe danced around impatiently in his saddle oxfords. No way was he going to kill a good day of racing if something could be fixed and he could run some more. No way.

Joe Banker climbed down off the stand and came over to the pit where Bubba and the others stood.

"We ready for the stop?"

"Ready as we can be. He really is running good, Joe. How's his times?"

"Pretty quick. There's a couple of cars I don't know if he can catch. Gurney in the 121 car and Fireball's number 22. They're a couple of tenths faster right now. We'll see if they can last. Us, too."

"The 121 is going to be tough," Bubba said, still watching the Bud Moore crew doing surgery behind them on the crippled Mercury.

"Unless some of those cars start breaking and giving up the ghost, we may be lucky to get us a top five."

Joe had to yell to be heard over the hammers banging on metal and the stream of curses from the men beneath the car. The hot underbelly of the race car was clearly not much fun to work on.

"Don't worry. Some will break," Bubba said with a nod toward Little Joe's Mercury, its innards spread all over creation and men's legs sticking out from underneath like the tentacles of an octopus.

"Little Joe, you ain't going back out there, are you?" Joe yelled over.

"Just you wait and see!" the Virginian called back.

"I got to give your driver a run for his money. We ain't lost a lap yet with this red flag."

"Well, you be careful out there and don't tear that car up worse than you already have. It ain't worth it."

The yellow flag finally came out after about fifteen minutes, and the field of cars rolled off from where they had been parked. The wrecked cars had been hauled off and a few track crew members still swept up bits and pieces of wounded cars and tried to soak up oil and other liquids that had bled onto the track surface.

Bubba watched as the cars rolled beneath the green flag again and then were off, racing once more. Once the tight field rumbled past him, he started to get things ready for their first pit stop. Behind him, he caught a flash of Little Joe climbing back inside his racer even as the crew was finishing up. Bubba couldn't believe they had changed a transmission so quickly. They were only going to lose a couple of laps at worst. But even then, there was little chance of picking up any championship points.

Bubba shook his head. It was hard to understand why the man would even go back out there and take the risk of tearing up a good race car. But that was the way he and some of the others were. If there was racing going on, and if they could push, pull, or pedal their own cars, they'd be out there or be damned.

Off Little Joe went, uphill toward the esses, feeling out the gears in the new transmission as he went. And soon he was up to speed, driving, pushing the car hard, as if he was in line to win the championship again in the next few laps if he could only catch up to Gurney and Roberts.

Jodell's first pit stop was as good as they could have

hoped for, and they were able to get their driver in and out quickly. He had seemed pleased with the car, not signaling for any changes. They simply poured in the gas and swapped all four tires and sent him back out, still somewhere around tenth in the field.

Bubba studied the tires that came off the car like a jeweler examining the faces of a diamond. They were worn almost completely out. That meant that Jodell had definitely been running the wheels off the race car.

Joe yelled something down to the big man, and he picked up the signboard and chalked in the message "Minus 16." He stood on the wall and waved it as Jodell came by, informing him that he was running sixteen seconds behind the leader. Bubba could feel the power of the engine vibrating the concrete beneath his feet as the car flashed by him.

Back inside the car, Jodell was already feeling the race in his bones. Driving the road course was hard work. With all the steering and shifting and braking, there was no time to relax, to stretch and unkink strained muscles. The constant pressure of the restraining belts was making his shoulders ache from all the hard lefts and rights. Although he was constantly wrestling with either the steering wheel or the gearshifter, he knew that he had to handle it all smoothly. If he didn't, then he would be too hard on the brakes and they would fade dangerously. Or he could scramble his own transmission or kill a clutch. Or put even more wear and strain on the tires to the point that one of them would fail.

Catherine and Joyce had quickly settled into a routine in the scoring stand after the restart. When it came down to it, scoring was a lot easier here than at other places. With the length of time it took the cars to go 'round the track, they could actually sip on the sodas they had in front of them or stand and stretch their legs before the cars came back around. Catherine watched Jodell anxiously when she could, and she worried when he was out of her sight on the sections of the track that hid him from her.

She finally realized that the interval between Jodell's Ford and the leader was slowly but steadily getting greater. Unless something else happened to scramble the field again, there was no way Jodell could catch him. She caught herself actually wishing for a wreck so the field could get tight once more, then quickly felt guilty for having done such a thing. The last thing she wanted to see out there was cars crashing into each other or careening into the unforgiving retaining wall.

Then she wondered what was running through her husband's mind out there. Probably the usual. How is the car running? How can I get past that guy ahead of me? She touched her stomach lightly. Did he even have time to think of the new life she was carrying? Did she actually want him to be thinking about their child at this very moment, as he hurtled around that murderous racecourse at such dangerous speeds? She smiled and marked down another lap as he came past, picking off another slower car at the same time.

Jodell glanced in the rearview mirror, making certain nobody else was trying to outbrake him in the tight corner. He opened it up and roared down the long straight behind the pits, once more aimed for the tight 180-degree turn that waited at the end like a bad debt. He checked his gauges down the stretch and was pleased to see everything was in order. The Ford was running perfectly. Just not as perfectly as the leader.

The number on Bubba's sign was getting bigger

every time he held it up. At the same time, the laps remaining on the scoreboard were not coming off quickly enough to suit him. He could feel the fatigue relentlessly claiming his concentration, his stamina.

He almost got himself in trouble the very next lap. He smoked the brakes when he got too hard into a corner, then gave another Ford he was trying to get around a slight sideswipe before finally inching past him.

In the next turn the Ford's driver gave him a nudge on the rear bumper, simply to let him know he did not appreciate the little move Jodell had made on him. Once they hit the long straight, the power of Joe's motor let him pull away from the miffed driver, and he set his sights on the seventh-place car. He'd have to pick his spots carefully. Passing on this track was hard enough even with the better car, but now, in the top ten, most everyone had a good mount beneath him. Outbraking a competitor in one of the corners was about the only way to get past him.

Little Joe was still running the number 8 Mercury brutally hard, trying to catch up. He had passed Jodell a couple of laps before, throwing up a silly wave after giving him a sharp bump in the rear end in the middle of the corner and then buzzing on past. Jodell had tried to hang with him for a while, but Little Joe was simply pushing the car too hard, driving out there on the raw edge. It wasn't long before Little Joe was almost out of sight, ahead of him by better than a turn.

In the short time he had followed him, Jodell had watched the line Little Joe was taking, then tried to mimic his line. But it was suicide, he quickly decided. Weatherly was braking much too deeply into the corners for any sane driver to match. Besides, Jodell's brakes were beginning to fade slightly if he got on them too hard. Weatherly appeared to be standing on the brake pedal as he twisted the wheel into the turns.

The vibrations of the car traveled up his arms from the steering wheel and into his body like a long, slow bolt of lightning. His fingers and hands felt as if they were asleep, tingling, weak. The constant repetition of pushing the clutch and tugging on the shifter was wearing him down. Jamming down hard on the brake and gas pedal a dozen or so times a lap had his bones aching. He could smell the burning tire rubber, the metallic odor of the hot clutch. Each smell tickled his senses, heightened his awareness that the car was under a strain, too, and if he didn't break soon, the Ford might. He tried to stop thinking about such things and to concentrate on running down the sixth-place car.

Little Joe, ahead of him, was charging to the front like he was on some kind of mission. The man was still running as if he actually had a chance of winning the darn race. He pushed the car hard through turn five. Shifting gears, he headed toward turn six as fast as the car would go. Little Joe got out of the gas as he went to set the car up to make the sharp right through turn six.

But when he hit the brakes there was nothing there. The pedal sank to the floor.

He tried to grab the shifter and downshift. The car slowed for an instant while Little Joe continued to try to pump brakes. It flew straight for the outside wall. Still traveling sixty-five or seventy miles an hour, the car slammed into the concrete wall with the driver's side of the race car. The impact sounded like a bomb going off.

Catherine and Joyce heard the impact from the scoring stand. She took her eyes off Jodell long enough to try to see who it was but there was too much dust and smoke to tell from where she was. She breathed a sigh of relief that it was not her husband. And maybe the resulting yellow flag would get him close enough to Gurney and the rest of the leaders so that he could make a real run at them toward the finish.

Jodell was actually in position to see the slight puff of smoke from the rear of the Merc before it was snatched toward the wall as if jerked that way by a giant hand. He slowed his Ford heading into six to allow himself a chance to steer clear of any debris or other cars that might have gotten caught up in the wreck.

"That'll serve him a good lesson," he muttered. "Runnin' that damned hard when he was that far down in a race. At least the car ain't tore up too bad."

The yellow flag was out, and Jodell could finally relax his throbbing arms and legs, stretching them as best he could. He thought of the cool drink that awaited him when he got back to the pits. He twisted his neck, trying to ease the strain on his shoulders where the belts had cut deeply into the skin and sinew.

He was ready when he rounded the corner and made the short run down to his stall on pit road. Joe dropped an ice-cold canteen of water into his lap, then set about cleaning the windshield. Bubba jumped on the jack handle, pushing the heavy car up with several powerful strokes. The others set about changing the tires and dumping in a couple of cans of gasoline.

Before he knew it, Joe was waving frantically for him to go. Jodell popped the clutch and tossed out the half full canteen as if it were a hand grenade with the pin already pulled. He smoked the tires as the car took off down pit road, then blended smoothly back into line, ready for the restart.

It took a while to clean up the accident, and Jodell welcomed the chance to catch his breath. He expected to see Little Joe running along behind the damaged car, making sure the wrecker crew didn't do more damage to it than he had already. The little Virginian would be hopping mad about how his day had ended, but that wouldn't keep the night's postrace party from being a lively one. Nothing ever did.

The rest of the afternoon was a blur as Jodell continued to wrestle with the car. The brakes were fading more quickly now, forcing him to use the shifter more as he steered into and out of the turns. He prayed that the clutch and transmission would hold long enough for him to finish the race.

"Tell you what, Nadine," he told the car. "I'll make you a deal. You hold on till the end and I will, too."

The car seemed to hear him and gave a little surge down the stretch. He smiled. Joe Banker's engine had not missed a beat all day. And Bubba's setup was perfect. He had a good car under him and they should have a good finish. He only wished it could have been up there, where the 121 was sailing.

Then, finally, more than five hours after they had started, the checkered flag finally waved over their heads. An exhausted Jodell Bob Lee was never so happy to see such a sight as he flashed by under the flag stand. He let off the gas and made the final cooldown lap around the track, already unbuckling the shoulder harness he knew Little Joe despised so much. Then, going through turn six, he couldn't help but notice the ugly skid marks and the garish red-and-black paint where Little Joe had slammed into the wall. He coasted on past, glad to put it behind him. He couldn't wait to give Weatherly grief about his lack of driving abilities.

He pulled in and parked the car next to their trailer, already dreading the load-up and the long trip back east. Bubba and Joe were nowhere to be seen. The boys who were helping them were already bringing some of the equipment over from the pits, but Bub and Joe must have gone on over to congratulate the winner. He shut the motor off and gave Nadine a pat on the dash, thanking her once again for bringing him around fast and safe and in the better money.

Jodell unsnapped the lap belts and slumped back in the seat for a second. He sucked in a couple of deep breaths while he pulled the helmet and driving gloves off. There were blisters on the palms of his hands. He pulled his feet up under him so he could leverage himself out the window, and as he climbed out, he could feel crunching under his feet the "good luck" peanuts Little Joe had dumped into the car.

"Guess they worked after all," he mumbled. "We're here in one piece."

"Huh?" one of the helpers asked.

"Nothing. Just talking to myself."

Jodell took an unsteady step or two, trying to get some feeling back into his legs. He looked over at the scoreboard and saw no surprises there. The 121 of Dan Gurney was first, while the 22 of Fireball Roberts was third, with Ned Jarrett bringing the 11 car home in fifth. Jodell was more than satisfied with his own top-ten finish. And especially considering it was his first trip to a road course.

He looked around for Joe and Bubba but still didn't see them. He got a Bubble Up out of the cooler and rubbed the cold bottle on his forehead, then took a deep swig and wiped his face with the rag. He strolled around the car, checking all the rub and scrape marks it had acquired during the race. There was the one

Little Joe had left on the rear end when he had passed Jodell that last time.

"So-and-so owes me a paint job!"

Then somebody was running his way. Catherine. And there were tears streaming down her face.

Something was wrong. He thought of the baby first, for some reason.

Or Joe Banker. Somebody had jumped on Joe.

"Oh, Jodell," she sobbed, and grabbed him, trembling.

"Honey, what's wrong?"

She tried to tell him but it wouldn't come out.

"Calm down, honey. What's happened?"

"It's Little Joe!"

He held her away from him and looked into her face.

"What did he do to you?" Jodell asked. Had he pulled one of his silly pranks on her and upset her? He had stepped over the line then for sure.

"He's gone, Jodell."

"What?"

It still didn't make any sense. He had just seen the little cuss a while back in the race. It looked like he'd hit the wall pretty hard, but he had surely hit many other walls a heck of a lot harder than that before, and he had lived to brag about it.

"The wreck. He was killed, Jodell."

"That can't be," Jodell said helplessly. The car had been in one piece. The side ruined, maybe. Some sheet metal and paint, maybe some frame work, and she'd run again good as new.

Nobody died in a crash like that one. Certainly not tough-as-whit-leather Joe Weatherly!

"It is, Jodell. We just heard it from one of the officials."

Jodell had no words left. He used his rag to wipe the tears from Catherine's face and didn't even notice he was leaving greasy black streaks on her cheeks. She suddenly looked him in the eyes.

"All I could think of all the way over here was that it could have been you, Jodell. Oh, God. What if it had been you?"

And she pulled him back tight to her, as if she might never let him go.

It was almost an hour later that they found Bubba, sitting on the retaining wall with Joyce. She was trying to comfort him but he was stunned, staring at the ground, slowly shaking his head from side to side in disbelief. The big man had developed a close friendship with Weatherly, even though he had many times been the butt of "the Clown Prince of Racing's" pranks.

Jodell and Catherine left them there alone. Joe was trying his best to get the equipment loaded up while he still had the help of the pickup crew. Jodell worked alongside him for a while but then he simply lost interest. He slid down next to the car and sat there for a bit, with Catherine close to him as he stared off into the lingering dust toward the purple mountains in the distance.

How could something Jodell loved so much have reared up and trampled someone he cared so much about? He didn't even realize he had asked the question out loud until Catherine answered him with a strange, peaceful look on her beautiful face.

"It would be the same if you had worked side by side with him at a foundry. At a construction site. If you were truck drivers. This could have happened anywhere. But look at it this way, Jodell. He died doing something he loved doing. How many people can say that? How many get to do the one thing in life they most crave doing? I'll bet if he was here right now, he'd tell you that if he had to go, he would have wanted it to be with him behind the wheel of that Mercury, racing toward the front of the field like a bat out of hell."

He kissed her then. She was exactly right. And Little Joe had told him that very thing himself several times before.

But it still hurt. Oh, God, did it hurt!

COME-TO-JESUS

The gentle sea breeze blew in off the emerald water like a soft, warm caress. The surf fondling the sandy beach whispered quietly, soothingly. It was the perfect prescription for what ailed Jodell Bob Lee, and he was gratefully soaking up the healing warm sun, the curative clean air. It helped, too, that Catherine lay on the beach blanket next to him, holding his hand, sensing perfectly when it was a good time to talk and when it wasn't.

The beautiful day had brought out a crowd of folks, many of them already down for the races, but they managed to locate a relatively secluded spot, far enough from the Daytona Beach hotels that it had so far remained their own private little sliver of sand. The constant stream of cars moving along the beach was far enough away to not cause them any problems.

Even Joe, Bubba, and Joyce weren't around. They would be coming down in another couple of days, bringing the car and all they would need to compete at the big track.

Being by themselves at last would be good rehabilitation after the last few emotional weeks. All that had happened in California had Jodell seriously questioning his commitment to racing. So far, it had been only in his own mind, but Catherine instinctively knew what had him so quiet, so morose. With a child now on the way, and with the perils of the sport so clearly highlighted for them in Riverside, it was obvious to both of them that it was time for a "come-to-Jesus" discussion. That's what Grandpa Lee had called it, but with him it had always been a rather one-sided talk and often involved a peach tree limb and a good whipping.

It wasn't only the baby and Joe Weatherly's tragic death. They had to face the cold hard fact that financially, racing so far was, at best, a break-even thing for them. Bubba still worked part-time at the mill, and both Joe and Jodell made up the shortfall by working on farm equipment for their neighbors and fixing a few cars on the side when they were home. With that, their wives' income, and what they won in the races, they weren't falling behind but they certainly weren't getting rich. It was clear, too, that the Bubble Up money wasn't going as far as it had five years before, when they had made their first trip to Daytona with the sponsorship.

Nowadays, they were having to pick and choose the races they could make. Instead of running fifty or more races this year, they planned on competing in only thirty or so. Of course, the actual number of races they would make depended on how many they finished strongly in and what Homer Williams and the Bubble Up people decided to do come May. Without them or another significant sponsorship, they would have to curtail their schedule even more severely, to only the biggest tracks, those closest to home, and those with the strongest paydays.

He turned over on the blanket and watched the sun on Catherine's face for a moment. She was so beautiful, so loyal, so deserving of more than he had been able to give her so far. He hated to break the calm, quiet spell that had been cast here in this beautiful place.

But it was time. Time for a "come-to-Jesus."

"What if I were to quit racing for a while and get a full-time job?" He paused and let the words lie there for a minute. He fully expected the waves to stop washing up on the sand, the seagulls to hush screeching long enough to hear what else he was about to say. Neither happened, and Catherine lay there on the towel, perfectly still, a fine bead of perspiration on her upper lip. She could as well have been asleep. He went on. "They're hiring at the new Ford dealership in Kingsport. Paying good money, too, for mechanics." She turned her face slowly toward his and opened her eyes slightly in the bright sunlight. But still she remained silent. She must have known that he was finally ready to talk and she intended to allow him his say. "We don't have enough money in the bank to last us a month if something happened to me. We need to have something put back to take care of you and our baby."

She closed her eyes again before she spoke.

"Jodell, why would you quit? I make enough at the law office to keep us going."

"But when the baby's born, you'll need to stay with him. Or her."

He couldn't imagine a mother not staying home with her baby. Mothers didn't work. Mothers stayed home and raised their babies. Most mothers, that is.

"Your grandmother's already told me she'll keep the baby while I work. And while I go with you to all races that I can. You got to have a scorer, you know. Besides, old Mr. Houston would have to close the office and go get a real job himself if I wasn't around. He would never make it to court on time without me," she said, smiling. It was true, of course. And Catherine had taken night courses and was practically a paralegal by that time, making her even more valuable to the old attorney.

"Grandma is pretty excited about the baby," Jodell agreed. "But we still have to be realistic about the future, Cath. I want the best for you and the baby. Maybe if we took the rest of the year off and saved up all we can, we could make a real run at it next season."

She opened her eyes again and switched on what Jodell called her "Darlington face." He kidded her about the way her beautiful features would instantly turn as hard and unyielding as the retaining wall at the track.

"Don't you think I consider the future every time you go out there and drive around at over a hundred miles per hour? You can make a living at this if a living is all you want. But correct me if I'm wrong, Jodell Bob Lee, but I thought the reason we have been working so hard was to win, not to try to get rich. And like you've always told me, if we win, everything else will take care of itself."

"Well, honey, I guess you're right about that," he

said sheepishly, idly watching the steady line of cars rolling by on the hard-packed sand beach. Anything but looking into the flinty depths of her dark blue eyes. "You know how bad I want to win. But things have changed now. I have to think about you and Grandma and our baby and Joe and Bubba and Joyce and the Bubble Up folks and everybody else that's depending on me."

"Well, I wish you'd tell me how you plan on winning for all those folks if you're camped under a rack changing the oil on old cars all day. Losers quit. Winners keep doing whatever it takes to win. Don't quit for me. The only thing I want is for you to realize your dreams, Jodell. Take a vote among all the others. I bet even Grandma would tell you to keep at it now that we're so close to something big." When he turned to face her again, her eyes were on fire and she had risen to prop herself up on one elbow. "And do you want to have to convince your son or daughter one day to chase a dream even when the odds are stacked and it would be much easier to abandon it? To go after that dream with all his or her might and not quit like Daddy did?"

"I just want to do what's best for—"

"Then let's do what we started out to do. Let's be the best at this as we can be. Let's win ourselves some races!"

Jodell reached over and pulled her close to him. Someone in a passing car gave a long, low wolf whistle, but they both ignored it. He kissed her and felt her wiggle even closer.

"I love you," he whispered into her ear. "And I love you even more for understanding why I have to do this."

She drew away for an instant and looked up at him.

There was still a hint of steel in the hard set of her jaw, the determined look in her eyes.

"I'm not 'understanding,' Jodell. Not at all. I just crave winning as much as you do."

And Jodell Lee knew it was absolutely true.

DUELING THE HEMIS

The couple of free days at the beach were like a tonic to Jodell. Still, by the time Bubba, Joe, and Johnny showed up the night before the track opened, he was itching to go racing. Catherine told him he was like an old drunk, dying to fall off the wagon. He had awakened her the last few nights, talking in his sleep about the high banks and long, fast straightaways.

He was ready. And he knew the race car would be. They had spent endless hours over the winter, building the car to fit this track, this race.

The big unknown was what impact the new Chrysler "hemi" engines would have on the race. Joe had spent the winter working on the motor they had dropped into this car, tweaking it to get just the right formula they had decided from experience was perfect for Daytona. They even brought with them a spare engine, similarly tweaked, just in case, no matter that they couldn't really afford such luxurious redundancy. When Bubba finally steered the truck and trailer through the crossover gate into the magnificent speedway, all of them were brimming with confidence.

It took a long while to get checked in and to have the car inspected. As they finally pushed the Ford out to the pit road to await the start of the first practice, Jodell suddenly felt an odd wave of melancholy wash over him. He had subconsciously looked around the pits for Little Joe Weatherly's car, for the man's broad, smiling face. He finally spotted the Mercury, and it wore the right number, all right, but now there was a stranger standing next to it, ready to climb in and drive it away like a common car thief.

"I'd give anything to see Little Joe and his danged old 'mongoose box,' " Jodell told Bubba.

"I never thought I'd say so, but I sure would, too," Bubba replied sadly.

The "mongoose box" had been one of Weatherly's best tricks on Bubba Baxter. The time he had pulled it on the big man had been the stuff of garage-talk legend. They had been in Charlotte for the "600," and Little Joe had been telling Bubba for days about his new pet mongoose, how vicious it was, how hard it was to control.

"Big 'Un, that thing is so wild and mean, I can't hardly keep it in its little box," he had reported with a sincere, straight face.

"Little Joe, I was raised in the mountains. I've fought everything from 'coons to civet cats to black bears. Let me have a look at that thing. I bet you I can tame it. I ain't afraid of no goose."

"Mongoose."

"No kind of goose. Lemme take a look at the thing."

"Naw, Bub. I don't want that little old thing to hurt you and embarrass you in front of all these folks."

And he had patiently refused to allow Bubba to see it, baiting the hook perfectly, biding his time until he had set up the ultimate trick. Finally, the day before the race and between practice sessions, Little Joe had approached Bubba in the garage holding the mysterious box carefully at arm's length.

"Mountain Man, reckon you could hold my mongoose for me while I go to the bathroom? I'm scared to death he's gonna break out and hurt somebody."

"Sure."

"Now, be careful and don't open the lid or he'll be out, and I don't want to be responsible for what that thing might do. Okay?"

"Sure, Little Joe."

"Now, squeeze down on the lid like this or he'll get loose. We don't want that."

Bubba didn't even notice the crowd of mechanics and drivers who had begun to accumulate once Little Joe had disappeared around the corner. Or that they had begun to subtly egg him on to take a look at what was inside the box.

"Come on, Bubba. We won't tell him."

"I thought you could handle anything, Bubba. You ain't scared of that thing, are you?"

"Bubba, you afraid of a little old goose?"

"How big and mean could something be that fit in that little bitty box?"

"Look, y'all. I ain't gonna get it out. If she got loose, Li'l Joe would knock me cold as a wedge."

"Aw shucks, Bubba. Just let us have a peek!"

"Yeah, I ain't never seen no mongoose. I want to

see what one of them critters looks like."

It had been Joe Banker who finally convinced him to open the lid. Somehow Joe had managed to keep a straight face as he spoke.

"Little Joe wouldn't have given you the box to hold if he didn't think you could handle the thing if it got loose."

"Well, I guess that's right," Bubba said, still unsure of himself, but his own natural curiosity was clearly winning out. "Y'all stand back and let me see how to get a hold of this critter and we'll have ourselves a look-see." He waved the crowd back and brought the box up to eye level, then cautiously raised the lid a tad. "I got to get a peek at him so I know where to grab him without hurting him."

Suddenly, the top of the box jumped off and out popped the "mongoose," springing right into big Bubba's face. He screamed, whooped, danced, and slapped at the wiggling ball of fur that seemed to have designs on his nose. He knocked over several of the men, who were already hooting with laughter as the big man tried to escape the clutches of the critter. He finally managed to knock it away and began stomping it, not caring a whit whether he killed Little Joe's precious pet or not. All he knew was he was saving his own life and that of those gathered around, even if they were ungraciously giggling and hooting and howling at his life-or-death struggle.

It hadn't taken Bubba long to realize the "mongoose" was only a ratty old foxtail on a spring that had been loaded into the box, ready to pounce on anyone who dared to open the lid. Little Joe had sneaked back to hide at the edge of the crowd, and his cackle had been the loudest of all. He had laughed about the trick for months, called Bubba "Goose" for the longest, and guffawed even harder when the nickname made his big friend turn bloodred beneath his crew cut.

Jodell shook his head and smiled at the memory, but then forced all thoughts of Weatherly from his head before he climbed into the car and started to buckle up the belts. He never allowed the ghost inside the car with him.

Settling in the seat, he strapped himself in and began to focus on the track. The next thing he knew, the official at the front of the line was waving the cars out onto the racetrack. Jodell hit the starter switch, shifted up into gear, and commanded the car to begin its roll down the pit road and out onto the gigantic track.

He loved Daytona. No two ways about it. Her wide, sweeping turns and long, linear straightaways were built for speed. Wide open all the way around was the only way to go. The feel of the power pushed him hard back into his seat as he accelerated down the chute, aiming his rocket ship off toward the first turn.

The four-hundred-plus horses beneath the hood seemed ready to kick as he worked his way up through the gears. Out of turn two and onto the long straightaway, he glanced at the car behind him in his rearview mirror, then scanned the gauges. All was well. Foot to the floor, he steered the car down the backstretch.

The Ford was fast. *Real* fast. Jodell knew by the end of the third lap that the car was already set up perfectly. That made his confidence soar. And the way the car handled through those first laps of the initial practice session reminded him of how much fun racing could be.

At least until Richard Petty and his light blue Plymouth almost blew him off the track. Jodell had a good head of steam, running high through turns three and four with a broad grin on his face. He pointed the nose of his Ford down toward the start/finish line in the middle of the dogleg.

Then, from out of nowhere, the 43 car came roaring past like a misguided rocket had somehow escaped from down at Cape Canaveral. Jodell had to shake his head and look closely to manage to catch who and what it was that had just dusted him.

Petty was already in the center of no-man's-land between turns one and two as Jodell entered the corner. That was Jodell's first encounter with the Chrysler "hemi" engine. If this was any indication of the motor's strength, it was going to be a long season for the other manufacturers' cars. At least on the big tracks.

The hemispherical engine was Chrysler's remake of an engine first introduced in the early fifties. It had had an unfortunate habit of burning valves when driven at slow speeds, but with a few modifications it was a perfect power plant for the bigger racetracks.

"Well, Lucy, it looks like Cousin Joe has his work cut out for him," he told the Ford. Joe Banker was going to have to try to find something under the hood for Jodell or it was going to be a long week at the beach. All he could do right now, though, was to kick harder on the already floored gas pedal, trying to coax another ounce of speed out of the car. But it was futile. Richard Petty continued to pull away from him.

Jodell pulled down to the inside of the track coming off turn four. He headed down toward the pit road, scrubbing off speed as he went. He rolled onto pit road and pointed the car to where Joe, Bubba, and

Johnny waited with glum expressions on their faces.

"Man, did y'all see Richard?"

"He was a couple of tenths quicker," Joe confirmed, still staring at his watch as if he wasn't sure it was telling the truth. "I thought you were running good laps but those hemis are tough. The only thing close to Richard is Junior Johnson in that Dodge."

"Well, while you're resting, you'd better find us a whole bunch of horsepower or we're gonna spend all week gettin' lapped by all them Chrysler cars."

"We got time to find some more speed," Joe said with more confidence than Jodell could manage. "How'd she handle?"

"Perfect. High, low, wherever. I could take her anywhere I wanted in the turns and she stuck. It was like she was on rails."

"Well, we better start looking under the hood, then," Joe conceded, already popping the lid.

All around them, other crews were clearly involved in their own frantic, desperate search for speed. The rest of the day, Jodell and Joe huddled after every run out on the track, trying to find more power in their engine. Bubba and Johnny concentrated on getting the changes made as fast as possible so they could go back out and see if they had happened upon something magical. Slowly but surely, the times dropped as they would find a tenth of second here, a couple of hundredths of a second there, but they were still not up to the Chryslers.

Of course, the Pettys were not sitting still either. They couldn't rest because Junior Johnson was just as fast in his own hemi-powered Dodge. Fireball Roberts, Ned Jarrett, and some of the others continued to pick up speed as well.

As they continued to tinker with the Ford's engine,

Jodell worked to get the car comfortable. The g forces in the turns were fierce. If they couldn't match the Dodges and Plymouths with raw speed, they would win with a steady, consistent race, and he needed to keep his stamina to make sure he drove as smart as he needed to.

The hundred-mile qualifying races confirmed the obvious. The Fords were no matches for the power and speed of the hemi-powered race cars. It was all Jodell could do to keep up in his qualifier. The Chrysler cars took the top three spots in each race, but at least Jodell made the 500 field. Some didn't.

They would continue to look for more power any place they could find it right up until the green flag dropped on Sunday.

"Shocks, springs, you name it, we've changed it," Bubba had said that morning at breakfast. "We need to steal us one of them hemis and stick it in the car when they ain't nobody watching."

"If I thought we could get away with it, we would," Jodell responded, not speaking totally in jest.

Then they had dived back into their gravy, biscuits, and grits, each man silent, thinking, wondering where else they might look for a precious dose of swiftness.

SPEED, PRECIOUS SPEED

By nearly race time, the crew was in somewhat better spirits, even if they were no happier with the car than they had been at breakfast. It had run beautifully in the last practice, fast enough that they would have been ecstatic in a normal year or at another track. But this was the year of the hemi.

Jodell tried to talk Catherine out of scoring the car, insisting that she rest in the infield instead, but she would have none of it.

"I might be pregnant but I'm not fixing to miss this race," she emphatically told him. "I didn't come all the way down here to sit in the car and listen to the race on the radio. And if I'm watching, I may as well be scoring."

She fussed at them, too, about all the negative talk. Bubba joined in. They both maintained that the car would be good enough to win. That they would have the best driver within miles of Daytona Beach, Florida, that day. That nobody knew if the hemis could even last five hundred miles or not. And if they were so danged sure they were beaten before the green flag dropped then they'd better get busy loading the car back up on the trailer and head on back to Chandler Cove right then and there.

And that put an end to the bad attitudes. At least, the talking-out-loud part of them.

Jodell talked briefly with Richard Petty as they stood waiting for the drivers' introductions.

"Richard, I hope you'll at least wave at me every time you put a lap on me today."

"Hah!" Petty scoffed, showing his trademark wide grin. "I'm just gonna be out there driving in circles trying to keep from running over any of you cats that get in my way."

"Well, unless we miraculously found another twenty or so horsepower since last night the rest of us'll be racing for position behind you and Junior."

"You cats are gonna be fine. I think y'all are just sandbagging me."

"I wouldn't be startin' halfway back in the field if I was sandbagging, Richard. If this old Ford would run any better, I'd be up there in the front row with you!"

Finally, the introductions and accompanying cheers finished, the drivers were ordered to their race cars. Jodell was ready to get going, to see how this thing would play out on the big track. He often wished they could show up ten minutes before the green flag, crawl into their cars, and go racing, not having to wait for all the prerace festivities.

"Hey, Fireball. You ready to go get 'em?" Jodell

asked Roberts as he passed him climbing into his Holman-Moody Ford.

"I reckon I'm as ready as I'll ever be," he answered. "May be a long day for us Ford jockeys. We'll probably be glad just to get out of here when this thing is over."

"I suspect you're right. We've about worried ourselves sick, and I guess we'll still be short of what we need."

Jodell quickly looked around to make sure Bubba or Cath had not overheard him, wished Fireball luck, and ambled on back to his own car.

Jodell was still adjusting his helmet when Joe stuck his head in the window. They reviewed their pit strategy though it had long since been committed to memory, regardless of how the cautions might fall during the race.

"Go flat-out, Cuz," Joe said, and gave him a wink. "But try not to run up the tailpipes of them hemis when they blow up out there."

Jodell grinned back. It did make him feel better to be behind the wheel of the car, to feel the solidity of it beneath him, the snugness of the belts. It was a fine race car, plenty good enough to win this or any other race. And all he had to do was drive it home and let everything else take care of itself.

He focused his thoughts in on the track itself, on the high-banked first turn that he could see shimmering in the distance. Since he would be running wide open all the way around, he wouldn't have any marks to worry about. No spots where he would be getting out of the gas or have to brake, let alone downshift. He would simply pick a line and run full throttle, even through the turns.

Flat-out! That was the only way to run Daytona.

Finally, the command came to start the engines, and he could hear just the beginning of the roar of the massive crowd before it was washed away by the throbbing engines igniting, coming to life like a herd of long-dormant beasts. This was one of the best times for Jodell Lee. He could feel the latent power of Joe Banker's engine when he first fed it gas and eased out on the clutch. Like a thoroughbred bucking at the reins, the car was itching to go.

"Be patient, Betty Lou," he told her. "We'll run directly. We'll run."

Then he grinned at the silly thought of a racehorse named Betty Lou. Or a powerful race car either, for that matter.

The gauges reported back good news. The car rolled smoothly, shifted up cleanly, bucked only slightly as he hit the next gear. The smell of exhaust, of warming rubber, of hot metal already filled his nostrils. The thunderous roar of all the cars had already numbed his ears and he wasn't even through the first turn yet.

The pace car led the way, already building speed, but even then, it felt as if they might tumble right off the high banks because they were going so slow. All the competitors were lined up behind the pace car like a pair of parallel freight trains. As the cars came back around to finish the first parade lap, Jodell glanced up into the packed grandstands lining the front stretch for his last look at the crowd.

"All them folks here to watch us, Betty Lou," he whispered, but the car seemed to hear him and gave a little surge forward, right up on the tail of the Chevy that rolled along in line ahead of him. "Let's show 'em how it's done!"

Then they were off, long before Jodell could even

see the flagman giving the go-ahead. When he saw the line of traffic ahead of him surge, some diving low to gain position from the start, fanning dirt, sand, and rubber dust, he knew it was time for him to join the fray, too. He danced hard on the accelerator and fell back deep into the seat when the force yanked him hard.

As they zoomed past the flag stand, the phalanx of cars was already building speed, roaring down toward the first turn. Jodell saw his first opening quickly, gave the wheel a twitch to the left, and powered by the car on the inside, pulling down in front of him to take the spot before they ever hit the first curve.

He felt a burst of elation, but then wondered what was happening up there at the front of the field. No doubt the Chryslers were holding on to their lead, holding down the first couple of spots. And behind them, all the rest were feeling out their cars, some working for position already, others discovering they had overtweaked, had gone past the mark, or had simply made the wrong call, and were already in trouble.

In the early laps, Jodell found he could keep picking off cars that had somehow qualified ahead of him. That meant that his team had found a bit more speed in their final adjustments—or that the unfortunate ones had actually done more harm than good in their frantic need for locating more speed, precious speed.

Before he realized it, he had moved up onto the rear deck of the Ford of Fireball Roberts. He settled in behind Roberts, tight on his bumper, and allowed him to pull his own Ford along behind him in a tight draft. Together, in tandem, they seemed to be markedly stronger than most of the others, and they managed to slip easily past several more cars.

Lap after lap, locked together, Jodell and Fireball ran hard, giving chase after the Chryslers. Richard Petty had powered his own Plymouth to a strong lead with Junior Johnson pressing him hard. It wasn't long before the dominance of the 43 Plymouth became even more obvious, the new engine tugging Petty to an insurmountable lead.

Jodell and Fireball continued their waltz, swapping the point back and forth, one leading the way for a few laps, then the other taking over. Never mind that the leaders were practically out of sight by now. Jodell had the accelerator shoved to the floor, felt the car holding tightly no matter how hard he attacked the corners, but still, there was no catching the leaders. Even at 165 miles per hour, he felt as if he had an anchor thrown over the side when he compared his own track position to that of Petty and Johnson.

Joe stood on the pit wall timing Jodell and the leader every lap, but it was a painful experience. The story the watches told was frustrating. They had a powerful race car, probably the best they had ever built, and they had no hope of winning the race unless the hemis suddenly expired.

Their first green flag pit stop was a quick one. Bubba and his crew got the car in and out beautifully, plenty fast enough to win. It made no difference. The Chrysler-built cars quickly made up any advantage they might have lost in the pits once they were back out on the track, motoring unimpeded.

Bubba joined Joe on the wall after the stop.

"How's he running?" Bubba yelled.

"Faster than we ran last year, but it don't matter one bit."

"I bet Jodell is fit to be tied in the car. He don't like having no chance at a win."

Joe nodded his agreement. As frustrating as it was for them, he could only imagine how it must have been bothering his cousin to be out there in such a good car and still not be within hollering distance of the race leaders.

"These Mopars are gonna win every race this season. There's no way I can squeeze that much power out of the Ford engines," Joe shouted. Bubba scowled, but he knew it was true. "Well, maybe I could, but it wouldn't be legal for nothing but hauling white lightning."

Bubba didn't have the strength or the voice to remind him that technically that, too, was illegal.

Jodell decided to simply do what he could do and not worry about what he couldn't. He maintained the draft with Fireball Roberts as both of them settled on passing what they could. Up front, Petty had begun to leave behind the entire field while Jodell and Fireball raced like it was the last lap. They were *racers*, after all. That's what they did. Raced as hard for thirtieth as they would for first.

The private battle Jodell had been waging with Fireball Roberts finally got settled, of all places, in a wild and woolly pit stop. Jodell beat him out of the pit with an especially good stop and then drove away. Meanwhile, Petty managed to lap the entire field in an amazing show of strength.

The crowd was on its feet, showing their appreciation for dominance instead of a tight finish. The Petty-blue number 43 Plymouth flashed under the flag stand to take the checkered flag while Jimmy Pardue brought his Plymouth home in second place, a lap down. Paul Goldsmith, also guiding a Plymouth, took third, while Marvin Panch somehow managed to take fourth in his Wood Brothers Ford.

Jodell didn't even bother to check the big scoreboard in the infield to see where he wound up.

He took the cooldown laps at close to race speed, reluctant to slow what had been a remarkably strong race car, but he finally braked and headed onto pit road. He parked in the fenced-off garage area right next to an equally frustrated Fireball Roberts.

"It felt like I was going backwards," Roberts said, grinning. "I've seen it happen before, though. Somebody finds some way to get a leg up and guess what. We all go back to the garage and figure out a way to beat them."

"We better find something, or one of them hemis is gonna win every race this year."

"Hey, we might have eaten 43 dust all day today, Lee. But we had ourselves some fun drafting like that, didn't we?" He showed his handsome smile, and it was once more clear why he was one of the most popular drivers in the sport's history. "You got any idea how much those folks up in those stands would have given to swap places with you and me today? They wouldn't have cared if Petty lapped them a dozen times as long as they got to drive one of these cars at Daytona."

Roberts was right. They had both won money that afternoon, plenty more than what it had cost to come down and spend a week at the beach. They had been doing something they were born to do. They were among the best in the sport. There was hardly room to complain.

Still, Jodell hated to lose. And anything but first place was a loss, far as he was concerned.

He tried not to allow it to eat at him as they loaded up and headed for home and the next race. Richmond, Bristol, Atlanta, North Wilkesboro, Martinsville, and a half dozen places in between all went by in a blur. The good news was that they were consistently finishing in the money this year so far. They even picked up another win, and the press was now starting to take notice of Jodell, figuring he was a threat to win anywhere.

Before he knew it, Jodell had shoved the doubts he had been having out of his mind. He missed Joe Weatherly, but nowadays several races would go by without his hearing what sounded like Little Joe's laugh in the garage, or catching a glimpse of someone that looked just like him bounding down pit road toward him, big as life.

"We're almost there," he announced to Catherine one night during a rare moment alone together. They were enjoying the warming temperatures on Grandma's front porch.

"Yes, we are," she confirmed with a smile.

"Thank you for not letting me quit."

She gave him a hug but didn't bother to say "You're welcome."

She knew something that likely had not yet occurred to her husband. She knew that Jodell Lee would rather die than quit racing.

DASH DOES IT AGAIN

It felt so much like old times as Jodell lined up with the other cars, ready for the gates to open at Hickory Speedway. He had always enjoyed driving the track, and not simply because it was the site of his first win ever in serious racing. It was the same spot where he had outdueled Ned Jarrett in a close race the locals still talked about. Never mind that when he won he had killed a perfectly good race car in the process. It had led directly to something bigger, too. That's the race that had caught the attention of Augustus Smith, the old bootlegger, and had given Gus the idea of giving Jodell the money to run the first Labor Day race at Darlington. After that, they had been on their way.

Their luck continued to be as up and down as a stretch of mountain highway. They had been at Darlington the week before, and Jodell had blown the motor in the car they planned to take to Charlotte in a couple of weeks. It had especially hurt since the other Fords had run well on the famed Darlington track, taking the first couple of places. Fireball Roberts had raced for second behind Freddy Lorenzen in their Holman-Moody Fords. A frustrated Jodell had caught up with Fireball after the race in the back side of the pits.

"Good race, Fireball. It's nice to see somebody put a hemi in its place on a big track, even if it can't be us."

"Hey, Jodell," Fireball responded. "We just had the right combination under the car today."

"You and Freddy were both tough out there."

"Thanks! What happened to you? Blow up?" Fireball asked as he wiped his face with a cold towel.

"Darn motor blew. This is the car we're taking to Charlotte, too. I guess ol' Joe will have his work cut out. We got three races coming up this week with the dirt car."

"You'll be ready for Charlotte."

"You'll be there, won't you?" Jodell asked. He knew Roberts had cut back on the number of races he was running this year.

"Charlotte for sure."

Fireball was gone then with a wave and swallowed up by a mob of fans and autograph seekers. It was well known that Roberts liked to race, then go home, unlike some of the other more flamboyant drivers, who preferred lingering to bask in the attention of the race fans or to unwind with a postrace party. He didn't necessarily enjoy his celebrity. But it certainly had not hurt him with the fans. He was easily the most popular driver out there.

Now, it felt like time for their luck to turn once more. Jodell normally didn't care that much for a dirt track anymore, but Hickory was different somehow. It was as much the challenge of the track, most likely, as it was the nostalgia. Jodell Bob Lee did relish a challenge. Hickory was one of those tracks that could make a driver crazy one minute and ecstatic the next, leaving him either in the throes of a temper tantrum or dancing a happy jig once the race was over.

Besides, there was something special about this tight little racetrack that always allowed Jodell to run well. He could never figure out what it was, but somehow when he got on this track, he could navigate it like a man possessed.

As he sat waiting for the gates to open, he reflected on his chances this time around. With the likes of Junior Johnson, Ned Jarrett, Tiny Lund, and Richard Petty in the field, and with other young drivers like David Pearson and Buddy Baker competing, a victory could be ellusive this time. But that's why he raced. He knew that if he beat these guys he had beaten the best. And the thought of matching up with them already had his blood pumping.

This was the second race in as many days for Jodell and the crew. They had finished ninth at Langley Field in Hampton, Virginia, the night before, and it had been a frustrating run all the way. They easily had the best car on the track, but the radiator had gotten clogged up with dirt and the engine kept running hot. Every few laps Jodell had had to come in and cool the car down to keep from burning it up. Jarrett had taken the win and the thousand-dollar purse in the Bondy-Long Ford, while Marvin Panch, Buddy Baker, and Wendell Scott had taken the next three positions.

By the time they had gotten the car and equipment packed up and had made the drive down to Hickory, it had been well past midnight. Exhausted, the four of them had squeezed into a single room at a motel, one in each of the twin beds and the other two on pallets on the floor. And they had been so tired they didn't even argue about who drew the floor. Jodell, Joe, and Johnny Holt had staggered directly to a bed or a pallet and were asleep instantly. But Bubba lay there for a while, tossing fitfully.

"Shoot," he finally announced to the other men's snores, "I can't sleep with that car out there broke."

He pulled his jeans back on, went outside, unpacked a new radiator and got busy changing it out with the damaged one on the race car He had wanted to crank the car up and check it out when he finished. That was the best way to find leaks or loose clamps. But he figured the other guests at the motel would have lynched him, so he went on to bed and waited for morning to give it a try.

Jodell's first runs on the familiar dirt track felt as if he had come home. The first time he threw the car down into the initial turn at full speed and then power-slid all the way through the corner, he felt as comfortable as he might have in his own bed back in Chandler Cove. He grinned broadly and slapped the wheel with his open hands. He absolutely loved the feel of power as the motor pulled him along lap after lap, obeying his every command.

When he finally parked the Ford, Bubba got busy adjusting the screening in front of the radiator to make sure it was completely protected. A single stone could ruin their race in an instant. Joe, too, had a few new things he wanted to try out with the motor and in the gearing to see if he could help the car circum-navigate the track a bit quicker.

Tiny Lund slapped Jodell on the back.

"She running okay for you, Joe Dee?"

"All right. Sometimes I think I'd rather have a bull-dozer on these little old dust bowls."

"Yep, speed's not necessarily what you need here. I might prefer a tank myself."

Lund was hardly tiny. At six-five and 270 pounds, he looked every bit the football player he had been when growing up in Iowa.

"Especially when we have to run against nitwits like that one," Jodell growled, nodding toward Dash Rockford, who was entertaining his crew and a few fans a couple of stalls down. "That so-and-so must've found a new car owner to sucker in. I expect they'll be hauling that shiny new car off in a wrecker before too long."

"And some innocent old boy's car like you or me, too, Lee. I thought after he totaled that car the other week that we might be rid of him for a little while," Lund said, sadly shaking his head.

"I don't care if he tears up his own cars. Just don't hurt old Donna Sue here." Jodell gave the Ford's fender a tender, heartfelt fondle.

"I'm not gonna let him cramp my style one bit," the giant Lund stated matter-of-factly. "If he gets in my way, I'll just go ahead and shove him into the fence before he hurts me or somebody else."

The look on Tiny's faced showed no hint of humor at all. He would do exactly as he said he would if he got the chance and saw the need. And with his ex-pertise on short tracks, there was no doubt he could get the job done quickly and efficiently if it came to that.

"Me, too," Jodell agreed. "Maybe somebody else'll do it before we have to. Or he'll barrel roll the thing all by himself."

"If we're lucky," Lund said, still without a smile. "That son of a gun will wreck one of us, though. Just you wait and see. And I don't plan on it being this old fat boy neither."

"I expect I better make sure old Bubba brought his boxing gloves, 'cause we'll most likely have to fight the peckerwood again before it's over."

Tiny suddenly broke into his familiar grin and threw a playful punch in Jodell's direction. Jodell staggered backward as if it had landed full force. He wished Lund luck as he headed back for his own car.

Still, Jodell kept a wary eye out for Rockford, even during the practices. The contemptible car jockey had even been known to tear up somebody else's car before the race ever started, simply to establish his intimidating image. Jodell didn't mind beating and banging to take away a spot on the track in the heat of racing. Nor did he shy away from letting someone know in an unmistakable way that he was less than pleased with a move the other driver might have made. But he certainly didn't try to wreck someone for the hell of it. There was too much hard work and expense wrapped up in his and the other drivers' cars to risk tearing them all to pieces for no good reason.

Lord knows there were enough bad crashes out there without some yahoo causing them on purpose!

Jodell shook off his concerns about Dash Rockford and went out to run a few more practice laps on the tail of Ned Jarrett, the acknowledged master of Hickory Speedway. Even though he had beaten Jarrett here a time or two, Jodell was never so vain as to think he couldn't learn something from him. He carefully noted the line Jarrett took into the corners, the points where he eased off on the accelerator, knowing that all the while Joe Banker was timing both cars.

Sure enough, Joe knew by then that Jodell and Jarrett were running close to the same times. Only Junior Johnson had run a faster lap in the practices.

Bubba Baxter stood like a monolith down by the first turn, his clothes and face and flattop haircut already covered in a fine layer of dust. The big man loved the vibration of the ground beneath his feet as the powerful race cars rumbled past, only a few feet away. That's one of the reasons he liked these smaller tracks so well. This was what racing was supposed to be. Close quarters, tight corners, tracks where drivers could drive and not just run flat-out the entire time. Not like those big tracks where it was more like a roller coaster ride than a race. And they were places where the spectators could be close to the action. He would have stood right out there in the middle of the racing groove if he could have and let the stream of race cars part around him like he was a sapling in the creek. He watched Jodell slow down and head for the pits when the red flag came out, ending the practice, then he turned and trotted back to the pits to see what else he needed to do.

Then, ultimately, with everything set and the cars lined up in front of the grandstand for the race's start, they could rest for a few minutes. After 250 laps tonight on this tight, dusty four-tenths-of-a-mile oval, they would have to pack up and drive most of the rest of the night, headed for South Boston, Virginia, and the next opportunity to win a race.

At the drivers' introductions, Jodell stood talking quietly with some of the others, but he also watched

Dash Rockford, standing a distance away with a few of his black-shirted entourage. The man was bragging to them about something or another he had done that had forever turned the tide of stock car racing. Most of the crowd booed when his name was called, but he seemed to bask in their scorn, sticking his chest out and waving happily as if it were a welcoming ovation they were giving him. He had done a good job of establishing the perception by the fans that he was the villain, the one they despised but watched nonetheless to see what evil act he would perform that night.

Hardly fifty laps into the race, Jodell found out for himself. Jodell was already frustrated, sweating and cursing, as he continually had to push slower cars out of the way. The younger, sluggish drivers were all over the track, effectively blocking all the driving lanes. The only real way to get around was to ease the front of the hood right up on their rear ends and gently shove them aside. He never hit them hard enough to wreck them. That is, if the inexperienced driver didn't panic. But he did butt them with enough force to move them out of the way so he could drive on and try to catch the leaders.

Typically, a couple of taps to the rear bumper was all it took to let them know a faster car needed to slide past. But tonight, for some reason, the "chrome horn" wasn't as effective as it usually was. There were constant spins as someone would get impatient and push a bit too hard, or surprise an inexperienced driver with a solid tap, sending the slower car pirouetting like a clumsy ice skater. Tempers were soon running as hot as the dirt-clogged radiators.

Jodell did the only thing he knew to do. He continued to push hard, but he knew he was falling farther and farther behind as the slower cars kept boxing him in. He lost track of how many times Jarrett, Johnson, Lund, and some of the others had lapped him. Finally, he simply locked onto the rear bumpers of the leaders and followed them around the track in tight formation, like a covey of jet fighters.

He soon noticed the lead cars had been having the same problem with the slow cars as he had. But they were being a good bit more aggressive about jostling them aside. He held his position and scrambled through the holes they would punch before they closed back up.

There was so much dust in his face as he followed close that he couldn't actually see that the lead race car was about to put a lap on Dash Rockford. But he watched as the leader tapped the jet-black car hard in the rear a couple of times and then put a fender up alongside Rockford, clearly establishing a line going into turn one. Anybody with an ounce of sense would have let the faster car ease past. That description, though, had never applied to Dash Rockford.

As the leader slid past into the turn, Dash jerked the wheel sharply to the left, trying to force the faster car to ease off, to turn downward. The two cars banged together hard, but the race leader had enough momentum and speed to hold his line after an initial wiggle on impact, and quickly drove on past. His blocking move having failed once, Dash tried it again anyway, veering downward to cut in behind the leader and shut off the second-place car. But that driver had no intentions of letting Dash squat in his way, of losing sight of the lead car, and he didn't appreciate being cut off either. He gave Rockford a substantial jolt in the rear just as the cars were entering the second turn. That's all it took to send Dash

Rockford spinning, careening in a wild loop-de-loop coming out of the corner.

The next three cars, with Jodell bringing up the tail, were lined up on the track in single-file order. They tried to hit the hole that was there ever so briefly before it was closed by the spinning car bouncing back down off the fence. The two race cars in front of Jodell made it through and drove away safely. When he got to the spot, Jodell gunned the throttle, trying to get through the opening, too. But in the process, he must have fed the Ford a tad too much gasoline. He felt the rear end lose some traction, and he had to oversteer the car to try to keep the rear end from breaking loose and sending him whirling after Rockford.

Fast as lightning, the hole closed on him. The fraction of a second it had taken him to gather the car back up beneath him was all it took. Jodell's foot was still in the gas as he plowed into the side of Rockford's Chevrolet. There was the hard crunch of crushing metal as the two cars collided. The right front nose of Jodell's Ford punched the door bars of the Chevy, sending it once again spinning upward toward the wall.

Jodell struggled mightily and managed to keep his own car heading in a straight line as he eased up on the gas only for an instant. He caught his breath and stomped the accelerator once more, ready to run down the others and try to get a lap back before they got to the inevitable yellow caution flag.

But then he heard the racket of screeching metal, and with the dust from Rockford's spin now behind him, he could see the crumpled sheet metal on his front end and the telltale mist of steam from beneath his hood.

"Please just be the hose," he prayed as he limped the car around to the pits. "Please. Not the radiator. Just the hose."

It didn't make him feel any better when Dash Rockford roared past him, still racing despite a big dent in the driver's-side door. The bum who had caused it all was still running!

Bubba set to work trying to open the crumpled hood, finally resorting to a crowbar from the toolbox. Steam billowed from the engine compartment when he finally got the hood sprung. The front grill had been shoved rudely back into the radiator on impact. The hood was bowed up, and the right front fender was pushed almost into the tire, rubbing badly when the wheels were turned much in either direction.

Jodell easily read the look on Bubba's face and climbed slowly out of the car. The day was over for the Ford.

"Two radiators in two days," Bubba said. Jodell had to read his lips over the engine noise of those lucky enough to still be circling out there on the race-track.

Now all they had to do was find a parts store or junkyard, change the radiator, fix the crumpled body, and check the front end for other damage. Oh, and they had to do it all, then drive to South Boston in time to race the next day.

Joe walked around the car with Jodell, sorrowfully viewing all the damage much as he might have an old friend in final repose in a coffin.

"I was timing somebody else and missed most of the excitement. I looked up and you were running all over that other car. What happened?" Joe asked.

"Aw, that idiot Rockford!" Jodell answered, pushing the words through gritted teeth. And that was all he had to say to give Joe the picture.

"Looks like the radiator got the worst of it," Joe observed, stating the obvious in a voice loud enough to be heard over the hissing steam. "I guess we can beat everything else out with a hammer."

Bubba was already swinging the hammer, pounding out the dented sheet metal, the muscles in his powerful arms flexing with each strike. Jodell winced at the force of the blows. It was painful for him to have to watch such radical surgery being performed on his car. Instead, he turned away to watch the race wind down. Ned Jarrett easily took the win, with David Pearson and Richard Petty finishing two and three, both a lap down.

Joe, Bubba, and Johnny got busy stripping out the busted radiator, trying to get as much work done as they could before the race was finished and they could push the car out of the track's infield and to the truck. The more they could finish tonight the less time they would have to spend tomorrow trying to fix the car before they could race.

Tiny Lund walked up just as they were buttoning up the hood. He, too, had had a long day.

"What'd I tell you, Jodell?" he said with a wink. "Rockford got one of us."

"You called it, Tiny," Jodell replied, offering him a cold Bubble Up. "You got any other fortune-telling you want to do? I'd love to know how we're gonna do at South Boston. And in Charlotte. Yeah, Charlotte for certain. You got a feeling about it?"

"Reckon not. Y'all break anything crucial?"

"Naw, mainly just got the radiator. Nothing we can't fix."

"Well, I am out of here, boys. I think I'm gonna

head to the camp and see if the wife still recognizes me. If I can remember the way home, that is."

"Seeing the wife sounds good to me, too. See you in Charlotte, Tiny," Jodell called as the giant man turned and headed off.

"Yep, I'll be there with bells on. Y'all drive careful."

Jodell passed Bubba a tool he had requested and stuck his head under the hood to check the progress of the work. He half noticed the loud voices of some of the lingering crowd heckling someone not far away, but he figured it was only a few rowdy fans who had gargled too much beer during the race.

But suddenly, someone yelled Jodell's name on the end of a string of curses. Then, before he could pull out of the engine compartment of the Ford and see who was making so much vile noise, whoever it was grabbed Jodell roughly around the neck from behind.

He tore at the sweaty arms that had a choke hold around his throat, and tried to pull them away even as he jumped backward, attempting to buck off the sneak attacker who was trying to wrestle him down to the ground. The voice in Jodell's ear was raspy with anger.

"Wreck my car, will you? I ain't gonna let you get away with that, Lee. Nobody gets away with wrecking up Dash Rockford!"

Jodell should have known it was Rockford when the scoundrel had sneakily grabbed him from behind. That was, after all, his usual way. They quickly ended up scuffling in the dirt, first one on top, then the other, in a whirl of arms and legs. Dash was grabbing and pulling at vital areas but Jodell, once he got over the shock of being ambushed, was gaining ground, landing a few strategic blows himself.

Bubba came scrambling from beneath the hood, then watched the fight to make sure Jodell was able to hold his own and that none of the other scoundrels who hung with Dash was going to jump him, too. Finally, with the scuffle mostly over, he grabbed Dash Rockford by the collar of his racing suit and yanked him to his feet. Rockford was still flailing away, trying to land a blow on Jodell, Bubba, or anybody else he could reach. Jodell quickly scrambled to his feet to finally meet his adversary face-to-face. He landed one more nice, solid punch to the side of Rockford's head before Bubba jerked Rockford out of Jodell's reach.

Several of Dash's crew made halfhearted moves as if they might want to try to rescue their driver, but one scowl from Bubba Baxter backed them away. He finally threw Rockford in the general direction of his crew as if he were tossing aside a candy wrapper, then faked a kick to his backside. The bunch of them were a hundred yards away before they turned and tossed some more curses and threats back to Bubba and Jodell. Bubba stomped his foot and pretended he was going to give chase. Rockford's bunch scattered, disappearing into what was left of the crowd.

"What was that all about?" Bubba asked.

"It's just Dash being Dash. First he wrecks you, then he wants to fight about it after the race." Jodell answered as he slapped the dirt and grass off his racing suit.

"I done lost count. What is this? The tenth or eleventh time we've had to whip his butt?"

Joe came running up then, close behind several security men checking on the commotion. Joe had been trying to buy a spare radiator from one of the other Ford teams so they wouldn't have to track one down the next day. His quest for a radiator had been successful, but he was still clearly disappointed at having missed all the action.

"Every time I turn my back you and old Dash are dancing with one another."

"I guess we gotta beat him on *and* off the track."

"So did you nail him this time?"

"Not hardly. He jumped me from behind like he always does. I got a few good licks in, though. That jaw's gonna be sore for a couple of days," Jodell answered, idly rubbing his own bruised neck where Dash had tried to choke him. "I don't mind a fight. I just prefer to see it coming."

They finished tearing down the car while Jodell patiently signed autographs for a few lingering kids. Then Bubba recruited some helpers and they pushed the damaged car out to where the truck waited. Bubba started pulling off the spare tires that were stacked up on top of the trunk and began loading them on the truck. Joe carefully leaned the radiator against the truck.

"Y'all want to go ahead and put that radiator in now while we got all the tools where we can get to them?" Joe asked.

"Sure," Bubba answered. He was ready to get the job done. It pained him to see a race car that wasn't ready to race. And especially when it was *their* race car.

Jodell had another idea, though.

"How about we just load this thing up and get out of here?" he said. "We got a long drive, and I promised Catherine I'd call her tonight before it gets too late. Besides, I don't know about you cats, but I could use something to eat right about now."

That, of course, did it. Bubba's vote had been

swung over instantly, and just like that, Joe Banker had been outpolled.

"Now that you mention it, I could get up early and get that thing put in quicker and better when it's daylight and all," Bubba reasoned. "What you got in mind for supper, Jodell? I'm thinking fried chicken. Or barbecue. I ain't had no barbecue since . . ."

The moon had dropped well behind the mountains and it was pitch-dark by the time they had loaded up everything and headed off in search of any café that was still open. It should have been a dully disappointing night for them. But somehow, they were all four in high spirits when they left Hickory. Never mind there had been little purse money tonight. Races like this one had become the exception rather than the rule lately. They all felt they had turned the corner. Better days were ahead.

Now, they'd go win South Boston the next day and then go home for a few days to get ready to go conquer Charlotte in a little over a week.

And they'd be on their way. God willing and with a good run at Charlotte, they'd finally be on their way.

The lone howl of an accelerating race car rattled the condo's plate glass window overlooking the first turn at the Charlotte Motor Speedway. The engine groaned even louder approaching turn one, as if it was complaining that the driver had not yet blessed it with a shift to a higher mesh of gears. A lingering ray from the dying sun glinted off the colorful car like a flash of white lightning as it thundered off into turn two. With a roar that echoed all around the speedway, the car was gone, tearing boldly down the long backstretch, the Doppler effect making the noise waver as it quickly moved away.

Soon, another boldly bedecked car followed the first out onto the track. Then yet another one made its way out, set to practice. It looked like a regular race weekend at Charlotte except for one thing. There was no swarming crowd in the grandstands. Only a few folks watched from a small section of the massive scaffolding near the start/finish line. The arc lights that surrounded the speedway had just clicked on automatically, bathing everything in a false ghost light. It made the place look more like a football stadium or a shopping center parking lot than a shrine given to the worship of speed.

The practicing cars swelled in number, and packs of them drifted together so their drivers could get a feel for how their vehicles reacted to each other in the draft. They knew the effect of the stiff wind from the lead cars would be critical in getting their vehicles set up perfectly for the eventual race. The clumps of cars exited turn four and rolled down the D-shaped front straightaway, running deeply into turn one, once again passing directly beneath the cold, blank stare of the big condominium windows.

If the drivers had looked up that way, they might have seen the silhouette of a tall man standing perfectly still as he watched the practice play out. If they had had a chance to watch him for a while, they would have noticed that he seemed to almost be in a trance, to be mesmerized by the hypnotic drone of the race car engines. The man's only movement was to occasionally lift a can of soda he held in his right hand to his lips to take an idle sip, but his eyes never left the track below. They couldn't have known that he didn't taste the drink at all, was not even aware he was swallowing it.

He was clearly alone with his thoughts. Farther down the way, his wife was in another of the trackside condominiums, visiting with some of the other wives, talking about everything else but racing. But she, like her husband, never tired of coming to the track. Not this one or any of the three dozen others around the *country to which they trekked like Gypsies from February to November each year.*

Even as he watched the darting, dashing cars, the old man knew in his heart that he should have been down there in the garage, overseeing the preparation of his own car, getting it out there to rehearse, too. But instead, he stood exactly where he was, all by himself even though he liked being with people, listening to the hollow roar of the cars inside the nearly soundproofed room, feeling the vibration of their power in the floor beneath his feet.

Just then, a pack of five cars bellowed off down the front straight, their speed approaching two hundred miles per hour. Two cars abreast led the way, then came two more, also side by side, and finally a fifth car, trailing a car length and a half back in the inside groove. The three inside cars went low into turn one with the ones on the outside running high into the corner. The outside cars found they had a slight advantage as the track cooled and that allowed them to pull slightly ahead of the cars to their left.

Then, as they freight-trained through turn two, the car in the inside middle eased up the track a few feet and, in the process, took some of the air off the rear spoiler of the car running in front of it. It certainly wasn't intentional. It was an explainable phenomenon of the aerodynamics of big-track high-speed racing. With the air pressure suddenly lessened on the surface of its trunk end, the front car wiggled almost imperceptibly, then squirmed even more, and the driver suddenly found himself having to fight the steering wheel to maintain control.

But there was little he could do. The rear end of the car had begun to swing around on him.

Inside the car, the rookie driver tried to bring to bear

his limited experience, all the things the veterans had told him when he listened to them, his own car-aiming instincts. But in the process, he cut the wheel a fraction too far, overcorrecting, and that caused the front tires of the car to try to grab a hold on the asphalt. Before he had any time to think about it, the car shot upward, banging into the side of the car that was running along innocently side by side with him.

The cars bounded together like a couple of giant magnets, opposite poles attracting. Together, now joined in the crash, the cars broke loose from their previous easy straight line and began to spin around. Smoke and dust boiled from beneath the two cars, and the squall of their protesting tires reverberated up to where the old man watched, teeth clenched, breath held. He squinted, tensed, then arced his back, bent his knees, as if he were gussied up inside one of those cars and was bracing himself for the inevitable impact with the track wall even as he worked the shifter, stomped the clutch pedal, and tried to reclaim the rebellious steering wheel.

The second car on the outside had nowhere to go. With the track effectively full of skidding automobiles, that one bulldozed hard into the first two vehicles before its driver could even begin to react. The second car on the inside line scooted by the melee. The trailing car's pilot kicked the accelerator hard, trying to drive through the ever-so-slight hole before it closed right back up.

The two spinning cars were well on their way to the outside wall, while the car that had tagged them spun down to the inside. The trailing car didn't quite make it through the smoky hole. It was clipped in the right rear by one of the gyrating race cars. If this had been a smaller track, the cars wouldn't have had enough straightaway to allow for any serious speeds, the spin-out would have likely slid to a stop, the cars involved none the worse for the tangle-up. But at such a rapid pace, the tap to the car's tail was plenty enough to send it brutally head-on into the inflexible outside wall.

The old man winced as he watched the car smash into the barrier. Immediately, a giant, ugly ball of bright orange fire rolled out from under the car as if, in its spin, it had somehow ripped a hole in the roof of hell. It was likely the oil cooler, tucked into the left front of the car, had broken loose and dumped oil all over the white-hot exhaust headers, creating an instant black-smoke inferno. As soon as the careening race car had slid to a stop, the flames billowed all around the crumpled hood, the left fender, and from underneath the race car.

The old man closed his eyes tightly. Even from hundreds of yards away, he thought he could feel the blistering heat of the fire, burning his hands, singeing his eyelashes, sucking the air right out of his lungs. Without realizing he had done so, he dropped the soda can, the brown liquid spilling all over the carpet.

Just like that, it was thirty-four years earlier. Charlotte. Fire. Fire everywhere. Somewhere inside that wicked wall of licking, roaring flames was a 1964 Ford.

Eyes still shut, he put his hands to the cool glass of the window, palms flat.

"Get out! Dear God, get out!" he pleaded, mostly in a whisper. "Come on, Fireball. Climb out of there!"

He shook violently, as if racked by a chill, and in his mind's eye, he could see the licking flames devouring the car, claiming his friend as its own, greedily taking something it could never give back. His ears were filled *with the hungry slurping and smacking of the ravenous fire.*

He never heard the door opening behind him.

"Jodell! Jodell! Are you okay?"

Catherine. Dear, sweet Catherine.

She stepped to where he still stood, hands on the glass, body quaking, and slid her arms around him. At her touch, he finally opened his eyes. The flames around the car's front had died down, the oil quickly consumed, and the safety truck had just arrived. They immediately aimed fire extinguishers at what was left of the blazes. The driver had climbed out and was now walking dejectedly down the banking, already looking for the rookie so he could give him a piece of his mind, if not a good sock in the nose.

"It's okay, honey," Catherine whispered, trying to hold him tight enough to stop the trembling. "It's the ghosts again?"

"Yeah." He turned to embrace her. "They seem to be showing up a lot lately."

Lord, he was tired.

He shot a glance back out toward where the crash had happened. The dark smoke had mostly drifted away already. A wrecker had hooked up and was towing away the scorched car.

1964.

What a glorious year it had been.

What a terrible year.

GONE AGAIN

The late-spring breeze blowing up from the southwest was pleasantly warm as it found its way across Chandler Cove and up the mountains on the other side of town. It promised another fiery, hot summer was not far behind. The sun had only been up a short while, and a few stubborn crickets were still refusing to hush their fiddling.

They finally got quiet, though, when Bubba Baxter cranked up the grouchy truck engine and guided it backward to the open doors of the barn-turned-race-shop. He whistled tunelessly as he hopped out, ran back to the rear of the truck, and hooked up the trailer that had already been loaded with tires and tools and other equipment, leaving just enough room to roll the race car aboard.

The truck's gears grumbled slightly as he eased forward to pull the trailer out into the new, bright sunshine. The touchy brakes locked when Bubba stepped on the pedal, bringing the truck to a sliding halt in the gravel of the driveway. He killed the engine, hopped out again, and disappeared into the darkness of the shop.

Only a minute later, the brightly painted nose of the race car emerged, propelled by Bubba, Jodell Lee, and Joe Banker as they slowly pushed it out of the shop and up to the back of the trailer. All newly painted, waxed, and polished, the car fairly gleamed in the sunlight. The new bright red and yellow Bubble Up logo jumped out from the dark blue background of the rest of the car.

The three men stood there for a moment admiring their handiwork. Lord knows they had seen plenty of her over the last little while. They had devoted at least fifteen hours per day the last few days to getting this car ready to go to Charlotte and to getting the short track car fully mended and ready to race again.

Now the Ford looked sleek and powerful, plenty good enough to win some races merely on appearances alone.

"Ain't nothing prettier, is there?" Bubba asked no one in particular.

"Especially this part," Jodell said, giving the sponsor logo an appreciative caress.

He and Catherine had gone out to the Bubble Up bottling plant two days before at the request of Homer Williams. Still flagged from the three days of hard racing at Langley, Hickory, and South Boston, Jodell had not even had a chance to dread whatever news Williams might be about to deliver.

"Don't worry," Catherine had told him several times during the drive over. "If he was going to cut us off, he would have told us on the phone. Not invite us out to the plant for lunch."

Turns out she was right. Business had been good lately, much of it attributed to Jodell's success on the track and his willingness to visit with and sign autographs for various important customers prior to races. Williams wanted to assure them that the sponsorship was secure at least through the Labor Day race at Darlington, and it looked good beyond that for the rest of the year if Jodell could manage a few up-front finishes.

And to top it off, Williams had talked with a friend of his who owned a big Ford dealership up toward the Tri-Cities. He was willing to kick in some cash if Jodell would park one of his cars out front of his store for the weekend and come by and sign some autographs for customers. A decal on the fender facing the crowds when he raced sealed the deal.

Somehow, the Bubble Up splotch on the hood seemed even brighter and more beautiful this morning. Bubba gave it one more loving swipe with his rag, then got the ramps to the trailer in place.

"Ready to load her up, Bubba?" Jodell asked.

"If you're ready to guide me."

Bubba climbed into the window and kicked off the four-hundred-plus-horsepower motor. Joe Banker stood there, chest out like a proud papa, listening to his handiwork growl. He had spent every spare moment when they had been at home the last three weeks trying to rebuild and coax more power out of that mill.

Jodell waved Bubba up onto the trailer as he eased the car up the ramps, then, the engine shut off, they set about fastening her down securely, then covering her with the big canvas tarp. It took them another couple of hours to get everything else loaded up, and it was near midday when they finally pulled away. They still had to run by the garage where Johnny Holt worked and pick him up for the run over to Charlotte.

"Y'all don't mind if we make a quick stop, do you?" Jodell asked.

No one did. Bubba wanted to get a sack of cheeseburgers from the pool hall grill, and Joe was already half asleep against the passenger door.

When she heard the rumble of the truck's engine, Catherine Holt Lee came bounding down the front steps of the law office to meet them, a big grin on her face. Jodell winced when he saw her running, pulled to an abrupt stop, and hopped out to slow her down. At better than five months pregnant, she wasn't quite as graceful as she once had been.

"I didn't know if you would have time to stop by or not," she said after giving him a big kiss.

"I couldn't leave without checking on . . . uh . . . everything," he said, pulling away just far enough to be able to give her bulging middle a tender pat. "How are things going?"

"Mr. Houston is in court all day today, and it's been pretty slow around here. I don't think he's coming back, so I should be able to leave early."

"Good. You rest up the next couple of days, especially if you and Joyce are still planning on riding over to Charlotte with Mr. Williams."

"It'll take a lot more than a bad case of the pregnants for me to miss this race. You think I'm going to let you win it without me being there to give you a big kiss in Victory Lane?"

"Well, that pretty, blond Miss Charlotte Speedway will be there to do it for you if you don't make it." She gave him a mock scowl as he pulled her close to him once more, ignoring the smiles of the people passing them by on the sidewalk. Everybody in town knew Jodell Lee and his wife and were kind enough not to interrupt their good-byes. "Besides, I'm glad you plan on me winning. That's the kind of attitude I married you for."

"And I thought it was my beauty and my biscuits."

"Well, those, too."

"Jodell, be fast but please be careful," she whispered in his ear, suddenly going serious. "I promise not to worry if you promise to be careful."

"Tell that to Bubba. The most dangerous part of it all is the highway from here to Charlotte, and he'll be driving."

Catherine stood on the little porch of the law office and waved as they pulled away. The early-afternoon sun danced off the truck's rear window like a flash of white flame as they made the turn onto the road that led out to the highway. She stood there for a while, leaning against a support post, watching the spot where the truck and trailer had disappeared around the corner. She ignored the incessantly ringing phone inside the office.

They'd just have to call back.

TOURING CHARLOTTE

Waiting. That's what they were doing. But surprisingly, Jodell didn't mind this time. They were parked in the middle of the red dirt road that led to the competitors' entrance to the sprawling Charlotte track. A long line of trailered race cars snaked out ahead of them, waiting to get through the gate and into the track complex just as they were.

But Jodell was reveling in the excitement he had felt the first moment they had caught sight of the racetrack. He loved the giant new speedways like this one. Simply anticipating the speeds he would achieve inside there, the side-by-side racing they would do in the broad, sweeping turns, the sheer joy of hurtling down their smooth stretches, all combined to get his competitive juices flowing. He had never experienced anything else that could compare to flying full throttle into a turn, feeling the car dig down into the corner and miraculously stick there, no matter that it seemed to defy all logic that it could actually do such a thing. And nothing could compare to the elation he would feel when he was hammered hard back into the seat as he stomped the gas pedal coming off the turn.

Sitting there in the stifling truck cab, sneezing from the dust that spilled in the lowered window, back aching from the long ride, he could feel other sensations that were yet strong in his memory and were only a short while away from being reality once more. He couldn't wait!

It was hard to believe that Curtis Turner had been one of the people most responsible for this place's being built. Turner had described many times for Jodell and his crew and anyone else who would listen the trials and tribulations of carving out the speedway, of all the rock that had had to be dynamited out of the way so cars could circle in front of rabid fans. They had discovered solid granite beneath the soil where the track was to be built, and it had cost a fortune to clear the rock. Curtis blamed the track for claiming one of the several fortunes he had won and lost over the years. But he loved the place, too. All the drivers did.

Finally, credentials in hand, they followed along as the slow-moving line began to inch along through the crossover gate and into the speedway itself. Bubba inched the truck along in first gear, straining to catch his first look at the inside of the track. Like a tourist catching his first sight of water after a long journey to the beach, the big man always looked forward to his first sighting of the surface on which they would eventually run.

Once inside and parked in the fenced-off garage

area, they spilled out of the truck and tried to stretch out the kinks.

"I love this place," Jodell, Bubba, and Joe all said simultaneously, then giggled like school kids before getting busy unloading and easing the car off the trailer.

All around them, the other teams were doing exactly the same thing. The Pettys, the Wood brothers, the Holman-Moody team. The excitement was palpable, breathable, like sweet air. Soon it not only looked like a big-league racetrack, it sounded like one, too. There was the music of powerful, finely tuned engines being run through their paces, being revved as talented mechanics fiddled on their settings.

Once the inspectors had cleared their car, the four of them slowly pushed the Ford back to their stall. Joe Banker went under the hood, laid a fistful of tools on top of the radiator housing, and began to unscrew the air cleaner. Once it was out of the way, he inspected everything he could see beneath where it had been. Getting down into the top of the carburetor, he took a wrench to it and began to take it apart.

Like a diamond cutter carefully but efficiently working on a precious stone, he stripped the carburetor down, thoroughly checking each piece before setting it aside on a clean rag. He adjusted the jetting expertly, doing his best to get it set just right, never mind that he had done the identical thing the day before back in the shop and the engine had not been fired once since. Then, once he was completely satisfied, he reassembled the carburetor and double-checked everything he could still see for fit and tightness.

Bubba Baxter worked just as efficiently but thoroughly underneath the car's front end while Johnny Holt and Jodell changed the rear springs. On the trip

over, Jodell had convinced the other three that it
would be best to start out with a little stiffer set than
what they had put on the car back at the shop. If they
didn't work, they could always go back to the softer
set, but Jodell was certain that he wanted to try the
more rigid setup in the first practice. They had to
work quickly, though, because they didn't want to lose
any of the precious practice time out on the track.

Once on line to pull out onto the track, Joe and
Jodell talked strategy for the first run. They wanted
to get a feel for both the car's setup and the track
itself while trying to establish baselines off which they
could make changes.

"These are the guys I expect to be fast from the
get-go," Joe said, showing the car numbers he had
written on the clipboard. "If you get a chance, try to
run with them some so we can see how we stack up."

None of the numbers surprised Jodell. The usual
suspects, most of them driving Chrysler products with
the Mopar hemi engines.

He climbed through the driver's-side window and
strapped himself into the seat like a jet pilot tying
himself into the cockpit of his fighter. He worked to
clear his mind and concentrate on the track itself, on
his memories of past experiences out there on its long,
undulating surface, and how he was going to attack
it.

Mentally he ran a lap around the track, visualizing
where he needed to place the car over every inch of
her. He had been here before. He had finished well
at times and he had looked like the rawest rookie at
others. Now was the time to put his past learning experiences to practical use.

Bubba pulled him out of his deep thoughts.

"These good and tight?" he asked, giving the belts a testing tug.

"Yeah, they're fine."

"Good. Can't have you flopping around in there like a just-caught sunfish."

Baxter wiped the windshield one more time, even though it was perfectly clean already. Jodell grinned crookedly at the big man.

"You gonna wear a hole right through that glass if you don't quit wiping on it."

Bubba gave him a sideways look and pulled on the shoulder belts one more time. Since Little Joe Weatherley's tragic accident at Riverside, Bubba had become a safety fanatic. He insisted on double-checking every single thing himself.

"You check them lugs?" he'd ask Johnny Holt.

"Sure did, Bubba. You saw me."

"Well, I better check them again." And he'd grab a lug wrench and do that very thing while Johnny would wander off, shaking his head. "Some of these jacklegs might forget being safe while they look for speed. Not this team. No sir. No-sir-ee-bob! Not this team."

The way Bubba looked at it, they wanted to make the car go as fast as they could. But when the inevitable happened, when there was a crash, he wanted to make sure his driver walked away from the wreck. Joe Banker built the engines for the cars, Jodell drove the things, and Bubba built the actual cars themselves. And since he was in charge of building them, he was convinced it was his charge to make them as safe as he could.

"Okay, let's do a fifteen-lap run and give this baby a chance to trot so we can see if we got a thoroughbred or a nag," Joe yelled to be heard over some of the other cars that had already cranked up their motors.

"Got it. Have Bubba show me some times on the board and count down the last three laps," Jodell said as he cinched up the strap on his helmet.

"All right! Go and get 'em, Joe Dee." Joe looked back at a couple of Plymouths that sat in line behind them. "Let's see if we got a thing or two for these Mopar hemis this trip."

"I hope so. I'm gettin' damn tired of watching their back bumpers!"

That's about all the view he had had of those cars at Daytona, Atlanta, and some of the other big new speedways. He could only hope that Joe's magic touch with the engine would be enough to offset some of the big-track advantage the Mopars had enjoyed so far this year.

The Ford built speed as he steered it into the first turn, then past the steep banks of turns one and two; the car rolled along on the apron of the track as it moved faster and faster. Out on the backstretch, past the crossover gate, the car roared as Jodell held the gas pedal hard to the floor. The car found more velocity down the backstretch as its jockey spurred her to go full bore into turn three. The Ford sat down tight running into the turn, then drifted upward toward the top in the center of the corner.

Coming out of the fourth turn, Jodell put the car right out near the wall, close enough that another coat or two of paint might have been too much. Joe's freshly built motor hummed happily as Jodell fed it more gas and the car roared down the D-shaped front straightaway. Jodell flashed by the entrance to pit road, drove down almost to the edge of the grass at the bottom of the racing surface, and then headed across the "short chute" toward turn one again.

This time through, he took the high line around the track. He rolled the Ford up toward the outside railing, keeping the RPMs in the engine high. Through the exit of turn two he kept his foot hard on the accelerator, daring the car to break loose, to let him down.

But she didn't. She gripped the track as if she was as much a part of it as the paint striping.

Standing on the wall in the pits, checking his stopwatch, Joe Banker couldn't suppress a smile. The times for the first three laps were better than any they had ever run before in this place. Bubba pumped his fist in the air and gave a mighty war whoop every time Jodell roared by.

Joe held fingers in the air for Bubba to see, and Bubba scribbled them down on the chalkboard. Then, when Jodell came past, he held the board high for him to see. The numbers seemed to spur the driver and car to push even harder, to go even faster on the next orbit around the place.

It was clear that Jodell Lee was having himself some fun out there. The car under him was fast and he knew it. Whether he went high or low on the track, the Ford stuck right where he aimed it. As he caught up to other cars on the track, he could pull up on their rear ends, then immediately swing down to their inside and make the pass on them, leaving them quickly in his exhaust.

It was clear they had a car that could win this race. And that was a heady feeling indeed!

The two Petty cars were extremely fast, of course, along with most of the rest of the Mopars. But it seemed that several of the Fords had found extra speed in the months that had passed between Daytona and Charlotte. In addition to Jodell, Ned Jarrett, Fireball Roberts, Junior Johnson, and some of the others had obviously closed the gap and should be competitive with the Chryslers on Sunday.

That's one of the things Jodell and his crew loved about this sport. Once somebody seemed to have found an edge, the other competitors would go back to their shops and look for a way to get back even once again. It took hard work, some smarts, and lots of experimenting, but there was always a way to get back into the hunt, and it was certain that somebody would eventually find it. It was a chess game played out at over a hundred miles per hour.

Jodell roared down the front stretch once more, flashing past the mostly empty grandstands. As he sailed high into the first turn, the car climbed the banking and the g forces yanked him hard, pulling him deeper into his seat. He could feel an ever-so-slight dip in the track as he started to come out of turn two and he knew he was near flying, as surely as if he were piloting an airplane instead of a landlocked vehicle. The bump made him take an even tighter grip on the steering wheel. His heart jumped but he felt a burst of adrenaline, too, a wonderful sensation washing over him as he sensed the raw power and speed of the car as it obediently shot down the backstretch toward the next turn.

It seemed as if he had just pulled out onto the track when he saw Bubba waving the signboard high over his head, signaling him to come in. He almost ignored him to stay out there and fly his aircraft for a few more laps. Besides, he was afraid he would lose the magic he and the crew had found if he slowed down now. He raced through the first and second turns, then decided he really needed to go on in and let the guys check the car over. He pulled low going down the backstretch, got out of the throttle, and eased down onto the apron as he rolled through three and four, then pointed the Ford's nose down onto the pit lane to brake it gently to a stop.

Bubba went straight for the tires all around. Joe stuck the clipboard in the window so Jodell could see the times for himself. Sizing up a couple of columns of figures, Jodell could see that he was running within a couple of tenths of a second of the fastest car out there. With a little adjusting on the car, he knew he stood a good chance of overcoming that gap. He grinned when he passed the clipboard back out the window to Joe.

"Times look good."

"You were right up there with the guys I figure will have a shot at winning this thing. Lots of fast cars out there, though."

"Yeah, but we can run with them. That's better than having to start from scratch. How about some water?"

Joe grabbed a paper cup and filled it with ice water from a jug and handed it back.

"You want a rag? It's gettin' awful hot."

"Naw, I'm okay right now."

Jodell poured some of the ice water down the front of his driving coveralls, and it felt wonderful. He knew he would be a lot hotter by the time this first practice was finished. Joe was still studying the clipboard.

"Petty and Pascal are quick. See if maybe you can catch one of them and run some laps with them. If you can, then I think we will have a good idea of where we stand."

"Okay. How did the tires look?"

"Hey, Bubba! How the tires looking?" Joe shouted

across the top of the car to Bubba just as another formation of low-flying race cars came screaming past them.

"A-okay," he yelled back, or something to that effect. At least he was giving a thumbs-up, and that was a good sign.

With that Jodell pulled back out to join the fray for another dozen or so laps. He knew that Joe had a long list of things he wanted to try before the practice session was finished and he needed to run to try them out. But mainly, he simply wanted to be back out there, driving the wheels off this fine machine, feeling the wind roaring through the open window as he passed the other cars.

A couple of hours later, the session behind them, they rested beneath an umbrella in the infield, talking over sandwiches about what they had learned. Joe and Johnny plotted, drawing in the dirt as they went. Jodell was sprawled back against a propped-up tire, a bottle of soda balanced on his belly, occasionally offering a thought but mostly just unwinding from the day's activities so far.

Bubba was too involved in his own lunch to do much more than merely grunt at the appropriate places in the discussion or when someone dared to ask him a direct question. He had already killed off a sandwich Joe had described as being roughly the size of a '57 Chevy hubcap. Now he had constructed two more that were even bigger and had one in each hand, taking huge bites from each in turn. Empty soda bottles littered the ground around him like spent cartridges around a machine gun nest.

Fireball Roberts passed by on the way back to his own car. He stopped to watch Bubba in disbelief.

"I'm glad I don't have to feed that one," he exclaimed, wide-eyed.

"Just don't get too close. He's been known to devour anything in a close radius, and I'd hate for you to lose a hand or foot," Joe warned.

"I believe it!"

"How's the car?" Jodell asked.

"We've gained quite a bit on those Chryslers but we're not quite there yet."

"Same here. I can get within a couple of tenths of them, I can draft with them okay, but at the slightest bobble they can still can get away before you know it."

"We're running into the same thing, but I think by race day we'll be fine."

"We sure plan on it," Jodell said. "We don't have any intentions of conceding the race just yet."

"Naw! Us neither. Well, I better get going. How about loaning me one of those sandwiches, Big 'Un?"

Fireball made a move as if he was going to try to grab one of the massive sandwiches. Bubba only sat there and growled like a dog about to lose some hard-won prey. Fireball stepped back and pretended to be counting his fingers just to make sure they were all still there, then disappeared into the crowd that milled around in the infield.

By the time the last practice of the day had been flagged to a halt, rumors of a big party at Curtis Turner's house were running rampant throughout the garage. Curtis was notorious for his parties, strung-out affairs that usually lasted most of the time from when the first car was towed into town until the very last one had headed off for the next race. It had been a while since Jodell had made one of the affairs, and he was actually looking forward to it. He needed to unwind some and it would also give him a chance to talk with some of the other drivers and crew members about who else was fast besides the Plymouths and Chryslers.

Joe Banker was itching to get the car put to bed and be gone, too. He lived for Turner's parties. And most of the afternoon, an especially attractive blonde had been hanging around the fence talking to Banker. She had taken an unusual interest in carburetors and how to set the timing on a Ford race car, and Joe had been more than happy to explain it all to her. That is, if she would accompany him to the night's soiree, of course.

Joe fussed irritably at Bubba and Johnny, trying to urge them on faster as they tried to buckle everything up for the night. They fussed right back but picked up the pace anyway. They, too, looked forward to Curtis's party and were more than ready to get finished, get back to the motel, get cleaned up, and be on the way.

When they were finally ready to pull out, Jodell paused for a moment, leaned back against the truck, and looked around the track that encircled them. The sun had fallen down behind the grandstands now and a dusky mist had rolled in over the last few minutes. It served to soften the colors and smooth off the edges of the place. Someone had hung a set of wind chimes from a nearby tent pole, and the slight breeze had them tinkling quietly. That was the only sound he could hear. There was an almost eerie feel to the speedway now, so deathly still and quiet where mere minutes before it had been all alive with bustle and noise.

It almost felt to Jodell that something was out of kilter here, that the world was slightly off its axis. For an instant, a powerful sense of foreboding washed over him, and he felt a strong need to get to a phone and call Catherine and make sure everything was all right with her, with Grandma.

"You gonna stand there wool-gathering till we miss the party?" Joe scolded.

Jodell shook his head and climbed into the cab beside the others. Johnny had already found some rock and roll on the truck radio and had it cranked up full blast.

By the time they were outside the gates, Jodell was feeling better already, was primed for the party, and was even singing along with the rest of them to a silly Beatles song. He didn't think any more about the strange feeling that had come over him back there in the track infield.

CURTIS AND ELVIS

The three men, all freshly showered and in clean clothes, rolled up and parked at the ranch-style house that belonged to Curtis Turner. Johnny Holt had opted out of going with them to the party, choosing a movie instead, although they suspected he really wanted to talk on the telephone to his new girl-friend back in Chandler Cove without their listening in.

There were cars parked everywhere, all over the front and side yard and up and down the street. A jukebox was blaring and thumping from somewhere out back, its voice so distorted it wasn't clear if it was playing country music or rock and roll. It was just some kind of generic, static-racked music. People were all about, laughing, singing, talking, drinking. Some were well dressed, in party clothes. Others appeared to have come straight from the garage or farm without bothering to change.

Bubba carefully parked the truck in the yard in a place where he hoped someone arriving later would not block it in. They did not want to be stuck here until sunup waiting for someone to show up to let them out. At least Jodell and Bubba didn't. Joe probably wouldn't have minded at all. If events spun out as usual, he'd hitch up with a pretty girl and they would not see him until tomorrow—typically, minutes before the start of the first practice.

They followed the noise and most of the crowd around to the back of the house. Sure enough, the party had not waited for them. It was already in full swing. Jodell quickly spotted several drivers, a number of crew members, and just about every newspaper reporter who followed the circuit on any kind of regular basis. There also seemed to be a plentiful supply of pretty young women everywhere, some already attached to boyfriends or husbands, others clearly not.

Jodell and Bubba ambled over to where a big washtub held a good year's supply of iced-down beer for normal folks. Jodell fished one out for himself and then passed one to Bubba. He grabbed a third one for Joe and turned to hand it to him, but he was not there.

"Where did he go already?" Jodell asked.

Bubba nodded in the direction of the patio. Joe Banker had already located two friends, one a tall, slender redhead, the other the blonde from the track who had been so interested that afternoon in internal combustion engines.

Jodell pushed the third beer back down into the tub of ice. Just then, he spied a couple of drivers talking with one another over to one side, away from the bulk of the melee. He stepped over to join them. Bubba headed off to find some of the other mechanics.

Both men had observed a valuable benefit to Curtis Turner's parties. Alcohol flowed generously, and that tended to loosen tongues. And that had allowed them to learn valuable information that could help them unravel the mysteries of this track or that, tips that might not have been so easy to garner if the source had not been so well lubricated first.

Curtis himself was nowhere to be seen. When Jodell asked someone where he was, there was only a shrug of the shoulders or a shake of the head. He'd been there earlier but no one had seen him in a while. Besides, the party was rolling along quite nicely without him anyway.

Someone had pulled a jukebox out onto the patio, and it continually blared out one tune after another. Its speaker was horribly distorted since the volume was cranked up as loud as it would go. What with all that noise, a rowdy mob of people who were clearly drunk, and the cars parked on lawns and blocking driveways all up and down the block, it was a sure bet the neighbors would call the cops before the night was out. But so far, the party was proceeding unabated.

Most of the guests had moved away from the blaring jukebox so they could carry on their conversations. But suddenly the racket from the thing stopped cold. Jodell was talking with one of the Plymouth drivers when the music died, and he found himself yelling in the unexpected silence. Embarrassed, he turned with everyone else and looked back toward the patio.

There stood Curtis Turner holding the plug to the

jukebox high above his head, a serious look in his eyes.

"Sorry. Party's over, folks," he said solemnly. Some of the guests groaned and protested. Others who knew Curtis only smiled and waited for the next shoe to drop. A sudden grin cracked his broad face. "But the next one is beginning in 'bout five minutes!"

He plugged the jukebox back in, and it resumed in the middle of the fuzzy, throbbing song in which it had been halted. Turner, ever the gracious host, picked up the tall glass of almost straight Canadian Club from the top of the jukebox and began making his rounds. Eventually, he strolled up to Jodell's group and offered him a fresh beer.

"Sorry I don't have no white lightnin'," Curtis apologized. "I know that's your drink of choice."

"Beer's fine, thanks, Curtis. I just used to haul it, not drink it. What you been up to?"

"Aw, not much, Tennessee. A little timbering, a little of this, a little of that. You know me. I'm always gettin' my fingers into something or another." He used one of those fingers then to stir his drink. "How's that old hunk of junk car of yours running? Reckon it'll last for six hundred miles on race day?"

"It's plenty fast but maybe not fast enough."

"You're just not driving it hard enough, Tennessee. You gotta push the thing if you want to win races."

"I drive her any harder I'll be in the wall all smashed up."

"Well, sir, that's what I would do. I'd run the wheels off the darn thing if I was driving it." He paused and gazed wistfully into the drink he was holding, as if he was looking for something in its murkiness. "I sure miss being out there racing you boys."

Curtis, along with driver Tim Flock, had been

banned from racing for life after a series of events that involved the Teamsters, Jimmy Hoffa, and a possible union for stock car drivers.

"Well, why don't you do something about it?"

"Aw, Lightnin', all they're doing is trying to keep me from winning *all* the races."

"Yeah, I'm sure that's it, Curtis." Jodell grinned.

"And boy, do I miss Little Joe." Was that a tear in the corner of the man's eye?

"We all do, Curtis. We all do."

Turner suddenly shifted gears.

"Did I tell you about me and Elvis Presley gettin' together and partying a couple of months ago?"

Jodell immediately smelled a rat.

"Elvis? Come on, Curtis. I saw you get that kid from Freddie Lorenzen's crew to take all day trying to find you a left-handed axle puller. But I'm not quite that gullible."

"Naw, listen. We sure as heck did. We had ourselves a ball. Why, I even got E's private phone number right here."

He retrieved a book of matches from his trouser pocket. There actually was some smeared writing of some kind on it.

"Curtis, I do believe you are trying to pull a fast one on us."

"You don't believe me?" Curtis said, leaning in a little closer and squinting.

"No, I don't believe I do," Jodell said, ready for the inevitable punch line to get thrown his way.

"Well, then, come on and let's go in the house and we'll just call him up and invite him to come on over and join us. You'd like him. He's a nice guy. And he's from Tennessee just like you. And besides, even Elvis ought not to miss one of Curtis's parties."

Turner already had Jodell by the arm in a powerful grip and was dragging him toward the back door of the house.

"Okay, okay! I believe you, Curtis. Why don't we just stay out here and have ourselves another drink? I'm sure Elvis is busy. Besides, we don't want to miss any of the party ourselves while we're in there talking to Elvis."

That's when Curtis looked down at his glass and noticed it was almost empty."

"Lord, looka here. I'm about to run dry."

And he wandered off toward what must have been the door to the kitchen, where the bar had been set up.

Jodell found Bubba over in a corner, still talking to a couple of mechanics he knew who worked on Junior Johnson's car. They divided up and each went off in a different direction looking for Joe. Jodell found him in the living room, the blonde planted on his lap, and they weren't wasting time discussing how to set the jets on a carburetor. Jodell sneaked up and popped his cousin on the back of the head.

Joe never broke the lip lock he had on the blonde, but simply gave a wave of his hand to let Jodell know he would be a little while. Quite a little while, apparently.

"He coming?" Bubba asked when Jodell joined him at the truck.

"What do you think?"

"Let me guess. The blonde in the short shorts?"

Jodell only grunted. He had grown used to Joe's not showing up at the track until the last minute after a full night's catting around. So far he couldn't see that it had hurt them, but there would be the day when his womanizing would get in the way of their racing. And he dreaded it. Cousin or not, he couldn't allow Joe's appetites to get in the way of what they were trying to accomplish.

They headed the truck back toward the motel, neither man saying much the whole way.

Apparently nobody could sleep. It was race day and they were all up and ready to head for the track by the time the sun finally, reluctantly, rose up from somewhere down near the coastal plain.

Catherine and Joyce had shown up late the night before with Homer Williams. Homer and Johnny Holt had moved into a motel room with twin beds and a rollaway, while Bubba and Joyce and Jodell and Catherine split up into the double beds in their original room. Of course, the rollaway went unused. Joe had not been seen since they had left the track after qualifying the car the afternoon before. He was last seen escorting his new blond friend to another party somewhere.

Except for Bubba, everybody was too excited to eat

much breakfast. Their eggs and gravy and biscuits grew cold as they talked excitedly about the prospects for the race while Bubba finished off everyone else's plates. Jodell and the crew had managed to find a couple of extra tenths of a second of speed during the last practice, too late for qualifying but in time to get giddy about the prospects for the race. They were now able, they felt, to run with anyone else out there, and they couldn't wait to get to the track, get it cranked, and get a win.

They finally gave up on eating and got busy getting everything packed up for the trip over to the track. They made Catherine sit and rest on a bench in the shade of a blooming dogwood tree while they worked. It was heading for a hot day already, and they all agreed she should not push it so early. She sat there and scowled at them, wanting to be of help as she usually did.

"We better get going," Jodell finally announced as he picked up the last bag and wedged it into the trunk of Homer Williams's Cadillac. "Highway 29's probably at a dead stop already, and we can't let them start this thing without us."

Johnny rode in the front seat of the Cadillac, Jodell and Catherine in the back, while Joyce climbed up in the truck beside Bubba. Then their two-vehicle caravan moved on up Highway 29 toward the speedway. Jodell had been right. The traffic was already backed up, but Bubba blew the truck horn and held out the window the big sign with the Bubble Up logo and their car number on it and eased right on up the shoulder of the roadway, past the jams and on to the track. He acknowledged the honks and waves from the race fans and pointed with his thumb back to the Caddy, toward where his driver rode.

Jodell waved back and smiled when he had to but otherwise stayed quiet, slunk down in the seat, holding Catherine's hand. Homer Williams tried to ask him some more questions about the car but he only answered in short sentences, clearly in no mood to talk this morning. Williams sensed that the driver wanted to be left alone, so he talked with Johnny about what to expect, about how badly he wanted a win this day.

Jodell paid little attention to them. He preferred thinking about the moves he would make, where he would put the car in each part of the speedway, how he would react to various incidents and potential catastrophes should they present themselves. They had a perfect car for the race. It was so fast that it was almost scary. He knew how to drive on speedways like Charlotte. He loved these big tracks. It was up to him to steer them to their biggest win yet. And today was the day.

But something else had rendered him silent and reflective this morning. For some reason, since he had awakened wide-eyed in the small hours of the morning, he had been thinking about Little Joe Weatherly, about the senseless way he had died. He tried to shove the thoughts out of his head but they wouldn't go away for some reason.

"You okay?" Catherine finally asked, quietly enough that the men in the front seat couldn't hear.

"I was about to ask you the same thing," he answered, smiling, touching her swollen belly with the palm of his hand.

"I'm fine as can be. You're so quiet. Everything okay?"

"You know I like to think about the race when it gets this close. Run it through my head and everything."

"Jodell, I don't want you worrying about me or the baby or anything else. Fast as y'all run out there, I want you thinking about what's going on around you."

He gave her a quick peck on the cheek.

"You know I will. There's too much at stake here not to."

"I just remember what you told me one time. On the beach at Daytona that night. Remember? About how you can't drive scared, afraid of making a mistake or getting hurt? That that's when you are most likely to get in trouble. And when you lose the race for sure."

He squeezed her hand. It was the perfect time for her to remind him of how he felt about such things. And it was true. He needed to put Little Joe and his death behind him once and for all. And instead of fire and smoke, he needed to be visualizing a checkered flag flying over his Ford, a Charlotte trophy with his name on it.

He gave her another quick kiss on the lips, then turned and waved to a flock of honking, screaming fans.

The big Caddy and the pickup truck bounced into the infield of the Charlotte speedway only to find that the entire area was already filled with happy, milling race fans. The smell of barbecue smoke and campfires hung heavy in the early-morning air. Flags— checkered; Confederate; and red, white, and blue— were just beginning to flutter in the first hot breezes.

They were shocked to find Joe Banker already sprawled over the fender of the Ford, making some adjustment beneath the hood.

"Where . . . ?" Jodell started to ask but then

thought better of it. Joe was here. He was concentrating on getting the car ready to run. And there were hours to go before the green flag. He should be counting his blessings, not questioning his cousin.

Johnny and Bubba started in on their prerace checklist, four pages of things that had to be inspected before they would even consider cranking up the engine. Satisfied things were progressing, Jodell turned and started across the garage area to the mandatory drivers' meeting. He caught up with Fireball Roberts and several other drivers headed the same way.

"You ready to go get 'em today?" someone asked Roberts.

"Yeah, I reckon I got 'em all covered. How you doing this morning, Jodell?"

"Fine, I suppose. I'll be glad when we fire up and get rolling. I can't stand all this waiting around all morning."

"Well, you got to give 'em time to get here to watch us run. I bet the fans are backed up for miles out there on old 29."

The grandstands were already filling up for certain, slowly coming alive with early comers. Jodell knew there wouldn't be an empty seat when the green flag waved.

"I don't think I'll ever get used to these big crowds," he admitted.

"Me neither. I got to admit I've never been much for dealing with folks. I feel much more comfortable all by myself running around out there in that old car," Roberts said.

Though he had heard him say it before, it was still a surprising admission for Jodell to hear from the man. Fireball Roberts was far and away the most popular driver on the circuit. He seemed to have such a natural, easy style with the fans that everyone liked him. And if someone had taken a poll, most of the spectators at today's race would likely be pulling for him to win.

"I know what you mean, Fireball," Jodell said. "But you still have to spend some time with the guys who buy the tickets. Without them we'd still be out in some old cow field somewhere churning up dust for a ten-dollar purse."

"Yessir, things in this sport have changed more than somewhat since I started running way back when."

"You're starting to sound like an old codger," one of the other drivers said, laughing, mimicking an old-man voice.

"At thirty-five, a man is old in this business. I'm already looking to retire from this stuff."

"Retire?" several of the drivers said in unison.

"A fellow can't aim a race car forever. I got to grow up and get a real job someday."

"We do make a living," Jodell countered. Fireball Roberts had to be doing well financially with all the races he was winning these days. But Jodell winced when he thought of the constant juggling act that Catherine had to perform to get all the bills paid each month.

"Just think what the baseball players make. And they're not running a car into a wall at a hundred and sixty miles an hour!"

"He's got you there, Jodell." The other driver laughed and walked off.

Jodell shook his head as he held the door open for them to step into the little meeting room.

"I guess I never really thought of it like that. I love to drive and I want to win so bad I never give much thought to the money."

"You will. That young'un gets here, you will," Roberts said. "I've been talking to one of the big beer companies about maybe being a spokesman for them or something. You have to have a plan for when you can't do this anymore."

"Well, I got a lot more races to win before I can give up on racing," Jodell stated confidently, then nodded toward the meeting room door. "And the next one starts directly right out yonder."

They sat down together on folding chairs and acknowledged the howdys from the other drivers and crew members. Fireball pulled the zipper down a bit on his one-piece cotton driving suit and fanned himself with a big hand, trying to cool off. Jodell knew the man didn't wear the flame-retardant suits like the other drivers did. He was allergic to the chemical with which they were treated. It had taken a special waiver from the sanctioning body to allow him to race without the suit.

After the drivers' meeting, Jodell walked back to the car by himself, pondering the things Roberts had said. Having a wife and with a child on the way, he knew there were about to be a lot more financial responsibilities in his household. Bills for far more than just another set of tires or the parts to fix a busted engine. Once finished with today's race, he needed to think some of what Fireball said. He always appreciated his candor.

Fireball was a thoughtful man, a true deep thinker, and a gentleman to boot. Only in the last couple of months had Jodell been able to break through the veneer of Fireball's personality and to finally start to get to know him. He considered most of the drivers out there to be his friends, with the exception of Dash Rockford and a few of the others who raced dirty.

But the Pettys were all business and not much else mattered to them but racing and winning.

Curtis Turner and Little Joe Weatherly were a hoot to be around, but they had only lived for the next party.

But drivers like Fireball Roberts and Ned Jarrett seemed deeper somehow, looking at life as far more than a series of left-turns. They would race as viciously as anyone out there, but they had a more contemplative side, too. Jodell respected them for that and vowed to be more like them.

Bubba, Johnny, and the pickup crew were just about done with the car when he got back.

"We got you a good car today, Joe Dee," Bubba said as he squeezed his giant frame out the driver's-side window. He patted the car lovingly on her roof. "She's a winner."

"Good, 'cause I feel like winning today myself. What do you say we treat ourselves to a big old steak dinner tonight after we take this thing?"

"Now you're talking!" Bubba exclaimed, and his stomach grumbled right on cue. "Rare with a side of fries and a chocolate milk shake!"

"Why don't you take a break and go get us a couple of hot dogs? I'm buying. I don't want to have to listen to your stomach growl all the way up to race time."

Catherine and Joyce sat nearby, relaxing with some of the other drivers' wives beneath a large tarp set up to shade one side of an old school bus. Catherine was still a bit miffed at Jodell because he had expressly forbidden her to climb up into the booth and score the car.

"I want you to relax and enjoy the race," he told her.

"But I came to help," she said. "I'm not used to

sitting around in the shade while everybody else helps get ready."

"Humor me. I'll drive better if I know you're out here."

And considering the mood he had been in all morning, she had not argued with him anymore. Not even when he had asked Joyce to forego scoring, too, and stay with her. She even told him good-bye two hours before the race. Normally she waited until the last possible moment, but she didn't want to be any more of a distraction to him today.

Thank goodness we're on a good, safe track today, she thought. He'll be fine. Once they fire up those engines, he'll be fine.

The Ford was sitting poised on the line. Bubba watched over it, eyeing the competition up and down the line. He continued to wipe and shine the car with the rag from his pocket.

"You gonna raise sparks if you rub any harder," Jodell teased.

"Aw, pshaw, Jodell. I just want her to be clean and sleek out there."

There had already been one setback today. One of the men who was supposed to help crew the car during the race had failed to show up so far. That meant Joe Banker was going to have to change the front tires if the guy didn't make it.

As race time neared, Joe and Jodell met over the toolbox, their heads together, planning the pit stops. Homer Williams stood nearby, soaking it all up. Thank the Lord, he loved all that was racing. Otherwise, he might well have dropped the sponsorship over the last few years when things had not gone quite so well. And he had even provided them with some valuable guidance on running their team more as a business than the hit-or-miss way some of the gypsy race teams they competed against did theirs.

When it became painfully obvious the last of their pit crew would not show up, Bubba walked over and pulled Homer aside.

"How would you like to help crew the car?" he asked.

Williams almost jumped out of his wing-tipped dress shoes, and they could have likely seen his smile from the press box.

"Of course I would! What do you want me to do, Bubba? Just show me. What you want me to do? Gas? Tires?"

His job would be to keep the windshield clean and pass water or anything else Jodell needed to the driver during the pit stops. Bubba took Homer over to the car and showed him the part of the windshield that had to be clean, whether he got any other section of glass wiped or not. And he pointed out where Jodell's drinks were lined up and to the stack of rags he would need to keep wet with cold water so the driver could wipe the sweat from his face. Homer took it all in, as excited as he might have been if Bubba had told him he would have to drive the car today instead of Jodell.

Then Bubba pulled the crew's Bubble Up shirts out of the car and passed them around to everyone to put on over their T-shirts. Homer Williams loosened the tie around his neck and skinned off his white dress shirt, then pulled the Bubble Up route driver's shirt on and began to button it up and tuck the tails into his dress slacks.

The grandstands were full already, the fans burdened down with picnic baskets and coolers as they poured in and found their seats. Festivities that involved visiting dignitaries and a flock of local beauty queens and such were wrapping up down by the start/finish line. The national anthem was sung, the last two lines erased by the tumultuous whooping and hollering of the anxious crowd, ready to see some serious racing break out.

And finally, the drivers were ordered to their cars, setting off a mad scramble among the crews up and down the roadway that ran along in front of the different pit stalls. Jodell walked quickly to his own car, happy to at least be climbing inside and getting ready to race. Joe grabbed him and mentioned a couple of things they had discussed a half dozen times already. Johnny and the others helping him were stacking tires and already getting things set up for the first pit stop. Bubba checked the air pressure in the tires one more time, while Homer Williams polished the windshield, making sure there was not a speck of dirt or the hint of a smudge anywhere on it.

Catherine started to get up and climb the ladder to the top of the bus to see the beginning of the race, but Joyce stopped her.

"Cath, Jodell would drive that car right off the track and come over here and whip both of us if he saw you up on top of this thing! Let's walk over to the fence and we can see them coming out of the fourth turn to take the flag."

Catherine reluctantly agreed. She still wasn't comfortable with everyone making such a fuss over her being pregnant. She knew her limits and wanted to enjoy the race. But even more, she hated being at the track and not being able to see every move Jodell made out there, as she usually could from the scorers' booth.

At that moment, Jodell was getting settled inside the car, surveying everything to make sure all was as it should be. He was finally in his element—his "office," as he sometimes termed it. He reached up and pulled the shoulder belts down, locking them into place, and strapped on his helmet.

All the hoopla surrounding the race immediately vanished once he was strapped into the cocoon of the race car. So did the doubts, the bad thoughts, and the moodiness that had plagued him for the last few months. He felt his heart quicken, his nerves calm, his confidence soar. His hand was already on the starter switch when the command came to crank the engines. With a loud *"roomp,"* the engine rumbled to life in front of Jodell. He glanced quickly over the gauges, checking for oil pressure and the right amount of amps out of the alternator.

Bubba stuck his head in and made one last check around the cockpit, then shook Jodell's hand as he did before the start of every race. He had his game face on, all serious, all business.

The idling engine vibrated the race car gently; the promised tremendous power was there, ready at his command. Jodell could smell the hot exhaust coming up off the headers on the cars surrounding him. It was sweeter than any perfume he had ever inhaled before. The noise of those cars was deafening, too, numbing his ears through the cotton ball plugs. But it was as beautiful as any song he had ever heard sung.

The crews along the pit road finally scrambled back over the wall away from the race cars. The officials in front of the line began to wave the cars off. Jodell pushed the shifter up into first, let off the clutch, and began to roll forward.

He held his place in line as the first parade lap was made. The car seemed to buck in anticipation, ready to fly. And Jodell Lee was ready to let her soar.

He sawed the steering wheel from side to side, cleaning the tires of any debris they might have picked up on the pace laps. He wanted to make certain that he got a good grip when they roared off down into the first turn on the start. No need to send the car sideways in the middle of the field if it lost traction.

Joe had found something in the motor before the last practice, and Jodell was confident he could move to the front quickly once they were under way. The front was the place to be. That would keep him out of trouble if some sort of holocaust broke out in the middle of the pack. And besides, he loved the view out the windshield of nothing but an empty racetrack all the way to the turn.

Catherine and Joyce stood by the inside fence waving wildly each time Jodell went by on the pace laps. They knew he couldn't actually see them but they cheered and waved anyway until he had moved on down and out of their sight. Then they'd wait until he came around again and do it all over.

Joe stood nervously on the wall, waiting for the cars to come around to take the green flag. He fiddled with his stopwatch while he strained to see up toward the fourth turn, to get that first glimpse of the leaders as they raced down toward the start/finish line for the beginning of the race. He was proud of what he had done with the motor. So proud, in fact, that he had come to the track extra early just to double-check everything one last time. He knew what a hairline difference there was between being real fast and having an engine, stretched a tick far, blow up in his driver's face.

Like Jodell, Bubba was past ready for the start. Until they were under way and set for the first stop, he was simply a spectator. But when the stops started coming, he had as much to say about how the car performed, about whether they had a good chance of winning the race, as anyone else.

Homer Williams stood behind the pit wall soaking in everything, beaming from ear to ear in his Bubble Up route shirt and baggy, pinstriped suit pants. He was ready to help do his part and had vowed that Jodell Lee would have the cleanest windshield and coldest water of any driver at Charlotte.

Jodell rode along in the inside line of cars as they strung out down into turn one for the last time before the start. A Plymouth roared along to his outside, another Ford rumbled along directly in front of him. A couple of rows ahead were the cars of Fireball Roberts, Ned Jarrett, Junior Johnson, and the others who had been only a split second faster than he had in the qualifying session. But Jodell knew now that he had a car that could match or beat theirs and he fully intended to do just that.

Then he could see it through the windshields of the cars ahead of him. The green banner waving wildly above the head of the flagman. Jodell jammed his foot to the floor and the powerful engine leapt ahead, dragging the car along with it toward the first turn. Jodell came up quickly through the gears, jumping down to the inside of the Ford directly in front of him. By the time they were exiting the first turn, he had put the car behind him and had set his sights on the next car blocking his way to the lead.

The crowd in the grandstands stood as one, on their feet screaming as if trying to outdo the engines in the cars as they came up to power in front of them. The stands themselves quaked with the stomps of the people, from the rolling thunder of the motors as the pack went freight-training by to take the green flag.

But in a flash, the cars were gone, snaking off into the first turn, and then, before the crowd could grab its collective breath again, setting sail off down the backstretch. And already cars were breaking out of line, racing for position.

And that was especially true up front, where the drivers were apparently confused, thinking it was the last lap instead of the first. Fireball Roberts, Ned Jarrett, Junior Johnson, and another car or two were in a furious skirmish, each one determined to lead the first orbit, to show the others that his was the car everyone else would have to beat this day.

Jodell was no exception. He was pushing the Ford hard, trying to get up there where they were, to get in on some of the fun. In the process, he was knocking cars off running low, steering to the high side, or going just about anywhere else he could pick one off. It was apparent the car would stick and hold wherever he directed her. The extra power Joe had found the day before allowed him to put the nose in any place he wanted and then zoom on past anything that got in his way.

What a wonderful feeling! To know he had the power and the setup to win. He couldn't wait for the rest of the race to play out.

Joe Banker stood on the wall timing the cars as they came roaring by to finish the first lap. The times were stellar, the race fast from the very beginning, but he couldn't help but scowl as the bunches of race cars roared by in such close quarters.

"Looks like the last couple of laps on Saturday night at a short track," he mumbled to himself. If they didn't string out pretty soon, there was going to be trouble. Big trouble.

He had to smile, though, when his driver came by.

Jodell was moving up well through the field and the car was clearly strong. The stopwatch confirmed it.

By now, there were only a few cars running along between Jodell and the four-car pack that included Fireball Roberts, Ned Jarrett, and Junior Johnson. Freddy Lorenzen had fallen back on the start but had somehow managed to put his car ahead of that bunch in search of the lead. But Johnson was clearly itching to get to the front and mix things up.

For the next few laps, those four cars chased Lorenzen like a pack of hounds bearing down on a fox. Jodell had worked his way up so that he followed several car lengths behind, closing in fast, ready to make his move past the bunch, then set his sights on Lorenzen. Using their draft, he was sucked right up toward their rear bumpers as they headed into the first turn. He knew he would have the power to catch them and maybe even to get by them as they lit off down the backstretch.

Jodell licked his lips and gave a whoop. There was nothing to keep him from second. And he knew instinctively that he was running faster than Lorenzen. It was a matter of a couple of more laps before he would lead this damned race!

Bubba Baxter's head might as well have been on a swivel as he followed Jodell and the other cars. He had watched Jodell pick off the cars in front of him in ones and twos, seemingly without effort. With a satisfied grin, he watched the car he'd spent so many hours working on stretch out and begin to show its legs. Then, as Jodell started to close in on the rear of the four cars dueling for second, he pumped his big fist in the air. He fully expected to see that Jodell had worked his way past them when he came back around again. He only wished he could see what was about to happen down the backstretch when his driver would blow right past the rest of them. It would be a glorious thing to watch!

Bubba glanced up at the scoreboard and saw that only six laps were done, that they had just begun the seventh. It seemed like they already had run a dozen or more at least. He leaned over to Joe and hollered, "What's the times looking like?"

"He's as fast as the leader, maybe even a tick better. It's hard to tell with all this traffic. Once he clears them we'll see."

"Man, he's fast. We need to get out front quick. Big wreck coming. Big wreck."

Another horde of side-by-side race cars bellowed by, a couple of them touching and rubbing slightly as they passed the pits.

"I think we're far enough ahead now to stay out of trouble. Good drivers up there with him. We oughta be all right," Joe yelled. It was a big advantage to be with the lead bunch, ahead of the trouble and riding with guys who knew what they were doing up there.

"Hope so!" Bubba said, almost like a prayer. "I sure hope so."

He stood on his toes, trying to watch Jodell and the car as far into the corner as he could.

Catherine and Joyce were still standing by the fence, watching the cars roar past and waving at Jodell each time by. They tried to listen to the broadcast of the race on a small transistor radio Joyce held in her hand, but the noise made it impossible to hear much. Meanwhile, Joyce was trying to keep Catherine from getting too excited as they watched Jodell move up farther, closer to the lead each time he had swept past. Catherine could tell that the car was as fast as the boys had said at breakfast that morning. Maybe faster. But there were still the "ifs."

If the car held together . . . If there was no wreck that got him caught up . . . If everything finally worked out . . . Victory Lane could be theirs.

Joyce cranked up the volume on the radio then she and Catherine turned with the cars, following them as far as they could see down toward the first and second turns, until they had disappeared going into the corner. A few slower cars went by and it was almost quiet for an instant, the announcer's distorted voice chattering away excitedly on the tiny speaker.

But then they heard a distant screech and a sudden concussive boom from somewhere over toward where they knew the second turn to be. They twisted around, looking to see whatever it was that had caused the horrible thunder. And suddenly, a massive smoky column of fire erupted above the far side of the track, as if someone had dropped a bomb. As they watched, the flames grew into a huge roaring inferno.

Catherine's hands went to her mouth and she felt her heart stop, her blood go cold.

Bubba and Joe were still watching the last of the cars head into the turn, trying to see who else was moving up fast to try to challenge Jodell. Johnny and Homer and the pickup crew stood just below them, looking back the other way to see where Jodell would fit in the tight pack of cars when they eventually roared out of turn four once more. They instinctively turned in unison with the boom, and they saw the smoke and fire, too.

"Whoa! What in hell . . ." Joe started to ask, but then he saw the massive ball of fire climb the sky and it hushed him like a sharp slap in the face. Then he thought of his driver. "Can you tell if he made it past?"

"I can't see anything," Bubba called back, trying to look right through all the vehicles and obstructions in the infield.

The fire and smoke grew worse, clearly spreading, burning black and ugly against the blue sky. Freddy Lorenzen came roaring out of turn four and headed down to take the caution flag that was already being waved frantically from the flag stand.

But there was no one else trailing Lorenzen closely. No one at all.

"Where is he?" Joe shouted.

"It looks bad, Joe. Real bad," Bubba said, now pivoted around and looking back to the fourth turn, praying to catch sight of Jodell's Ford Galaxie coming their way. Homer, Johnny, and the rest of them had joined Joe and Bubba on the wall, half of them watching the smoke and fire, the other half peering hopefully to the turn in hopes of seeing Jodell and the others come into view.

The big man could wait no longer. Without hesitation, he went sprinting across the infield toward where the flames boiled. Joe almost yelled for him to wait, that if Jodell came around with a damaged car or a flat tire they would have to try to get it ready to race again. But he knew he couldn't stop Bubba and contemplated taking off after him.

Meanwhile, Bubba was scaling a low fence and was gone at a dead run through the throng of cars and milling people in the infield.

Then several other cars straggled out of the turn, some with damage, others running slowly, seemingly unscathed. But none of them was Jodell Bob Lee. Where were Ned, Junior, Fireball, and Jodell? Now the thick smoke was being blown back toward them, and it was even harder to see what was going on over there in the exit to turn two. But they could still see the orange, licking flames.

Catherine and Joyce strained to hear the words on the transistor radio but they could only make out every few words.

"Fire . . . Junior . . . smoke . . . Jarrett . . . several cars . . . Roberts . . . fire . . ."

It was clear, though, that even the announcer was having difficulty figuring out who exactly had been caught up in the fiery crash, even from his vantage point in the booth high above the track.

Joyce noticed too that the cars Jodell had been racing behind had not come around yet. Catherine didn't. Her eyes were closed and she was praying quietly.

"Catherine, I don't see him."

"Don't worry, he'll make it through fine," she replied confidently, opening her eyes and managing a weak smile.

"He hasn't come by yet."

"He's okay. Even if he's in the wreck, he's okay. They build good, strong cars. He's okay," Catherine said determinedly, trying to convince herself as much as Joyce.

Joyce almost said something about the fire, about no matter how strong the car was, how well constructed it might be, that the fire could climb right inside one of those cars and claim whatever it wanted. But she thought better of it. She fought panic. For Catherine's sake, she fought panic.

"Well, let's head back to the truck anyway. They might need us."

She had no idea what they might need them for.

She only knew she needed to get Catherine back to where everyone else was. Just in case.

Lord, just in case.

Jodell had been enjoying himself about as much as he ever had inside a car. And that was saying a lot. His car was remarkably fast. He was closing in rapidly on the pack of cars in front of him that were fighting desperately among themselves for space on the track. Getting past them and challenging for the lead should be easy, but with only six laps done, he needed to be patient and keep his head. There was still a long way to go.

But going into turn one, he felt a twinge of apprehension. There was some hard racing going on several car lengths in front of him and it would be awfully easy for something disastrous to happen. But with the pace he was running, he should be able to clear them before all hell broke loose, and then it would only be him and Lorenzen for a while until they actually started to lap the tail end of the field.

Jodell had the best view in the place when he watched Junior Johnson jump down suddenly, getting inside of Ned Jarrett as the pack approached turn one. Ned moved over and gave him room, apparently conceding that it was foolish to run so hard this early. Jodell actually sighed with relief when he saw the move.

Bless you, Ned. Bless you.

Junior ran side by side with Ned all the way through turn one. Fireball Roberts and the fourth car were directly behind, almost as if they were in tow, hugging their rear bumpers. Jodell checked his mirror quickly, saw no one else was close behind, and actually eased off a smidgen, just in case.

Then, just as the cars hit the slight bump between

turns one and two, something happened. Whether it was the bump or the air just got sucked off his car's rear end, Junior's racer suddenly broke loose, lost its straight line, and spun sideways, hard into the left rear of Jarrett's Ford. With the contact, both cars began to spin, out of control.

Jarrett spun down to the inside of the track while Junior careened upward, toward the outside guardrail. The two cars, instantly sideways, effectively blocked up the track for everyone behind. And Fireball Roberts was close behind. Too close to do much of anything but hit the brakes and hold on for the roller coaster ride that was inevitably coming.

Whether the other car, trying to miss the spinning racers in front of him, hit Roberts, or whether Fireball simply lost traction when he hit the binders and tried to swerve past the melee, it was impossible to tell. It happened in a split second, and all the cars were so close together that the crash was in progress before anyone had had time to blink.

Ned spun around hard and backed into the unforgiving wall, crumpling the rear of the race car, rupturing the gas tank, immediately spilling fuel all over the track. A fraction of a second behind him, Fireball plowed his own car into the wall right next to Jarrett in a rough approximation of a backward parallel park. But his car had hit the gap in the wall where one of the crossover gates was, splitting the rear of the car open, slamming it brutally into Jarrett's wreck. Then the last of its momentum flipped it right over onto its roof.

Jodell saw nothing but spinning cars and blue tire smoke. He twisted frantically on the steering wheel, trying to find a hole to dive into that might lead to a way out on the other side. Somewhere in the fray he lightly tapped Fireball's Ford, but managed to get past most of the wreckage before he finally felt his own car get totally out from beneath him. He tried to steer it lower, to get out of the way of the cars he knew would be bearing down on him from behind. The inside wall came up to meet him quickly and put a sudden, hard end to his spin. Almost instantly he heard the unmistakable *"whuuump!"* when the spilled gasoline on the track behind him caught fire, then erupted with a rushing sound.

For a moment, Jodell sat motionless, still strapped in his car, half stunned from the impact. He had hit the wall a ton, practically knocking the front end off the race car. He was starting to move around, trying to collect his thoughts, get the wind back in his lungs, and get all his parts back under control.

Then he glanced in the mirror and saw nothing but tongues of vicious, snarling fire and boiling smoke. He could feel its searing heat. That quickly brought things back into focus as he realized he had to get out of the car and fast.

God! When he climbed out the window of the crumpled race car, it looked as if the whole world was ablaze.

Then, through the smoke and flames, he could see Fireball's car flipped over onto its top, and above the roar of the conflagration he could hear someone crying for help.

The car was already eaten up with fire, but Jodell didn't hesitate or even consider that other cars might come barreling blindly through the smoke right at him. He ran at a full sprint toward Roberts and his Ford, but the intense heat seemed to rise up and slap him back. He felt his eyelashes singe, the hair on his arms burn away, the skin on his cheeks tingle and fry.

But he could still hear Fireball's screams.

"Oh, my God, Ned, help me . . ."

Jodell put his arms over his face and rushed the flames a second time, trying to get to the trapped driver. He felt his face blistering, and he burned his hands badly in the searing flames trying to feel his way to the car's window. He was near panic when he realized that he was powerless to help Roberts, that he was going to have to stand there and watch his friend burn to death.

But he refused to give up. He dashed around to the other side of the car, only to find that Ned Jarrett had somehow gotten to the driver's-side window and was already pulling Fireball out.

At first, Jodell was elated. Fireball actually seemed to be conscious. Maybe he was going to be okay.

But then he saw that Fireball's driving suit was blackened, charred, almost burned away, that his skin was red, blistered. Ned was trying to pull away what was left of the suit while Roberts, dazed and obviously hurting, was attempting to help him. The flame retardant that Ned had used on his own driving suit had helped shield him from serious burns as he had struggled to help Fireball out of the car.

Just then, the rescue personnel rolled up, and along with Jarrett and Jodell, they helped move Roberts farther away from the hellish flames, then the crew went to work trying to get the rest of the tight-fitting driving suit off him. Others ran to the rest of the damaged cars to see if anyone was left in them. Anyone alive, that is.

Jodell stepped back then, out of the way of the rescue workers, to let them do their work. He knew that was Fireball's best chance now. He was out of the fire. He was obviously badly burned. The sooner they could get him to the hospital the better his prospects would be.

That's when he noticed the searing pain of his own hands. His face burned, too, and he could smell his scorched hair.

He stepped farther away from the burning cars and staggered over to the wall to try to steady himself. He suddenly felt light-headed and seemed to be unable to suck in enough air to breathe.

He shut his eyes and tried to fight off the dizziness, the blackness that was threatening to claim his senses. He didn't want to pass out. He didn't want to take any of the rescue crew away from Fireball, from any of the others who might be hurt.

But he was fading. Fading fast.

He imagined himself passing out, slumping back against the inside wall. He fought to keep consciousness. He worried about Fireball. About his own car. Could it be beaten back into shape?

But on some level, he knew he was on the verge of going under.

That's when he felt a touch on his shoulder. He forced open his eyes and saw a familiar face.

Bubba Baxter was standing over him, a worried look on his face.

"Joe Dee? You okay?"

"I reckon so."

It hurt his throat and chest to talk. He had apparently breathed in lots of the black smoke and super-heated air. His hands stung like crazy. His face felt like he had a bad case of sunburn.

But he was alive.

And then he realized that he needed to get back and let Catherine know he was okay.

"You feel like walking?"

"I think so . . ."

He stood up then with Bubba's help, deliberately turned his back on the still-burning mess of metal that had been, until a few moments ago, a couple of sleek, hurtling race cars. He started walking.

But he stopped then and turned to face Bubba.

"You think we can get that car back together for the next race?"

"Reckon so."

He nodded, then he put his helmet under his arm. Moving stiffly, he started walking again back toward the sanctuary of the pits.

Sometimes, no matter what had happened, the best thing to do was simply to go back to work.

In the Charlotte crash, Edward Glenn "Fireball" Roberts Jr. had suffered third-degree burns over almost forty percent of his body and first-degree burns over another forty percent. He lingered on for another five weeks or so, despite his severe injuries.

Jodell Lee learned of his death on July 2, 1964, as he and his crew readied the car in Daytona for qualifying. It was the same car they had wrecked in Charlotte.

Fireball was buried in Daytona Beach, in a cemetery almost close enough to the speedway that the roar of the engines could be heard on race days.

His funeral was on July 5, 1964, the day after the "400" had been run.

Since they had another race to get to, few of his

racing friends and former competitors were able to stay for the funeral.

In 1998, Fireball Roberts was named one of the fifty greatest drivers in NASCAR history.

Roaring around a banked track at
200 miles per hour, it's not a question
of winning . . . but staying alive.

On to Talladega

Book Four in the
Rolling Thunder
Stock Car Racing Series

Jodell Bob Lee loved being in this position, challenging good drivers in strong cars, but with a strong car of his own to do it with. He kept sticking his car's snout right up to the back bumper of Buddy Baker's racer, hoping to be able to give him enough of a push that they could clear Richard Petty and finally make it a two-car fight. One-on-one, Jodell was certain he could get a good run on the Cotton Owens Dodge, make it past it, and then go looking for David Pearson and his Ford with the worn-out tires.

Jodell got a glimpse of the sign Bubba Baxter was holding up for him in the pits. "Twenty," it said. Twenty laps to go. He would have to do it soon if he was going to try to move up. There would be no glory, no money, in passing anybody on the cool-down lap!

Baker drove deeply into turn three, nosing his car past Petty. It was clear the veteran driver had decided that he too needed to make his own move quickly. But by steering so aggressively into the corner, his car pushed upward ever so slightly, opening a sliver of racetrack near the bottom for Jodell to try to scoot into. There had been a time when Lee might not have recognized the opportunity that had just been presented to him. But a combination of experience and instinct made the hole look a hundred feet wide when it finally opened up.

He pounced like a leopard on a gazelle.

Even then, the fenders on the two cars rubbed briefly as they made contact before Jodell was able to safely get through and past the other two racers. Petty had seen the same bobble as Baker's Dodge pushed up the track in front of him. He tried to jump downward to the inside, to follow Jodell. Coming out of the fourth turn, Baker and Petty still ran side by side but Jodell had moved away from them, already setting his sights on the lead car.

In the pits, Joe Banker breathed a sigh of relief and studied his stopwatches intently. Jodell was picking up a tenth of a second a lap. Pearson's tires were fading fast. There was no doubt that Jodell was quickly catching up to the leader. Getting by him, he knew, would be a different story.

"How are the times?" Bubba yelled over the roar of the cars' engines as they passed the pits down the front stretch.

"A tenth or more a lap. We'll catch him for sure," Joe replied with certainty.

Bubba nodded his agreement, wiped the sweat from his face with an oily rag, and watched their driver dive into the first turn.

Jodell was flying like the wind. He had already put a dozen car lengths between himself and Petty and Baker, that two-car duel now nothing more than a moderately interesting vision in his rearview mirror. Jodell wouldn't try to watch any of that though. The next battle was out his windshield, and it was coming up quickly. He would surely catch Pearson within the next ten laps or so. And that would leave him ten or less laps to somehow get past him and into the lead.

Out of the turn, he gave the gauges a quick glance, saw they were reporting all was okay, then jammed his foot to the floor one more time as the car built speed down the long, straight backstretch. Then, in seconds, he was near the third turn. With another quick glance in the rearview mirror, he was off of the gas at his mark, allowing the car to drift into the turn, and then was back on the gas as he powered through the center of the corner.

It was all a matter of concentration and maintaining his rhythm, doing the exact same thing he had done hundreds of times already this race, scores of times in practice the last couple of days, and once during qualifying. But now, there was no one to get in his way and the rear end of the lead car was coming closer and closer to him with each lap. When he had finally closed right up on Pearson's Holman Moody Ford, when he could clearly see Pearson's eyes watching him in his own rearview mirror, Jodell caught a glimpse of Bubba's sign indicating ten laps to go.

"Ten laps. Please be enough," he whispered, and it sounded so much like a prayer that he added, "Amen."

He had caught up to Pearson. Now, the truly tough part began.